ORGAN MEATS

ORGAN MEATS

a novel

K-MING CHANG

ONE WORLD
NEW YORK

Published in the United States by One World, an imprint of
Random House, a division of Penguin Random House LLC, New York.

ONE WORLD and colophon are registered trademarks of
Penguin Random House LLC.

LIBRARY OF CONGRESS CATALOGING-IN-PUBLICATION DATA
Names: Chang, K-Ming, author.
Title: Organ meats : a novel / by K-Ming Chang.
New York : One World, [2023]
Identifiers: LCCN 2023015607 (print) | LCCN 2023015608 (ebook) |
ISBN 9780593447345 (trade paperback) | ISBN 9780593447352 (ebook)
Subjects: LCGFT: Fantasy fiction. | Novels.
Classification: LCC PS3603.H35733 O74 2023 (print) |
LCC PS3603.H35733 (ebook) | DDC 813/.6—dc23/eng/20230403
LC record available at https://lccn.loc.gov/2023015607
LC ebook record available at https://lccn.loc.gov/2023015608

Printed in the United States of America on acid-free paper

oneworldlit.com
randomhousebooks.com

2 4 6 8 9 7 5 3 1

Book design by Susan Turner

Contents

CONTENTS

"I had been taught by my mother to take my dreams seriously. My dreams were not unreal representations of something real; my dreams were a part of, and the same as, my real life."

—JAMAICA KINCAID, *Annie John*

"'How did all this begin? And where are the souls to be reborn?'"

—CAO XUEQIN, *The Story of the Stone*

ORGAN MEATS

Disparate Girls Discover that Doghood Is Not the Opposite of Godhood, and Anita Hsia Recounts the Ox-Boned Origin of Her Family Residence

In the center of summer, soft with rot, Rainie and I decide to be dogs. Cousin Vivian says you can't be a dogpack with only two dogs, Rainie and me, but I say she forgot to count our shadows, Rainie and me plus two shadows, which makes four dogs, which is a lot of dogs. The dogs we know are strays, and they always travel in pairs or in sixes, and they sometimes get hit by cars and crows pluck the meat from their bones, though mostly they leave the bodies of the dogs alone, because there isn't much meat on them. I decide that being a dog requires three main things: First, that we drink with our tongues, which is easy, because I drink out of bowls anyway, ever since Abu decided to grow flowers in all our glasses. The second thing is that we must have collars, because we are not strays. We belong to each other. We cannot be strays, because our ribs are not visible, mostly because we wear shirts. And we have names, mostly because we have mothers. Also, strays stink and have fleas, and we are required to bathe, though one time Rainie got bedbugs and she and her brothers wore rashes as long as capes down their backs and then Vivian and I got them too and Abu burned our sheets, bleached the carpeting. I halo Rainie's neck with red thread from Abu's sewing kit and make a knot where she swallows, then tie a symmetrical thread around my neck.

Now we're collared together, I say. I get the knot right only on the second try: The first time, Rainie's neck turns to steam, and I can't get the thread to grip anything. There is something in her that resists it, that doesn't want to bind herself to me. She lives by flitting. Even when she stands on the wrinkled pavement in front of me, she shifts from foot to foot like she's surfing something, turning the street into a sea she'll ride away from me. Rainie tugs at the thread, tries to wedge a thumb between the knot and her skin, but I tell her it has to fit us snug as a bloodline or else we can't be synonyms.

The third thing is that we must learn to bite, even though our teeth are crooked and easily uprooted. We practice biting our own arms first, leaving purple perforated circles, and then we move on to biting shoulders, which requires our jaws to unhinge wider. I bit my cousin Vivian while she slept, kneeling in front of her mattress and gouging my teeth into her shoulder and gnawing the sphere of meat, imagining that Rainie had called me to fetch it, to bring it back to her whole, a tennis ball of bone, except we do not answer to names. When I bit her, Vivian flopped like a fish and landed outside her dreams, gasping, and I had to return her blood in a bottle. Rainie and I practice stretching our jaws, widening them enough for a crow to fly in and roost, and when our mothers see us sitting on the sofa, gaping at nothing, drool draping our chins, they leap at us and ask if we've become melon-headed.

When Rainie and I feel that we have properly committed to our new species, we walk the streets as a dogpack, our shadows tailing us. When our knees are sore and bleeding and gravel-crusted from crawling, we decide that we will be two-legged dogs. We sit in the shade of a bald sycamore tree, its trunk like a drunk woman hooked over the fence of an abandoned lot, and in the corner of the lot are dogs sleeping in knots, panting loud in the heat, tongues chugging like conveyor belts. We bark at them, whine, but they don't recognize us, probably because we wear collars made of red thread, which mean we own our blood and they do not. When we lean on the fence, they leap up and foam white at the mouth, frolicking in their own snow. But they never come close enough for us to know. Rainie thinks the empty lot is full of dumped Styrofoam and exploding sofa stuffing and chunks of the moon's infected flesh, but I know all that whiteness is the cream of their dreams. I want to enter their shoreless sleep, to paddle alongside their tongues, but Rainie and I haven't yet convinced them that we are dogs too, and so they only watch us through the fence with eyes dark as doorways, their minds shining through like lamplight.

On the way home, we see two dogs on the street, one on top of the other, the one on top driving itself into the one on the bottom, and both of us stop, both of us watch. The dog on the bottom keeps trying to run away, its teeth barging out of its mouth. We have never seen anything move that way, the dog clambering on top, the hilt of its hips. It's Rainie who tugs me away and says, *Let's go home, quick, let's go,* as if the dogs have caught us, as if we are the ones being watched.

The next day, when I knock on the door of Rainie's unit, she answers with her red-thread collar on, her neck owned and boneless. *Let's be dogs,* I say. *Let's go back to the sycamore that leans over the lot and let's chew the leaves till our tongues dew with blood.* But Rainie says no. I know she's still thinking about what we saw, the dogs, the blond one, its balls swinging like apples, the sweet stink of them both. She looks behind her, as if hoping her mother might say, *Stay, clean the sink with me, tweeze the overgrown carpet,* but both our mothers are out at the factory, designing colors and collars to stitch onto babies. So she trots out with me, walks with me to the lot two blocks away.

On the way to the lot, the sidewalk bucks beneath our feet, meeting our steps midair, high-fiving our heels. I say the sidewalk is a skin, and trees are born out of it, roots pecking for air. But Rainie says no, it's the heat that causes the concrete to grasp at the cool of our bodies. We don't agree. One time, Rainie claims, she was riding a bus with her mother and she looked out the window and saw a big truck with a wasp's ass churning the bodies of gray slugs and pouring the jelly onto the street. *That's what the sidewalk is made of,* she says, while tripping on a crack as wide as a casket. Ahead, past the rows of duplexes and fourplexes jostling one another, the sycamore hooks a skeletal finger at us, beckons our breath, reels it out of our lungs. It's so hot that the street has dissolved into tea and tries to shore at our feet, so we leap. *That's a lie,* I say. *It's skin, not street. It winces if you lick it, though we can't lick it now or our tongues will be grilled well done. And it's called a sidewalk,* I say, *because you're supposed to scuttle sideways across it like a crab. It's not designed for our species.* I hook my arm through Rainie's and turn us sideways and shuffle us all the way to the lot, our ankles clanking like bells, our hipbones magnetizing in the heat.

Rainie says, *Stop it, quit ringing me,* and when we reach the fence, she unlinks from me and shoves me away. She says it's not fair that I always get to invent the rules of doghood and she has to sniff after me. *Fine,* I say, *you get to add a rule, but it has to be about wearing ourselves bare.* We will be skin-only, and no one at school will make fun of us for wearing matching horizontally striped shirts our mothers sewed for us that make us look like Ronald McDonald and are too tight at the armpits and rip when we raise our hands. We will achieve the freedom of another being. I summon up a fist of spit, frothing at the mouth.

Foaming is not the freedom of another being, Rainie says. *That's rabies.* She steps away from the fence and toward the shadow of the sycamore. *If we have rabies,* she says, *who's going to give us dinner?* Rainie only believes what she can eat. Her mother says she has to be fed every day at the same time or else she will swallow her shadow and skin herself. Already, Rainie is scraping bark from the sycamore tree. While her mouth is dissolving the sycamore's scalp, I squat among the roots and tickle the sidewalk with a stick. It shivers and nips off the tip. *Fine,* I say, *then what's your rule? Being part of this dogpack is a lot of work, and you have to do your share.* There is one dog tightening the screws of its teeth in the far end of the lot, its head the color of crusted blood, and its job is to pee on the sycamore and fertilize the lot in all four corners. At least it's trying to contribute.

I'm trying to contribute, Rainie says, spitting out bark. *But you keep interrupting.* She squats with me between two roots and says she's thinking. For Rainie, thinking and eating are synced activities, and her molars are gritting like the gears of her mind. When she's finished sipping up a ribbon of bark as long as our arms, she stands and gestures at the rusted fence, says she's decided. The red thread around her neck is glowing, and I know she's going to test me. *Try,* I say. *Whatever you've invented is already inside me.*

My rule, Rainie says, her head turned toward the fence, *is that you have to poop in the lot like they do.*

I swallow all the foam in my maw and walk up to the fence. In the holes of it, dogs are curled in sleep. Some of them are missing ears, and someone has been sewing for them: The blood-colored dog is closest to the fence, and its right ear is a sycamore leaf stitched to its skull with red thread. The other is a lobe of Spam. Ten feet from me, the dog is humming static in its sleep like a radio. If I climb the hot fence and crawl into the lot, the red one will wake, so instead I eye the diamond-shaped peepholes and identify the one that aligns with my intentions.

Quiet as I can, I turn around and grill my back on the fence. I shimmy down the jeans my mother sewed belt loops onto, even though I won't wear a belt unless it's red thread, unless it's a fate I can wear around my waist. When the jeans puddle around my ankles, I bend forward and jut out my hips. Rainie runs forward, mouth pursed with a warning, but I shuffle back and push out a slug of shit, threading it through the hole in the fence, making a mouth of it. It dangles on the other side, wriggling like a flooded-out earthworm. The red-headed stray must be a beacon, because it wakes and rings its teeth in alarm. I hear the dirt dance as the dog bounds up to the fence and barks, the other strays waking behind it, howling. Rainie grabs my shoulders and yanks me away from the fence as the red dog charges. This is how Rainie describes it: the red dog surging, piloting its teeth, leaping up and snipping the strand of shit from my ass. *Like a soft-serve machine*, Rainie says. *The dog cut it off perfectly!* In a past life, I tell her, the dog must have been ice cream.

In my time: I collapse on top of her as the red dog batters the fence, shoving its snout through the hole. It tosses the shit onto the soil and stamps on it like a snake, snapping at its prey. On top of Rainie, I slot my face into the space between her neck and her shoulder, nosing the flap of her earlobe. Whisper that I did it. Rainie laughs and I laugh too, releasing a fart that will flavor a neighboring city. Her laugh is brittle as bark, flaking fear. *Can you believe it*, I say, leaping up and pulling her under the sycamore. *That red-faced stray saw my insides. It looked all the way inside me, the way we look at the sun through a bendy straw and expel it like a spitball. It probably saw all my organs juggling themselves, all my blood a big ball of yarn.* Shaking her head, Rainie says we'll never see inside anybody, roadkill not included, but her voice is vapor to me.

Your turn, I say to Rainie. Behind us, the strays sheathe their legs again, tethering themselves to sleep, except the red one who saw inside me. It flickers between being red-faced, red-snouted, red-headed, and red-bodied: the different stages of tunneling through a body. It can't decide how stained it should be, how clean. Pawing at the remains of my waste, it flattens my poop into a patty and then a field, spreads it like a warm sheet on a bed. It must be lonely being the only rusted dog. Curling on my mattress of mud, it tucks its snout under its tail. *You know me,* I say. *You put on your blood like a dress, just like I do.* I show the dog my red-thread collar, and I know its veins run in the same circle.

Rainie watches me. It's my turn to test her. Her shirt is swamped, cleaving so closely to her spine that I can see the exact curve of it, like a silver spoon cuddling my tongue. Her chest cresting with breath.

Another rule is only fair, I say, yanking on the red thread around my neck. *I risked my asshole for you!* Rainie swallows, her thread thrumming a nervous note.

Let's be dogs the real way, I say. The final rule is that we will try what those two dogs were doing yesterday on the street. Hip to hip. We will be real dogs and we will give birth to puppies, litters of them, and we will get to keep them all and feed them the livers of liars.

Rainie sits down to think about it, her back resting against the trunk of the sycamore. She rakes her nails down the trunk, the bark glittered with ants. Its roots are exposed like bone, and I wonder who stole the skin off them. *Okay,* she says, and asks which dog I want to be. I say I want to be the dog on top and she can be the one on the bottom. Rainie looks down at her lap, the crotch of her pants mended so many times that the seams bulge with teeth. I remember when she used to itch her crotch in public during that summer of the bedbugs, her fingernails grated down to nubs. Out of sympathy, I scratched myself too, even though I didn't have any bites, clawing myself until I couldn't sleep and lay awake every night, stinging and thinking of our paired misery. I miss that summer of synchronized scarring. I miss the brazen way she used to flay herself for me.

I reach down to pull her up from the gravel. First, I tell

her, she has to run, and second, I will chase. *Okay?* Rainie runs and her arms are oaring the air back to me, the soles of her shoes slapping the street because the glue is dissolving in her sweat, and I lope slow behind her. The block before our duplex, where the houses tilt toward one another like women trying to hear better, I catch her. She stops and bends, pleats at the waist, and I jump onto her back. Rainie bucks me off and squeals, flopping down on her back, her shirt curtaining open to show her belly, but I don't remember the dogs doing it this way, so I step off her shadow and run for home.

I wish Rainie had let me stay yesterday to watch the dogs so I'd know how they concluded, how they knew when they were done. Rainie runs after me, and when we reach our driveway with its gasoline stains and wrist-wide cracks, she tackles me to the pavement and straddles my back, pushing me facedown into the cement seams. Unlike the yesterday-dog, I don't try to run away. I don't want to buck her off, I want to bear her into brightness. The dog yesterday, the one on the bottom, bit its tongue and made some blood. I bite my tongue, and when Rainie gets off my back and turns me around, I spit at her. She bats it out of the air like a fly, and I flinch from the flat of her hand. Rainie doesn't realize that being a dog demands loyalty. Spit is the language of my longing, and she swats it away instead of answering.

She dodges me when I pucker my mouth again, runs laughing into the side yard. There's a door there that leads to the garage, where we're not allowed to go, and I follow Rainie inside with my arms around her waist. Inside the garage are bottles of pesticide with missing caps, the smell of citrus, a knotted jump rope with only one handle, a phone embedded in the wall, jars of pickles, leaves of extinct trees, a shuttlecock, and three pairs of scissors lying like a silver puddle, which must have belonged to the tenant who cut holes in her curtains for no reason we understood. Rainie says, *It's hot in here,* so we take off our clothes and lie naked and facedown on the concrete. Flipping herself over, Rainie asks if we'll always be dogs. *Of course,* I tell her, *as long as you don't snip the red thread around your throat, and as long as our mothers leave us every day and don't come home except to teach us how to tamper with the Weather Channel so that it might finally rain tomorrow, so long as they tell us every day to eat everything, leave nothing: The bottom of your bowl must meet the sky.* I used to say, *But there's no sky in here, there's just a ceiling, a popcorn ceiling that isn't even made out of real popcorn.* Abu would reply, *It's just something people say, popcorn ceiling. Now eat, eat.*

Don't you want to be a dog with me? I say.

If it means I follow you forever, Rainie says, *I have to think about it for at least a week.*

A week? I say. A week is too long. In a week, we could bite off each other's ears. Our bellies could blimp with worms and bad gas. In a week, we could start shitting live fish. In a week, the word *dog* could expire and get replaced by a terrible sound, like a car dying.

Okay, Rainie says, *then I'll decide after I weigh the pros and the cones.*

When I ask her what the pros and the cones are, and how I can help her shoulder them, Rainie says it means the good things and the bad things, though she doesn't know which word means good and which means bad.

The pros, Rainie says, *are when we're dogs, I always have someone to share my shadow. When I look down at the sidewalk, I'm never alone. The cones are I don't know what dogs eat, and I have to know what I'm getting to eat. Otherwise I can't commit.*

I say that the pros obviously outweigh the cones, because we can learn together what a dog eats, and besides, I've sutured us together with red thread. Now we share a fate more certain than shitting. Rainie says I don't make sense, so I have to wait for her to decide. I have to wait for the week to end.

It's been a week since my cousin Vivian introduced us to her boyfriend, who takes her to McDonald's almost every day, and sometimes I'm allowed to come too, as long as I don't say anything, especially in the back seat while they are kissing, so I lie down and pretend to sleep when really I'm listening to Vivian weave her tongue through his teeth like a loom. One time I opened my eyes and saw the boy sucking on Vivian's nipples, and she turned her head back to look at me, her mouth a hole punched into paper. When I tell Rainie this, she says she doesn't believe me, since only babies suck on nipples. But I say I saw it, and I say, *Rainie, lift up your shirt*, and when she does, I kneel over her. My foot swipes at a bottle of pesticide and knocks it over, moating us in acid, but when I bend over and sew my mouth to her nipple, I think of a scallop, salty and briny, and the time Abu bought fresh ones and pan-fried them in a sauce of ketchup and sugar and vinegar, the tang and the sweet, the purse of the scallop so secretively soft, blubber at first bite, then satin inside. I imagine Rainie as the innards of my teeth, the soft tissue in my roots. The throb in my jaw that makes me a dog.

The fortune teller says our house has a past life. In its past life, it was the skeleton of an ox we drove to death. It keeled over from thirst in the middle of plowing a millet field, and we clutched its hooves and dragged it to a gutter. To atone for our crime, we are tasked to walk on all fours, plowing the carpet with our knees, and we are not permitted to stand up or drink water until the house agrees we have paid back our debt, signs of which include: the walls relieve themselves of white paint, turning yellow as our teeth, or the sink-drains grow canines and tell us we are forgiven, or the roof furs like the back of an ox and kneels down, allowing us to board it. Until then, we seed the carpet with our sweat and throw off our thirst and practice our plod.

After the fortune teller drives away in his Honda Civic with the duct-taped headlights and statues of six gods krazy-glued to his dashboard, Abu walks the house on her knees and removes everything that could be used as a whip. Belts, scarves, clothes hangers, our bath towels. She burns it all in a tin bucket in the side yard, then places the bucket in the doorway and makes us all jump over the flame. *To keep the ghosts at our back,* Abu says. Vivian jumps first, launching off her hind legs and landing on her hands, her skirt hem dissolving into ringlets of ash, and I go last, backing up in the yard for a running start, my hands bare against the grass. The grass has never known rain and is the color of my earwax.

Because Abu does not trust me to jump high enough, she stands inside the doorway and grabs my waist as I leap, shoul-dering aside the smoke. Because my room is the ghost of an ox jaw, the walls grind against one another at night, orchestrating digestion. Other times, the carpet shudders with swallowing. *It is possible to be eaten by your home,* says the fortune teller over the phone. To insure against its hunger, we leave bowls of beef broth in the corner of each room, inviting the soup to evapo-rate and absorb into the walls, but then I remind Abu that the house was once an ox and will probably be insulted that we

are feeding it a broth of its own bones. So Abu drinks all the
bowls of broth herself and we leave peaches in the rooms instead. They wear shawls of black mold, waiting for the ants to
undress them.

Our electricity dies for two weeks because of several
downed poles—Abu says it was ghost oxen that knocked them
down and drove over them—but we find out that many of us
can make light with our mouths. My cousin Vivian is the first
one to do it: One night she lubricates her throat with soybean
oil, swallowing a whole teaspoon of it, and now when she
opens her mouth and tilts her head back like a wolf nuzzling
night, she barks out a beam of fragrant light. When Vivian
and I were little, we ate handfuls of sand in the side yard,
scooping it into our mouths like sugar, and because of this, our
stomachs are sanded smooth. You could skip us across the sea
like stones.

We teach the neighborhood girls how to eat sand too.
Rainie takes to it most naturally, since nothing sifts through
her fingers. She's the kind who holds on to everything, consid-
ering it seriously before deciding whether to keep it or discard
it. She doesn't filter anything automatically. I see her debating
the red thread around her throat, touching her thumb to it like
a pulse, counting the heartbeats of her other body. Calculat-
ing its weight. *Keep it keep it keep it,* I pray, but Rainie's mind is
mist, and I can't hold on to it.

Rainie eats sand more than I do. She doesn't like the way
grit gets caught in her throat, but we tell her it's the only way
to weigh herself down, to secure her hind legs to the surface
of the earth. Our mothers are dyeing denim this summer at
the factory, and their hands return to us blue. My mother's
hands lunge for color. She harvests blue things from the side-

walk and gifts them to me in padded ring boxes: robin's egg-shells, forget-me-nots, the blue-white wing of a dead moth. Unlike Rainie, my mother and I never discard anything. At night, we take our electric flyswatter outside and sauté the moths that sip light from our lamps, frying the baby crickets that climb up our walls, shattering the gnats into sparks. We treasure the dead crickets' wings, the oiled bead of a roly-poly, a ruby ring of ants. We hold the racket up like a hand mirror, an electrified fence framing our faces in feral light.

My mother is the sea-born god of adventure, her mouth a bowlful of pearls. Her teeth are so pretty, they disappear in pictures. It's a protective measure, in case any covetous people might try to steal from her jaw. Her favorite time is meantime. All the times in between doing "real" things and "real" work. *In the meantime*, she always says, *is actually the nicest time. Why don't they call it nicetime?* In many meantimes, she teaches me how to trap raccoons with peanut-butter-painted marshmallows. She teaches me inappropriate children's rhymes about a girl boiling her grandmother for soup and a man with a yam stuck up his butt. Her laughter is a season you want to stand in forever, golden leaves relinking with the trees, springtime fizzing out of a bottle. She has a dimple on either side of her smile, one lower than the other, and the asymmetry describes joy perfectly. Her smile is so radiant it makes me ashamed.

The way my aunts describe her: *She could enjoy life in a dank cave of corpses, so long as she had a pack of playing cards. She could make time stretch like a cat, languid and leisurely and unconcerned with humanity. She could produce amusements from the air, snag a fly out of the sky and make it perform a drama on her palm.* I cling like a flea to her back, content to sip and be full of her blood. If I do nothing else with this life, carrying my mother's blood is enough.

My abu never wanted to have children of any species, but my father dreamed of me. He begged and begged until her veins dried up, her blood no longer rushing to shush him. Brittled by duty, she carried me into being. One night, while my father was out with his friends, Abu had a sudden fever. She was knocked flat by torrents of sweat, unable to rise. When she called my father to come home, he merely sent a dog to her door with a bottle of ibuprofen in its jaws. After days alone, she pulled me out of her mouth, which had become the mouth of a river. Most people are born headfirst or feetfirst, but I was born directionless, a cord of gorgeous water, as Abu still describes me. For years I wanted to tell her I was sorry for stealing her solitude, sorry that I had been plunged into her like a dagger, an enemy desire. I tell her I will be anything she wants me to be, that she can course my life just as I had once swerved hers. But Abu shakes her head. *Your existence is enough of a tribute*, she says. At night she dreams of her body empty. I want to be free because she couldn't be.

We chase baby crickets around the house, jabbing our bladed hands into the cracks of the couch, fishing them out by the antennae. Like popcorn, they're reborn when I drop them onto the pan of the electric flyswatter, tossing them into the air like a tune. My mother and I laugh ourselves breathless, counting our kills, singeing holes in the wooden gate that are the exact size of a dog's pupils. Now she can gaze at me through the eyes of another animal.

Other times, our mothers come home without gifts, complaining that they were born near the sea and the color blue should always be free. Everything costs money, money, money, they tell us, except people. People are the only thing cheap. Every day, we cost so little to them. Should we pay for veins in our body to bring us our blood? Should we pay our bones to prop us up? But Abu is always indebted to her body. She owes it many lifetimes of aching. She is always asking me to oil her hands and her feet and her neck and I do, but there is sand on my hands and it sticks to her skin.

Rainie is so unfamiliar with rain, she forgets its name. We will be grown up before we realize that grass is supposed to be green, and not just on TV. Like me, she thinks a raindrop is sharpened on one end, like a knife. We sing her name and the sky snags in our throats, and we are so dry we peel away our skins like lizards and walk the street on our bellies. Cars drive over us, boys on bikes, seafood delivery trucks, cement trucks headed toward other cities, but we are never crushed. We know how to dart between the wheels and flatten ourselves.

In the garage, Rainie and I discover that the ceiling is leaking celestial secrets. There is a crack above us that twists like the wrist of a river, and it fills daily with a god's spit, a voice suspended in it. The voice loiters in our ears and sometimes coaxes out our own, and we can spend all day telling stories with it, a wet voice we lob between us like a piece of raw beef. In the hour between afternoon and evening, Rainie and I observe that a god dangles her chin above our garage and unravels a chain of spit that trickles down to our faces. Inside this rope of spit are suspended stars and glittered bits of chewed-up foliage and flecks of night. Rainie theorizes that the Milky Way is most likely this same goddess, that she sneezed one day and wiped snot across her face with the back of her hand, smearing us a sky. *This is why it is important for gods not to have tissues,* Rainie says, *because their bodies need to fully leak in order for us to have a world to live in.*

Borrowing the voice of celestial secrets, I tell Rainie the story of a dog whose feces fertilized a sycamore tree, living its second life in the sky. It spawns another story, this one from the island our mothers were born on. Rainie asks which island; I tell her there's only one island, the one they were born on, and she shakes her head. She says that each island is actually two. Each island is a coin, one side facing the sky and the other the sea, and the whole island flips over so that both sides can take turns breathing. But long ago the islands stopped flipping themselves over, and because of this, one side became permanently submerged and could only be visited with advanced scuba skills, military submarines, or transportation via the mouth of a whale. *Our mothers were born on the backside of the island*, Rainie says, *the underside.*

I ask her how she knows this, and she says she watches TV. TV people record just the topside of the island because the water would interfere with the camera wiring, and besides, it's hard to see anything underwater. She says that when she and her mother watch the island channel on TV, her mother points out all the things that exist on the topside but not the backside: actresses with pearled faces, shopping malls, dry clothing. One time the TV showed a flood where dogs rafted down a mountain on car doors, and her mother shook her head and said that only happened on the topside: On the backside of the island, where the sea was the sky and the cities were inhabited by gilled and finned dogs, people did not attempt to war with the water. It had the same texture as air, except that light was often misdirected through it and had to be chased down and caught. And the sun and moon were made of beached whales' bones at the bottom of the sea. Rainie tells me that, technically, all of us are sea-born. All of us emerged from water a long time ago, which makes me wonder why I don't know how to swim or float, why I'm not designed to return.

Rainie tells me that some people choose to drill holes through the topside of the island in order to access the backside and raise their children there, because no one ever bothers you on the backside, except for horned fish that might skewer your door. On the topside there were many men and bird droppings, which made it annoying. Rainie and I look up at the ceiling, at the stalactite of celestial spit that descends toward us, and I ask her if this means our mothers can breathe underwater. She says she's asked before, but her mother won't tell her, and one time when she filled the bathtub and tried to lure her mother in—she planned to grab her mother by the hair and yank her into the water and hold her head underneath for as long as possible—her mother had just looked at her and said, *Why don't you try it yourself?* It required belief, her mother explained, a faith that Rainie did not have, an ability to summon our original gills.

Above us, the spit is weaving itself into a silver chandelier, spattering the wall as it swings with our breath. I tell Rainie that I have another version of the story that's even older, in which we are the descendants of feces. I take Rainie's fingers and weave them through my own, making a basket of our blood. Abu told me that we are descended from dog feces. One day a woman born on a mountain carried her harvest basket home and discovered that it was pebbled with dogshit. She rinsed the basket in the river, but the next day the feces appeared again, silking the bottom, and this time she threaded rain through the weave. The third time she discovered her basket cradling a stone of poop, she made a fire to burn it, but this time the feces began to speak. It caved into a mouth and said that it was the woman's first mother. Long ago, a god rolled a fist of dog feces into a mouth-sized hole, and out of the hole climbed humanity, a woman with black hair that expanded into a banner, the stars pegged to it. *Our ancestors are poo?* Rainie asks me, laughing. *Yes,* I say. I roll away from her, undo the braid of our fingers, and fart in her face. She laughs and smacks my hip, leaning forward so that her chest chances upon my back, and above us, the ceiling is spackled with spit and streaks of dog feces, a galaxy of our beginning.

When Wives Were Dogs

MY MOTHER: You know, back when your ama was born, there weren't any women, there were only dogs. . . . You get what I mean? Wives were dogs. You beat the dog, it still follows you around. . . . Let me tell you . . . In my hometown I knew a man who had a mistress, and he made an appointment to meet her, but he got sick that day and couldn't make it. So he told his wife, Listen, I'm sick and I need you to ride my bicycle to the meeting spot and let my mistress know I can't make it. And the wife said, Why do I need to ride your bike? And he said, If you ride my bike, she'll know you're my wife and therefore a reliable representative. Proof of identity and that you belong to me. And let me tell you, the wife did it! She rode her own husband's bike to meet his mistress and deliver the message! If a man told me to do that, I'd ride his bike to the market and sell it! Bet she didn't even know how to ride the bike and just walked it over. . . . Back before IDs, there were bikes . . . Dogs, anyway, with no dignity . . . My ama really wasn't like that, she wasn't a dog at all. . . . When she found out about Agong's wandering prick, she severed the house in half, built a wall of her own dog feces (which dries harder than human feces), and cornered him in the lightless half and didn't talk to him until he died! She kept him like a rodent, rained the roof in two. . . .

ME: Well, did she talk to him after he died?

MY MOTHER: I wish she had just been a dog and talked to him. . . . Better to be a dog! The problem is, we've never had any dogs in our family, never, that's why no one keeps a man in this family. . . . Men want a dog. . . . They want someone who will need them, you know, who will never refuse them. . . . Dogs will take anything you give them. . . .

ME: So are you a dog?

MY MOTHER: No, we are women. Before that, we were women wearing the flesh of dogs. There's a distinction between that and a dog. Our mothers and mothers' mothers were true dogs, though they wore human flesh.

ME: When will I grow a prick?

MY MOTHER: Never. You won't ever grow a prick. Not a wandering one, and not a static one.

ME: Not even if I water my regions and expose them to sun? Not even if I promise to slice it off and sew it somewhere else?

Not even if I use it to skewer the moon and slot a penny into its place?

MY MOTHER: No, never.

ME: Does this mole look like it will grow into a prick?

MY MOTHER: No, and don't expose it to the sun.

ME: What if I want one?

MY MOTHER: A sun? You don't want one of those. Our neighbor has so many, and they're all idiots.

ME: A prick.

MY MOTHER: You can't have one, I'm afraid. You will never have a prick.

ME (disbelieving): Well, if I had one, I'd attach it to your sewing machine and use it as a forever needle.

MY MOTHER: A forever needle?

ME: One that never breaks or gets dull.

MY MOTHER: That's very generous of you. I too would like a forever needle.

ME: What do you want?

My mother: I would like to stop talking now. It's almost dark and the bugs will be coming out. Fetch the electric racket. If only it wasn't so dry here, we'd get some really juicy ones to kill.

Me: I'm glad I don't have a dog for a mother.

My mother: That's because we're women now. We came into invention. Into use.

Me: Do dogs dig?

My mother: They do. They can smell very deep into the dirt.

Me: How deep?

My mother: Very deep.

Me: As deep as under the bed? As deep as my armpit? As deep as the follicle of my hair? As deep as the roots of a tree?

My mother: Why do you ask? You haven't buried someone already?

Me: No, but I might be planning to.

My mother: My cricket, you're too small to bury someone.

Me: You're right. But I think there are dogs buried under the lot. I think they're running along the soles of our feet.

My mother: Stay away from those strays. They're starving, and anything in need should be a warning. Their bellies will indebt you.

Me: What do you mean?

My mother: Dogs are born with debts. If you feed a starving stray dog in this life, it will be reborn as your servant in the next life (inevitably, a daughter). Then, when your daughter is done paying you back, she will be reborn as a dog again. You see how fucked that is? The dog-to-daughter pipeline continues, a debt repeating endlessly, amassing into a giant mouth at the center of the universe. It will repeat until the entire planet is swallowed. And even that will be the dogs' job, utter destruction. This world will die, and the dogs will give birth to another dozen.

Me: Do I have to pay you back?

My mother: Never, never, never. I have died so many times to find you. I have cleared the account and cleaned out your earwax. I have done the work of worldbuilding so that you may be free. All you have to do is eat what I feed you, because I spent a long time making it.

Me: Thank you for being my mother. If I were a dog, I'd be your dog.

My mother: I've brought you more options than that. Before you commit to anything, take a while to consider all the lives you can loan.

Rainie Tsai Learns to Suspend Her Disbelief, Which Is Impressive, Given the Immense Weight of It, and Anita Hsia Presents Her Skeletal Assumptions

Rainie passed the empty lots where stray dogs steeped in their shadows, asleep. She hid her wrists in her sleeves. Once, Anita told her that getting bitten by an animal meant you were chosen by its species and would transform into one of its own. Since then, Rainie decided to shy from teeth and shelter her current shape. She preferred her borders not be breached. As she passed the shade of the sycamore, she did not step into its shadow, though she knew its shadow contained restorative properties, which she discovered once when she and Anita fell asleep with their legs knitted through its raised roots.

They woke up hours later with perfectly exfoliated skin and no eczema on their knuckles.

Still, Rainie avoided walking alone to any part of the tree, ethereal or physical. She walked up to the lot instead, pretending that she was not stargazing at the strays, indulging her fear of fangs. She told herself she was walking in a straight line to the grocery store to buy a pair of new flip-flops for her mother, who insisted on the sanctity of clean feet, which had been violated by Rainie's hourly regurgitation of sand onto their carpet. Rainie's mother disapproved of her eating sand, even after Rainie said (in truth, she was repeating Anita) that eating sand was actually good for certain birds, since it provided important friction in their digestive system. *Maybe in the next life you'll be birds, but not this one*, her mother said. *In this one, you have a bad chin and good manners. Buy flip-flops only.*

Before Rainie was allowed to go to the store by herself, before she was accompanied by the weapon of red thread around her neck, she used to go with her mother and brothers on certain free evenings. One of her mother's favorite stories, which were few—she tended to accumulate stories like seeds, but never planted any—took place when Rainie was little and used to sit in the shopping cart as her mother pushed her through the seafood section. The whole back of the store was bright with displays of fish, some filleted and some still zipped into their skins, others gargling in tanks. According to her mother, Rainie had pointed at every fluorescent display and mumbled, *Working. Not working. Working. Not working.* It took seven trips before Rainie's mother realized this was a precise system of classification: All the foil-bright fish swimming in tanks were *Working*, and all the fish flayed on banks of ice were *Not Working*.

Working, Not Working. Rainie didn't have a word for *living*. Whenever she saw Anita greet the sycamore by rubbing her haunches on its trunk, Rainie wanted to turn away. Even now, walking past the tree for the third time this evening, she wondered if the sycamore was Working or Not Working. She decided she didn't know the tree personally enough to label it anything. Another time, Anita asked her to classify their own bodies as Working or Not Working, and Rainie hadn't answered.

I don't know, Rainie would respond now, *how I would sort us.* She only knew that Anita was alive in a way that watered everything else around her, alive with such generosity that she gave it away without knowing, resuscitating the sycamore and the sidewalk and the walls of the duplex that cleaved them apart, and a part of Rainie wanted to not be touched by it. Wanted to function without feeling everything, feeding its history. Anita wanted to tackle those fish tanks to the ground, release the fish, and render the hallways into rivers, but Rainie was relieved to walk away from those shallow fish-eyes, their foggy jelly. Those fish-eyes gaped at her, pickled and unknowing, forever static in their tanks, safe where she stranded them. When Rainie left the seafood section first, threading herself through the dairy aisle, Anita stayed behind with the aquatic species, circling the same lobster tank, waiting for Rainie to return. Since they'd decided to be dogs, Rainie was at least comforted by the knowledge that Anita was waiting for her. Every morning by the door, just like a stray, her mother said. Waiting to be fed or pet.

Last week, Anita tugged her to the lot when the dogs were sleeping off the heat and curdling on the surface of the black-top. Yards away, the sycamore cast its shadow over them like a tent. Grabbing Rainie's wrist, Anita dragged her to the chain-link fence, pointing at their rusted mouths and claiming that she saw a boy pissing through the fence, his penis slotted through the hexagonal hole. *He was following your rule,* Anita said. *He was doing it in the lot, just like the dogs!* Anita sounded impressed, but Rainie said it sounded like a recipe for tetanus. Skin was thinnest on your private parts, she said; it was what her mother told her: *Scrub the folds of yourself gently and silently, and don't linger too long in your own shadow. Don't press your own pleats.* Touch was only a tool.

But Anita laughed and said it was true, she'd seen it, and even better than that, she'd spotted a red dog squatting on the other side of the fence, catching the arc of piss in its open mouth, bathing in it, rolling pearls of it down its spine. When Rainie said again that this was a lie—she'd never seen one of those dogs catch anything, and she'd thrown plenty of sticks and pebbles at them through that very fence—Anita shook her head and said, *You lack self-belief.* Rainie rolled this statement down her spine, but somehow it lodged itself, and even now, as Rainie walked past the fence yet again, she thought of what Anita said next: *Let's try it. Let's try being the boy and the fence and the dog.* Rainie asked which she was supposed to be, and Anita said, *You choose.* It felt like a test, so Rainie said she would be the boy, since he had amazed Anita first, delighting her with his ability to pierce the fence and stitch himself into it. She was relieved when Anita seemed pleased by this answer. *Try it,* Anita said, but when Rainie pressed the whole front of her body to the chain-link fence, which was neon-hot as a grill, she found that she had nothing to fit inside the holes of the fence except her fists, her wrists. Anita observed her posture, walking around her a few times, then tapped her own nose and said, *You need a boner first. That's what you need.*

As Anita continued to pace behind Rainie, stepping on her shadow until it was ragged, Rainie finally asked what a boner was and how to become one. *You don't become a boner, you own one*, Anita said, standing directly behind her. *Or is it that you carry one? I forget.* Rainie turned her face so that her other cheek hissed against the fence, bearing its share of the heat. She imagined herself patterned now, like those mottled dogs in the lot beyond her, who had no word for ownership, who craved it all the same. Until Anita released her, Rainie thought, she would not move. *Okay*, Anita said, *since we don't have a bone between our legs like raccoons do*—she'd once found a severed raccoon tail beneath a parked car, and inside its sleeve of fur was a bone, broken in several places and knuckled like a finger—*we will just have our shadows act it out.*

Standing beside Rainie, her legs a stray's length apart, Anita pressed her heels into the concrete and faced the fence. To her left, her shadow slanted across the sidewalk, slashing it in half. *Copy me*, Anita said, and extended her hand as if she was going to shake someone else's. She lowered her hand so that it seemed like a stalk jutting from her crotch, her fingers nudging through the hole in the fence. When Rainie glanced down, she saw that Anita had limbed her shadow, amending the body written on concrete. *See*, Anita said. *If you just looked at my shadow, you wouldn't even know that's my hand. I could call it anything.* Rainie, despite her instinct to dispute everything, couldn't help but agree. If you considered only the pavement, you might think Anita owned a beak instead of a crotch, that her three-dimensional body matched her shadow's flat anatomy. Later, Anita would use this as so-called proof that she could invent anything. For now, Rainie opened her mouth in wonder. For now, Rainie was not sick of Anita staring down at her shadow when they walked on the street or the sidewalk, hooking her fingers behind Rainie's ears to impersonate horns, or instructing her to lift her skirt so that their shadow could have wings, despite the risk of attracting perverts.

But when Anita's fingers pushed deeper into the fence, the dogs woke. Their tails snapped up like antennae, tuned in to the sky's bad mood. Rainie grabbed Anita's wrist and pulled her back. Dragging her home by the elbow, Rainie ignored Anita's protests about how she wasn't ready to leave, how she hadn't even finished peeing yet. *You know you couldn't actually have peed through that fence,* Rainie said, *unless your fingers are faucets and your palms are bladders.* Anita studied her hands so closely that Rainie regretted saying this, and when they were home, Anita asked if her palms could be bladders, or storage containers for prayers. *All skin is just a bottle,* Anita said, *so what can't I contain?*

Rainie reminisced on all this, as she was prone to do. Anita is action, Rainie is reflection, Rainie thought, though she knew Anita would snort at this and say, *What's the difference? Why sort us?* But Rainie had been doing it since she was a toddler in the seafood section, and it was difficult for her to stop. Giving up on the grocery store, she circled the lot three times each and then went home, counting the sidewalk cracks and crossing them out with her feet. At home, Rainie told her mother it had looked like it was going to rain, so she decided to turn back. Her mother didn't say anything about how it was clearly not going to rain, as it had not rained in years and the TV was contemplating the possibility of importing clouds. Rainie had no excuse for returning with empty hands, except that every time she neared the sycamore, no matter if she was walking sideways or forward, its shadow always seeped into her mind and redirected her intentions.

That night on the middle bunk of her bed, Rainie looked up at the slats of the top bunk where her brother slept, his toes tapping on the end of the bedframe like the percussion of rain. For as long as Rainie had lived here, she remembered only one rain. It had happened when she was very little. She felt no affinity for the wet, and though her mother said it was a relief to finally have rain after centuries of drought, Rainie threaded her head through the doorway and immediately retracted it: The rain was mouth-warm, and it felt like being relentlessly pelted by her brothers' spit, except the sky had no forearm she could bite in retaliation. But what she remembered best was the aftermath of the rain.

The next day, she and Anita stomped through the gutters and plucked earthworms, writhing like intestines, off the silver pavement. The sidewalk was veined with golden water, everywhere a mottled mirror. There was one puddle near the lot that was deep as a sleeve, wide as their torsos, and when they kneeled and reached their arms into it, they couldn't feel a bottom.

The puddle was so bright that Rainie believed she could pocket it like a penny. But Anita warned her not to remove it. *I'll investigate further*, Anita said, slipping her leg into the puddle's mouth, and it swallowed her to the socket. When Rainie asked her how it was possible, since there had never been a meteor crater here, no explanation for why the water gathered here so endlessly, Anita said it was clearly a portal. Something was waiting to emerge, to breach the skin of this sea. She made Rainie wait with her under the sycamore tree, and when it was afternoon, the puddle alert as an eye, Anita dragged her over to the water and pointed down.

When they looked in—even now, Rainie wondered if this

was some prank of the rain—they saw the faces of dogs. Rainie turned her head to catch the dogs craning over them, but they were not there. They existed only inside the sidewalk, their faces surfacing in the puddle. Their fur was patchy from years of licking one another roughly, and their ears were perfect corners. Water dribbled from their chins, a miniature rain. The skin of the puddle shivered, though Rainie was not stepping in it at all, despite her desire to smear those faces away, to turn from whatever fate was revealed. Anita didn't seem startled at all to see those dogs and instead wrapped her hand around Rainie's elbow and tugged her gently, as if to give them some privacy. As they backed away, their heels numb against the sidewalk, the surface of the puddle vibrated like a drum skin, and a paw punctured the membrane, then several paws, then dozens of paws, dogs bursting out of the water, a whole pack of them, streaming out onto the sidewalk, shaking out their fur like capes, water spattering everywhere. They nosed at the chain-link fence or lunged down the street. The pavement beneath Rainie's feet vibrated for miles, bruising her soles, and she resisted the urge to run toward the sycamore and climb its branches.

Anita stood her ground. *There are more about to be born*, she said. Kneeling, she pressed her palms to the ground and memorized the rhythm of the dogs as they ran along the underside of the pavement and gushed from the hole, hundreds more. Their paws clapped against Anita's feet through the concrete, meeting in applause, while Rainie felt them muffled, a distant stampede. Rainwater surged up from the puddle, cresting over them as the dogs geysered out.

The next day, when the world was once again crowded with overlapping droughts, the dogs gathered in the lot, bathing in saliva instead of rain. That was the beginning of their kinship with the strays. Rainie asked what the dogs were doing inside concrete in the first place, and Anita said it wasn't their choice to fossilize. They had to wait for the rain to make a door, for this world to grow pores.

A Dialogue Between Two Daughters

ANITA: Inside the lot, there are thousands of fossils. That's why the dogs spend their days there. They're sleeping on top of treasure.

RAINIE: The soil isn't deep enough for there to be actual fossils. Though sometimes . . .

ANITA: Sometimes what?

RAINIE: Sometimes I do look back at the sycamore and see a skeleton, a woman with her skin ripped clean off.

ANITA (crouching at the foot of the fence and picking something up): Aha. Look! A hollow bone. The femur of a phoenix.

RAINIE: That's a spork. A phoenix has red feathers, a long tail.

ANITA: Well, the feathers have all decomposed a long time ago—don't you know how a body goes?

RAINIE: That's not how it goes. Birds do not become utensils.

ANITA: If we were buried here, what do you think would be left of us?

RAINIE: We're too shallow to be buried here. I mean, the soil is.

ANITA: I think I'll decompose in my own order, an order I'll decide. It will be my bones and teeth first, all my hardest parts, and then my organs, largest to smallest, and then my tongue and hair and eyeballs, and then my skin, I'm going to rot from the inside out. Not the outside in. When they dig me up, all that will be left is what I think, what I dream.

RAINIE: You don't get to decide the order. The dirt does. It will catalog you completely.

ANITA: Not completely. Look at these jawbones I found. Who do you think they belonged to?

RAINIE: Those are soda-can tabs.

ANITA: Why can't you just imagine?

RAINIE: Why can't you be ashamed?

ANITA: It's your turn to find a fossil and bring it to me. I brought all of these to you already.

RAINIE: The only thing I can think of is the tree. But it's living, lunging out of the skin like a broken bone, and I don't think I can bring it to you.

ANITA: You're like a dog looking up at the moon, looking at that tree. So much longing.

RAINIE: Longing isn't enough to bring me to you.

Anita Senses an Impending Severance

It's been July for almost a century, a summer that dries our tongues into jerky, and I still wait by Rainie's window every morning, mushing my lips against the glass, leaving behind a slime that can only be loosened by the juice of limes.

All week I've been telling Rainie about my idea to rot in reverse order, starting from hard to soft, leaving behind my organs like almost-ripe fruit, but she says nothing, her eyes always avoiding the sycamore, trying to catch it slipping out of shape. Rainie doesn't understand that the sycamore doesn't just get naked for anyone, not when you aren't willing to do the same. I think Rainie wishes she could be hair everywhere, showing no skin at all, furry like the strays.

All day and night I spy on the sycamore, which I suspect is the secret and true home of the strays. In the day, the strays lounge around the lot and lick themselves into blades. Occasionally, when it rains, they return to the underside of the pavement, running the world below our soles. But at night, when all illusions dissolve, their heads soften and ripen into melons, heavy as women's skulls. They speak like women too, gossiping underneath the sycamore, the moonlight strained through the branches into a fine flour, and then the dogs retreat together, entering the sycamore at its base, squeezing through a slit the size of my thumb. The slit is typically furred by bees and wasps, stitched shut by wings, but they scatter for the dogs. One by one, the dogs nose their way into the tree, sipped by its straw into an invisible mouth. They dream inside the tree, braiding their veins through its trunk, giving blood to the roots. I know the dogs are widows, because they don't have husbands to call them home or make them stay put or tell them not to talk so long. They are unaccounted for and lick no one but themselves. I know they have done their duty and are now free.

Rainie doesn't hear the dogs talking with widows' tongues, or if she does, she pretends not to. She says, *Some things we're not meant to listen to; some languages are locked out of us.* But I hear the dogs talk through the cracks on the sidewalk and through the neighbors' open windows, through that slit in the base of the sycamore that looks like my own opening, and they tell me that they call themselves widows not because they were once married to human men but because they were once dogs. Widows are named for their losses, for what they're without, and the dogs beneath the sycamore say the same thing: *We were once another species, born from the bellies of mountaindogs, and because we can no longer return, we have been widowed from our bodies.*

Beneath the sycamore, where Rainie refuses to look, the dogs sing this prophecy to me:

Rainie will move away at the end of this summer, the same summer there's a wildfire that swats down all the houses in the hills and geckos slimy as tongues enter your lips at night and drop their tails in your mouth, plunging your throat until you choke. Rainie knows that she is moving away at the end of the summer, but she doesn't know how to tell you.

I tell the dead that what they say might be true, but I'll keep Rainie in my mouth if I have to. They howl inside the trunk of the tree, threatening me. Their widow-tongues retract in the mornings.

Rainie and I are not fully dogs yet. All summer we wait for the dogs to give us instructions, but they pretend not to speak. I still press my tongue to Rainie's window, hoping to keep her at bay, framing her in glass. She laughs but turns her head away. I still wear a red thread around my neck even though Abu says I'm outgrowing it and my neck is thickening into a trunk and one night the thread will strangle me in my sleep.

According to the dogs, Rainie will move away without telling me, but I hear her mother through the walls that are supposed to be soundproof, and I can hear them wrapping their bowls in newspaper. With my mouth roving the wall, I say to Rainie: *Stay and let's be bitches forever, let's eat a dozen plums as our litter. Stay and I won't make you eat sand anymore. Stay and Vivian's boyfriend, Mr. McDonald's, will let us eat his French fries, which we shove up each other's nostrils, dipping for boogers, because fries taste best that way, okay?* But Rainie doesn't answer or knock on the wall, and the door to the garage where we used to lie on the concrete to get cool is now bricked up with cinder blocks because Abu is afraid I'll drown myself in pesticide or choke to death on the dark.

———

Vivian's boyfriend doesn't take us to McDonald's anymore, but we do get his car. We find out Vivian is pregnant and that he owes Vivian some money, a skeleton for the baby, and three thousand years of apologies. Abu and Vivian went together to his apartment building's parking lot and waited three hours in a heat wave for him to come out, at which point they charged him with such rhinoceros-like aggression that he leapt into a dumpster. Then, while he was wrestling with garbage, Vivian and Abu drove his car away, Abu in the driver's seat, Vivian in the back so she could lie down. He owns two car washes, so his car is always as shiny as his forehead, and I could see them approaching from miles away. The dogs could too. They chased after the car, cackling as Abu circled the block a dozen times, accelerating past our house.

The car is dark green like horseshit and soft-looking, and the driver's side window only rolls down halfway, but the seats are slick and spotless. Vivian and I sit on the hood together and fry the backs of our thighs. We sit in the back seat with the windows rolled down and stick our heads out like dogs. One of us is the dog and one has to play the wind, blowing on the other's tongue so that it flaps a little like we're on the freeway.

I never see Mr. McDonald's again, but I tell Rainie that he must be a little good because he used to drive his dog around in the backseat of his car, and the dog was good. But Abu always says, *Did that dog have a name? Did he ever call it anything?* And I say no. Abu says, *See, there you go, that's how you know. What kind of man doesn't call his dog anything?* But I think maybe Mr. McDonald's didn't name the dog because that way it was free, all loyalty was voluntary, it didn't have anything to be summoned with. I think maybe it was a kind of mercy. But Abu disagrees with me and says I don't understand dogs. She also says my problem is that I forgive. *Forgiveness will show people you're boneless, and when you're boneless, people will think it's too easy to eat you.*

When Rainie leaves at the end of that summer, I don't remember her last name. It disappeared one night in a dream, growing wings. The red thread I tied around her neck must have replaced her original bloodline with my own, confusing our fates. Maybe we share a last name now. But Abu can't tell me for sure, can't remember Rainie's name either, and I don't forgive this.

The rumor around the neighborhood later is that when my cousin Vivian gave birth, the first thing she said to the baby was, *I forgive you, I forgive you,* though some of us couldn't figure out what the baby had committed, what crime in its past life had been pardoned by Vivian's existence. Vivian's baby will have tardy teeth, like all the dogs and dog-women and women before her. They won't grow in for years, the baby's gums all sloppy, and so we have to chew up its food and spit the mince directly into its mouth, and sometimes Abu massages its gums with her thumbs until finally a set of fins breaches the pink, though for a long time the baby forgets it has any and still gapes during mealtimes, swallowing the fine silt from our mouths and forgiving us later for all we fed her.

The Neighborhood Bitches (Bitches, Both Figurative and Literal) Narrate What Is Troubling Them, and Bunk Beds Are Ripe for Intimacy and Trickery

We are the bitches under the sycamore tree. Don't mistake us for strays, those dogs who don't have names, though that is how we appear in the day. We have names. At night, we lug around our human heads, carrying them low to the ground, searching for puddles to peer into like mirrors. So that we may be reminded: We were once women born from dogs. We straddle several species, and we can speak as many. For example, we are the widow Lin, who used to grow plums too hard for any of our teeth, but whose fruit could at least be salted and pickled and gemmed inside glasses of soda. We are the one who got hit by a car on the freeway at night, though why she was walking along a highway at night is a mystery to all of us. She used to spread out her underthings in front of the whole damn neighborhood. One week it was all bras. Another week it was all her underwear, beached on blankets like sunning birds. Some of us lifted our heads to the sky as if the underwear would launch into flight, a migrating flock. But she's dead now, the widow Lin or Lam or whatever it was, and her plum tree was cut down by the city, though we plucked it bare before the chainsaw could get there, not because we loved the plums so much, hard and green and sometimes more pit than flesh, but because we thought she'd want us to do that, to pluck the tree bald before all the plums were wasted in a wood chipper. And some of us buried the plums out of a sense of ceremony, plums in place of her body, and we wondered why she was walking along the freeway that night. If she did it every night, if she wandered the way we do now, if she was going to meet someone, but who, and was she wearing any underwear? No shame.

We swim in the thickest cut of shade under the sycamore, smoking a cigarette each, slobbering like the dogs we are. Dogs can see the dead—we come from generations of canines, so we know their ways, we still use our hind legs—and they aren't as interested in the living as you think. And we see the two girls, Anita Hsia and Rainie Tsai, red threads knotted at the plum of their throats, sitting together on the blanched roots of the sycamore, and we know after this summer they will never see each other again, not as daughters and dogs, and that only one of them knows this, the smarter one, Rainie, though both their mothers are fools, naming their daughters after singers, one of whom died early, and we know exactly the kind of woman who names her daughter in front of a TV screen or while dancing in the dark to nothing, and Rainie at least is better at belonging to her loneliness, inhabiting it like a house, ornamenting it with narratives of how she came to live inside it, her mother at work, her brothers out all night snipping the ears off dogs, her best friend belonging to a sycamore tree.

Anita is the one telling a ghost story. She is the kind of girl who grows up to be gone, so we watch her. We tug the thread around her neck and walk her home when we see her on the streets; we gift her fistfuls of salted plums, we plunge her mouth with a seed. Anita is telling Rainie about banana ghosts, the women who live in banana trees, and how dangerous it is to be sitting on the roots of something living like this. We know about ghosts: We were born in the belly of belief. Hair the color of scabbed blood, skin layered like a sea, eyes with the pupils broken like yolks and scrambled into the whites. Thorns instead of thumbs. They roost in the trees and eat unripe fruit and leave the rinds at the foot of our beds, glistening with the slime of their spit. Our mothers always said that banana ghosts only wanted to be free, but we asked why they couldn't just climb down the tree, why they perched in the branches, swathing themselves in shadow. And our mothers said, *Be careful, they are beautiful, despite the whisked yolks of their eyes, and the men, your brothers and fathers and uncles, have knotted a red thread around the trunk of the banana tree, tying the other end to the foot of their beds.* They plunge needles into the sponge of the trunk, burn the bark off with acid, and the banana ghosts are coaxed out by pain, descending from the branches, licking the rubies of their burned bodies, begging for the men to cut the red thread and set them free from their bruised trees. *In return for setting us free,* the banana ghosts say, *we will give you anything—the winning lottery numbers, the name of the dog that will win the next fight, land of your own, women—and when your wish has been granted, snip the thread around our trunks, retract the needles from our tree-meat. We will be grateful to you for letting us off our leash.*

But most often the men harvest their wishes and still do not sever the red string tied around the tree, and so the banana ghosts are trapped with no recourse, knotted and bound. They dream of the men's deaths, deaths that are worse than the widow Lam's, worse than the story of the boy who flew his kite into power lines and got electrocuted—whose son was he?—and the cursed men die the kind of death that involves entire skies, six days of rain made of nails, or they die in ways that don't refrain from shame, like an uncle who had a dream he was making love to a woman like a banana, skinning her with his mouth, readying for the first light-filled bite, except that it was a dream authored by a banana ghost, laid over his eyes like leaves, and in his sleep he bit off his own tongue. It slid down his throat and he died choking on its sweet.

We watch what Rainie thinks of this story, if she flees from the roots of the sycamore tree and doesn't return, afraid of what roosts in its branches, or if she's a girl like Anita, who needled her nails into the trunk of the nearest tree when she first heard this story, attempting to torture out the woman who lived inside it. But Rainie neither wounds the tree, drawing the sap out for the flies to thieve, nor does she flee: We should've known she was the kind of girl who looks at a ghost the way other people see electricity, as a necessity that costs too much, as one of many sources of light, as a way for the house to see clearly who lives inside its belly. She is not the kind of girl to go home and fetch thread, as girls like Anita would do, eager to wrangle a tree and shake it until a woman falls from its branches like a peach and begs to be freed. Rainie is unlike the foolish Anita. Anita, who will wear the thread around her neck until it is snipped away by years of scissor-like sunlight and someday by her own mother, who is afraid Anita will choke to death. (She is the kind of woman that tells her daughter not to wear necklaces to bed, because the chain will cinch like fingers around your neck and snap it, and for what, all because you wanted to wear something pretty to bed, but for whom, a man? No boys in your bed.)

We know now that that family is full of fools, Anita and her mother and that cousin. We all believe secretly that Rainie is right to leave, that she is right to stand in front of the sink the week before she moves, the red-yarn collar between her fingers, frayed from the friction, weakened by her sweat. She will cut it with a pair of bloodied scissors from the kitchen, and we all think it is only safe that the string is surrendered to the sink, water swatting it toward the drain, and that is the gravity of all things, leaving: The direction of all life is toward loss, and it is better for Rainie to know it now, to boil this truth to its bones, because a girl like Anita will never believe it. She would never let a banana ghost go, not because she lacks mercy but because she has fallen in love with the woman she's tricked down from the tree and believes that serenading some-one with string is a kind of love. She is a girl who believes that captivity is a condition of caring, and that is why she leashes dragonflies to her pinky fingers with string, until she inevitably tugs too hard and disintegrates the torso, and also why she traps geckos, even though her mother tells her not to, because geckos in the house are a sign of arriving wealth, and slips each one into her pocket and accidentally sits on it, staining the sofa with shimmering innards, a sin for which she is beaten. She takes a beating as land takes rain: with a sense of deep relief, a sense that she is being gifted by something too good, too divine. The problem must be with her, though we sympathized when she cried over the first gecko, sympathized when she waited hours in the heat for the banana ghost to appear, though she'd lassoed a sycamore tree, and we do not believe ghosts roost in sycamores, because there is nothing sweet about them, and even in death, ghosts seek sweetness, seek the shape of bananas, which they make love to and which accounts for the moaning produced by most trees at night.

And we know Anita would disagree with our phallic interpretation, though she too has holstered a banana in her underwear and walked through her house shirtless, pretending the banana is her erect penis, and when her mother catches her cupping it through her underwear, she is beaten and the penis splatters across her crotch, smashes into her pubic hair, so that in the shower later she scrubs harder than usual, and even then there are still shrapnel-bits of banana meat somewhere inside her, which she fears will impregnate her with a giant banana that will roll around inside her and rupture her organs, and she thinks, How can this be, how can pretending to be a boy be the thing that kills me, when my abu says being a girl is the fatal sentence? Which one? How many times can I die, how many bodies can I be exiled from? Her mother says, *I am preparing you for a world that will hurt you,* and Anita says, *I am preparing to eat this banana. I was just warming it up, the way you fry bananas in your pan, you see?* Her mother does not believe her, and neither do we, and we pray that she stays away from all phallic fruits in her future, that she someday learns the truth of trees and discards her banana dreams. Don't forget: A tree without fruit is good only for firewood. A daughter who doesn't bear children must burn.

Anita believes this is too dramatic. She says, *Actually, the body is mostly water. It can't burn.*

What about cremation? her abu says.

Well, Anita says, in a tone she believes reasonable, *don't drink water before you die. That way you'll be nice and crispy-dry. And also, remember to pee beforehand and afterward. Then you'll burn easy.*

Always we were taught: It's not a real story unless it begins *before you were born.* We cannot blame Anita for the circumstances of her conception and birth, and therefore we urge forgiveness of her hungers. We all know the story of before-Anita: Her mother, FeiFei, was born on the underside of an island and worked at a pearl factory in the island's largest and northernmost city, where it was her job to jimmy the knife between the oyster's lips and crack open the shells, extracting the farmed pearls.

FeiFei chose pearls over men. She loved loosening the oysters from their tanks, liking knocking the molars out of a mouth, and she loved the crack of the oyster as it opened, the gasping meat like a tongue seeking speech. Some of the pearls were mutant, double-headed or deposited in the shape of droppings, pearls like caved-in skulls. At the factory dormitory, FeiFei lived in a bunk between two other women, the one on top being a former fisherwoman turned aspiring garment designer, who described her idea of making lingerie out of fishnets, which FeiFei pretended not to hear, and a woman on the bottom bunk who was born to the mountains, like her.

The bottom-bunk woman never told FeiFei her real name, no matter how many times FeiFei asked, no matter how many times FeiFei offered her own, a name in a language she never

learned to speak. A name she'd never really used, having chosen *FeiFei* at the age of three. She didn't know the name of her
tribe, which had been intercepted midair, snatched like a bird
before it could land on anyone's tongue, and which was finally
and fatally dropped by the generation before her. Still, FeiFei
mouthed her name, wanting the bottom-bunk woman to be
the sole receiver of this sound.

The bottom-bunk woman possessed several unusual traits
that FeiFei never knew how to ask about, how to casually
bracket this bodily inquiry, shelving it in the space between
their bunks: For example, she had a single streak of red hair
that ran down the back of her scalp like a seam, and when she
wrung out her waist-length hair in the sink, it bulged like a
vein. FeiFei could not stop staring at it, wondering if it was
dyed or if it grew that way naturally, if it clotted in her sleep.
The strands were not true red, closer to rust than blood, but it
was brighter in the dark and throbbed with fluid, as if FeiFei
could thread it into her mouth and sip up the contents of the
bottom-bunk woman's skull. She was disturbed by her own
thoughts, and yet the red thread in the woman's hair continued to haunt her. She began to invent its properties: conduc-
tive of heat and electricity, capable of replacing an artery or
binding their two bodies together.

Besides this rusted streak in the woman's hair, FeiFei observed at the communal sink that she wore dentures, but only
on her bottom row. Standing behind the bottom-bunk woman
in line, she'd noticed a mosquito land on the woman's shoulder and reached out to slap it dead. The bottom-bunk woman,
misinterpreting this gesture, whipped around and opened her
mouth, perhaps to ask FeiFei what exactly she wanted, perhaps only to startle her with this uncanny sight: The top row

of her teeth was saw-bright and entirely without fillings, which FeiFei envied, given her own riddled history, but the bottom row was blank, absent of any teeth. For a second, FeiFei wanted to slot her head into the woman's mouth, crowning herself with that top row of teeth, but all she did was take a step back, her heels jostling the layer of flooded water that lined the dorm floor, her tongue feeling as pruned as her toes. She shriveled before that mouth, shrank from the bottom-bunk woman's silence, her gaze a challenge. FeiFei said nothing that night, but she later heard the top-bunk woman whisper that the bottom-bunk woman wore dentures she made herself from the teeth of an ox, cliffs of calcium. *Have you ever seen that woman open her mouth?* The top-bunk woman said. *No? Well, that's because the bitch's bottom teeth are as big as a cow's. You know the reason why she doesn't talk? It's because her cow-teeth will fly out of her mouth and smack you in the face.*

Didn't you say the dentures were made from an ox? FeiFei asked. *An ox is different from a cow.*

Shut up, the top-bunk woman said, spitting into the sink, which did not drain, allowing everyone's spit to churn together and solidify into a jellyfish with infinite limbs. *Of course you country girls know the difference between an ox and a cow. I don't know that sort of thing,* the top-bunk woman said, and FeiFei almost laughed in disbelief. She was as dirt-born as the rest of them.

Still, FeiFei continued to stand behind the bottom-bunk woman when they lined up for the sink, though she never again swatted a mosquito from her shoulder, even when she saw one grow ripe as a ruby, so fat with blood it couldn't fly. She wanted the bottom-bunk woman to turn around and reveal the two halves of her mouth again, the glowing row and the rind of ghosts.

At night, in her middle bunk, slotted between so many women, she experienced her only loneliness, floating in the moat of other people's sleep. It was then that she imagined a conversation with the bottom-bunk woman. If only she'd slapped another mosquito, found a way to face her:

How did you lose your teeth? And only the bottom ones? FeiFei would ask.

I fell off a roof when I was a kid. I was playing on it. There were grapes growing all over it, planted by my grandmother on an arbor. I fell and broke one leg and lost my teeth. My adult ones had just grown in, and I was so proud. I had them for so little time. The next day, I gathered the shards of them and buried them in the yard, dragging my splinted leg behind me. But it was raining, so I couldn't find all the pieces. I hoped that my teeth would grow back in crop rows.

Because FeiFei could not imagine the bottom-bunk woman's voice, she imagined her own:

And who made those dentures for you?

I made them myself. Well, I gathered the teeth, and we brought them to a denture-maker. The first time I went to the denture-maker, she asked me for teeth, and I said I didn't have any. She said she only made dentures from the teeth of corpses. Because I didn't own a corpse, I went home to pray for someone close to me to die, preferably a neighbor so I wouldn't have to walk far, but the only thing that happened was that a girl almost drowned in a rain-roused river, except her toes turned into tadpoles and tugged her to shore. I was very disappointed. But luckily I saw a dead ox one day, dragged away from the fields. The oxen are worked to death, and when they die, they can't even be eaten. They're worked till their tendons are thin as strings and all their bones touch. Luckily, I didn't need the meat. I broke the teeth out of its mouth. I put them in my pocket, and they jingled a song while I walked home. Later, everyone told me those teeth were too big. They would never fit my mouth. And I had my top row, and that was all I really needed. Some people have none. But then, look, see, they do fit. Somehow, in my mouth, they do fit. I must have a gigantic mouth. Do you think so? It looks normal from far away, though, right? You wouldn't know unless I said I had the teeth of an ox. Or maybe it was a very small ox. Or maybe the denture-maker carved the teeth down to my size. It worked out, didn't it? The only thing is, when I have its teeth in my mouth, I carry its memories. I feel the bones of my knees nipped by flies, my eyes pecked out, whippings, dirt displaced by my hooves, endless dirt—I envy its wetness, my tongue dry on both sides. I know the moment of death. I know exhaustion that no human can know. The kind of exhaustion an ox feels, it can't be described. It lies far past language. It's a birthright. It lives in my mouth, bludgeons my every bone, and it's a relief when I sleep and I put my dentures under my pillow and I know no one will steal them, not even as a prank, because they're afraid to touch ugly. Even though I broke the ground they grew from.

The bottom-bunk woman never spoke to anyone, not even when the top-bunk woman described the men she was fucking, men from the city, from the military base, one of them blond with freckles on his ass, freckles even in the cracks of his ass, can you believe, like sand had been scattered there, and sometimes when he was on top of her, she liked to slide her fingers between his ass cheeks and pretend to scrape the freckles out, as if she were scouring sand from his skin, and that's what she was best at, scouring, sanding irregular shapes into symmetry, spheres perfect as the idea of planets, and isn't that why women are drawn to pearls, because it evokes the fantasy of owning an entire world? The top-bunk woman said this in the boss's accent, mimicking the way he explained pearls in the showroom, where women bought brooches so heavy on their breasts that their skin beneath was bruised. (Only on the underside of the island were pearls capable of being shaped, whereas pearls on the topside of the island were predestined, tooth-hard. It was because the species of oyster farmed on the underside had been exposed to years of pollution from a leaking warship wrecked by the topside, and as a result the pearls were born unusually soft, some as viscous as balls of spit or snot, and all of them were capable of being carved, shaped, and solidified into new forms.)

The bottom-bunk woman was the only one who never laughed about the story of the sand-assed man, and later, when FeiFei was in California, she would think maybe that woman, still nameless like a god, saw something lonely beneath the surface of those stories.

When FeiFei finally heard the bottom-bunk woman speak, it was not in the factory but in the showroom, one night when the woman who usually maintained and mopped the floors was sick, which all the women knew just meant she was visiting her mother in a building at the center of the city where women are drugged like horses after doing things like biting off their husband's penis or dropping their babies out of windows. The factory showroom was twin-roomed, one carpeted in red, brimming with glass counters where tourists could point at necklaces displayed on velvet-coated mannequin heads—necklaces that catered to the space between your breasts, necklaces with pearls clustered like mosquito eggs, necklaces so heavy you couldn't lift your head while wearing one, forcing everyone else to bend to address you—pearl earrings that hung on strands of silver fine as spittle, near invisible, and even a tiara, pearls bulging like blisters beneath the showroom lights, as if they might burst open beneath a touch, spraying seawater. That was what pearls were, blisters, jewels forged by friction, and FeiFei didn't like the showroom, the light thrown into her eyes like sand, and she hated even more the second room, kept dim, full of tanks with farmed oysters inside, pulsing like exposed hearts.

The boss liked to bring tour groups here, showing them how oysters were farmed, inviting them to reach into the tanks, which glowed blue like the rim around the moon. It was the job of the tour guide to present two velvet mats: one plating a whole oyster, the other cuddling two pearls, one fake and one real. *Guess which one is fake and which is real,* the tour guide would say, placing them both in the outstretched palm of a stranger. When they were unable to tell which, the tour guide would scrape a small knife against the surface of each, showing that the surface of the fake one was smooth glass, while the real pearl produced a kind of dander, an iridescent dust. FeiFei disdained the knife trick: *Just use your teeth to feel its grit,* she wanted to say. *If you want to understand the reality of something, bite into it.* Then the tour guide would move on to the second mat, containing the oyster, and always the women gasped and flinched when they felt the slime of those shells. FeiFei hated to see those oysters petted for play. She slaughtered them, pried them open to the air, but FeiFei always believed they were hers to hurt, that they knew her when she slit her knife along their seams. They spoke her name by gasping, the way her mother could no longer say the names of her daughters, addressing them only with wordless wheezes.

That day while mopping up the slogged water, FeiFei saw the bottom-bunk woman leading a tour, walking backward through the dim aquarium room, the dark parting around them as she said, *And here we have the oysters. The glass in these tanks is magnified so that you can see them better—they're now three times larger than life size.* FeiFei dropped her mop. The bottom-bunk woman did not turn her head to FeiFei, did not acknowledge the sound of the dropped mop, and then the tour group was gone, the women with their hair mountained on top of their heads, their clothes the kind of white that existed nowhere in nature, white like exposed bone, like the time FeiFei's knife slipped from her fingers and skinned her knuckles.

That night in their dorm room, the woman on the top bunk was writhing in her sleep, having contracted a breed of insects that nested in her pubic hair. FeiFei reached up to punch the mattress.

Do that again and I'll piss on this mattress and you'll be drinking it all night, the top-bunk woman said. *Don't you know I'm suffering up here?* All night, the bottom-bunk woman had not returned, and FeiFei remembered the sound of her voice, low in the vowels, tilting higher at the end of a sentence, the quality of a question, a voice that contradicted itself, that begged to be contested. FeiFei thought of the woman's throat, how badly she'd wanted to stroke it, to pet it with the back of her knuckles the way you would a bird.

The top-bunk woman began to beat her head against the wall, her hand in her underpants, the thudding, the dent in the wall in the morning, the blood along her hairline that would drip like a necklace all the way to her chest, her moaning, her saying, *I'll tear out all my pubic hair, let's see where those bugs will live now, good god,* the mattress twisting like a tendon. FeiFei lifted her feet and pushed at the woman's mattress, lifting it a few inches, and said, *What happened to the woman below us? Did she leave the dormitory?*

It happened sometimes when women got married. But the top-bunk woman stopped drumming her head against the wall and sat up on her mattress, laughing. The top-bunk woman said, *Oh, that cow woman? Can't you guess how she got that new job of hers? Tour guide? That ox was cleaning our toilets before.*

FeiFei lowered her legs, almost sitting up in her bunk but remembering not to beat her own head against the wooden frame. *What do you mean?*

They all knew what the top-bunk woman meant. FeiFei would learn later, in the hallway line to the bathroom, on the factory floor even though they weren't allowed to speak: rumors that the bottom-bunk woman was the boss's mistress, that he liked her salted fingertips, the syllables of her name so easily scattered like pearls.

FeiFei didn't believe these rumors, though the bottom-bunk woman moved out of the bottom bunk soon after. Every night FeiFei undressed in the heat, positioning the electric fan between her legs, muffling the buzz against herself, thinking of the woman that had slept beneath her for so many nights, how she'd never once hung her head over the ledge of her bunk and asked for the woman's name face-to-face, how afraid she'd been that the woman would speak in a language she recognized but could no longer speak. The fan hummed between her legs, stirring a heat in her that mounted to her mouth, a humming so sweet she bit into her own tongue to fetch its salt, savoring its ache. The perfected pain of a pearl. She broke the fan with the force of her squeezed thighs, and in the morning, when the women panted awake in a heat stiller than pudding, they slapped and bit one another, trying to find out who had shattered the fan.

After that, there was no fan, and the women slept light as knives, poised to wake at one another's necks, and one morning they woke not to the heat but to the sound of crying, a wail as forceful as a fist. In the bottom bunk, the one that was going to be assigned to a new girl that week, there was a baby with its eyes open, pupils that were glazed like grapes, and because FeiFei was the first one to rise and touch it, lifting it into the sweet swing of her arms, the other women told her she had to be the one to take it.

FeiFei never confirmed it, but we are the dogs of your dead, and we know that baby was the bottom-bunk woman's, the one who spoke only to those who paid her (very practical, some might admit), and with a woman like that as her incumbent mother, and a woman like FeiFei as her newly realized mother, what kind of girl was Anita going to be? (You might think us too judgmental. And what does that make you?)

FeiFei bribed someone at a hospital to say Anita was born there. She obtained a birth certificate that listed Anita's name, but we all know the truth of that girl. No wonder she trusts only the knot around her neck, no wonder she basks in being beaten, knowing what the rest of the neighborhood says about her, the stray, the girl who was bathed in a dormitory sink, the girl who could never pass as a pearl.

We watch the two girls squatting beneath a sycamore, clasping the shade around their shoulders like a cape, believing in stories where ghosts can speak, when we all know most ghosts refuse to, since their mouths are too occupied by their own hunger. (We are the exception.) And who are these daughters, these dogs, these girls who deviate from death? Rainie is the one we want to save, to scissor out and paste to the sky, and Anita is the one who tucks her thumb beneath the red thread knotted around her neck, who says to Rainie, *You are the man who tied a banana ghost to the foot of his bed; you are the one to free me.* But Rainie sees only a mere string between them, dyed by sweat and fraying already, and by now she is imagining an upright life. Good. She will graduate from doghood. What we don't tell Rainie, and what she learns later anyway, is that red string is not only for lassoing banana trees: There is an Undermoon Deity whose job it is to knot souls together with leashes of red thread.

Before we were born, the only things on this street were sycamore trees painted white with insecticide. Before we were going to be married, our mothers tied red threads around our fingers or wrists or ankles, reminding us of the Undermoon Deity, the one who looks at all loves like a loom, who ties us to those we are destined to meet, to be. Anita knows the story, and though she says the red thread she ties around Rainie's neck is for the purpose of being collared like dogs, she knows the meaning:

Pay attention. Once, there was a boy who met the Undermoon Deity on his way home through his city of sycamore trees. The Undermoon Deity tells the boy: *I will show you the girl you will someday marry.* He points to a girl threading through the trees, a girl wearing red, but the boy says to the Undermoon Deity, *I don't want a wife or a woman, I refuse to be knotted to anything,* and so he plucks a stone from the soil and throws it at the girl in disgust and disdain. He watches in satisfaction as she flees the scene, running far away, too scared to turn back. Years later, when the boy is a man and must be married, he is pleased with the matchmaker's selection. On the day of the wedding, his betrothed lifts her red veil and her face is the moon. It is almost perfect, except for the pearl ornamenting the skin above her left eye, shining like a glob of spittle. When he asks why she wears it, the woman says it's to hide a scar she's had almost all her life, from the night a boy among the sycamores slung a stone at her face. She lifts the pearl to reveal her scar. The boy is shocked. He thought he had run from his fate, but the very stone he threw to ward away the girl only served to show him: Their union was destiny. He thought he'd scared her away, but he had written his name on her face. Every one of his actions returned as an injury.

It is troubling, the red threads around their necks. At least Rainie is testing its tensile strength, is always thumbing the length of it, searching for the place it may someday fray. Rainie is the one who searches for exits and entrances, while Anita willingly knots herself to the nearest doorknob. It is troubling how well Anita loves these stories of being bound. From afar, the red around their necks looks like slit throats, a seam where their heads were stitched back on. Anita thinks the story is romantic, the banana ghost bound, the boy who married the woman he wounded, but the sweetness in these stories is curdled, soft with rot. Anita thinks not of the girl's blood, not of the banana ghost who begged for release, but how, in the end, the boy and the girl were reunited. As if the sum of the story was love, not the desire to be severed from each other, to be given a true choice. Not straining against the strings that jerk us into the hands of men and gods. That is how we know Anita is both of her mothers' daughter, the one gone missing and the one who searched for the bottom-bunk woman's name in everything she touched. Anita's now-mother, FeiFei, has always had the habit of scratching her nails against the trunk of the sycamore, trying to surface that bottom-bunk woman's name.

FeiFei feared that Anita would never cry, that somehow the bottom-bunk woman's silence was the symptom of sleeping on the bottom bunk and bearing all other women's weight. But look at the way Anita cries and shouts and protests now, with no sense of a word as currency, and look at the girl who listens, how cautious she is, how she receives every word believing she must someday return it. And so it's Rainie who goes home first, who says her mother will be home soon. She knows they'll start packing, and though she doesn't know why exactly they're leaving, she is relieved to leave behind the string around her neck.

Okay, Anita says. *Go home now.* We shake our heads. We should have known since the day of the banana sliding slimy down her pants. We should have known she believes in the divinity of her demands. We know what she will say next:

Like the boy in the story, I will strike you with a stone and scar you, Anita says to Rainie, *so you watch out. You can't flee me. You better sleep away from the windows. Before you leave, I will scar you, right here—right here,* she says, her fingers butterflying to her left eyebrow. *That's the only way,* she says, *I can make sure we'll meet again.*

The Beginning of Anita Hsia's
Unsupervised Excursions
into Dreaming

Something Abu says: If you go to bed with a red thread gripped in your fist, you will never get lost in your dreams. You will always have something to follow back into your body. *Can't you just follow the path of your tampon string?* I ask. (No, Abu says; thread is most effective.) But the problem is trying to grip a red thread: If it slips out of your sweaty palm, if you don't hold it tight enough, if it slides onto the bed or strays to the floor like a floating hair, you have nothing to tether your soul to your body. You can't knot the thread around your wrist or ankle or neck and go to bed that way, because a ghost might mistake it for a leash, and when you wake you will no longer belong to yourself. It has to be something you hold on to, something you can let go of.

There was a girl Abu knew once, though I think Abu invented her to terrify me. This girl got locked out of her body because she wandered off in a dream and did not return. For three weeks she was asleep in her mother's bed, and each of her sisters had to take turns wiping her ass and flipping her over so that sores would not scuttle all over her body like roaches. To keep her blood wheeling through her body, they had to roll her down a steep hill, over and over, tenderizing her flesh.

I wouldn't mind being rolled down a steep hill, I say. But Abu glares at me from the sofa and says, *I'm telling you this as a warning. It's possible to dream so deep, you never surface again.*

Is it really so bad to wander away? I ask Abu. *Why occupy something so confined as a body when you could occupy night?*

Abu stands up from the sofa and yanks me close by the hem of my shirt. She says if I ever try to swim away from the shore of my ordinary sleep, she will reel me back in and staple me to the sofa. Reaching up, she plucks out a strand of her hair, long as my leg, and tells me to grip it in my sleep.

You're the kind that gets lost easily and willingly, she says, *so hold on to me.*

Abu knows all kinds of things about dreaming, and depending on how you die, she can dream you back to living, as long as you can describe your wants, the corners of your thirst. She dreams for other people, who pay her to sleep on our sofa and dredge up their dead relative. The dead present a desire, something that is preventing them from moving on to their next bodies. They require satisfaction, and Abu is excellent at customer service. Abu says she learned to hire out her dreams after getting bitten by a rabid dog, who gifted her with rabies and an ability to commune with the dead, since dogs can see ghosts. The dog that bit her, she said, had been ruby-toothed and pregnant, and it must have sewn its ghost-communing ability into her veins instead of transferring it to its young. *That's the danger of biting strangers,* Abu says. *You never know what hereditary ability you will accidentally imbue the wound with.*

Abu has also inherited, very ironically, a chronic case of insomnia. Her sleep can be stretched into only two-hour-long pieces. At night I hear her gnawing the corners of the kitchen, running the sink, sewing closed that leak in the ceiling, and repeatedly slamming her head into the wall to induce unconsciousness. Because of her nighttime symphony, I wake up too, and now we both sleep for only a few hours at a time, briefly diving into our dreams before leaping out again like dolphins on TV, framed against the sky, dimples of light. We cannot submerge ourselves in sleep for too long before our lungs empty out and we have to toss ourselves off the bed, beaching on the ground while we breathe, storing air for our return journey. Abu says, *Technically, we are not the sick ones, because sleep actually used to be extinct.* This was back when people had no bones, when we were featureless as fish fillets. When sleep was extinct, it didn't matter whether it was night or day, you worked anyway, seeing by the light of a dangling fish eyeball, and this meant we had to eat twice as much, which strained the sea's capacity to produce edible species. Sleep was bred back into our bones when a group of parents discovered that it could cut childcare costs in half because it required no supervision: You could simply lay the semi-grown child out on a sheet of sand and pull the tide up to their chin and leave them alone for a full six to ten hours.

But it still has the possibility of going extinct, and many of us still carry sleep only as a recessive gene. *If enough of us disappear,* Abu says, *we could all be awake again until the end of the world.* But I don't know why she's afraid of that, because we already don't sleep and are therefore living the end of the world. Abu blames her mother's night shifts (*because she worked nights while she was pregnant with me,* Abu explains, *my eyes were formed feline and my bones became nocturnal*), and other times she blames the institution of marriage, which has since gone extinct in our lineage. *If there weren't husbands trying to shove themselves inside you the moment it's dark,* Abu says, *then maybe I wouldn't have been born with a sleep deficiency.*

The widow Hua comes to our house every evening, and Abu sends her away until it's her turn. Taped to the door, Abu keeps a schedule of her professional dreaming appointments: Tuesdays through Sundays, in the evenings, the paper is filled with names and time slots, during which Abu will invite the mourner in, ask for an object that the deceased had been wearing at the time of their death (this is for the theater of it; she doesn't actually do anything with the object, maybe recommend they pawn it, probably), and charge a hundred dollars up front, plus fifty dollars per additional hour after the first (cash only, please). Then she will dream for up to two hours at a time, and in her dreams the deceased arrive wearing turtlenecks and car wrecks and shark heads. The deceased come with their desires belted around their waist or carried in their palms. They will communicate through Abu, begging their living relatives to take care of their children or feed their ashes to the dog or remember to lock all the windows at night. Their desires are widespread and varied, and Abu hears and communicates them so that the souls of the dead will be at peace, reincarnating with a sense of closure. I KNOW WHAT GHOSTS WANT, she writes in glow-in-the-dark finger paint on our door. EXPERT IN THE FIELD OF BENEATH-CONSCIOUSNESS. I WILL DREAM YOUR DEAD AND THEY WILL TELL ME WHAT THEY WANT FROM YOU AND THEN THEIR SOUL WILL MOVE ON TO OTHER LIVES AND FIND PEACE OR ANOTHER SUFFERING. The rain has scraped at her words, and now these are the only words that are legible: I   WANT.   DREAM ME   TO   PEACE.

Our door god is an electronic Santa Claus that hula-hoops his hips when you press a button on his butt. He dances frantically, like his bones are fish, and says, *Ho ho ho ho ho ho.* When Abu watered him with her hose, his hips short-circuited and he bent at the knees in prayer, his song reversing: *Oh oh oh oh oh oh.* We've had other door gods before, gods made of butcher paper that we pasted on either side of the front door, gods in the form of hummingbird nests cupped to our doorway, gods in the form of mailmen who stood outside all day and slapped any visitors in the face. But electronic Santa is our favorite door god—whenever the women come to sign their name on Abu's door, Santa's beard frizzes with electricity and he swings his hips, zapping whoever comes too near, whoever tries to cross out the name of the woman before her to obtain an earlier slot.

That afternoon, under the flayed hide of the sky, Abu dreams of mushrooms. First, a field of cleavers. Her feet minced up as she walks. The farther into the field she goes, the shorter her legs become, until she's walking with only her hips, until she's walking on her elbows, until she's bouncing through the field on the bones of her jaw. The field ends at a river shaped like a smile, teeth-stones showing beneath the water, a sun made of boiling oil in the far-right corner of the dream. Abu is only her head. A flock of gulls lift the river like a wedding veil and drape it over her head. Wet, she wakes in a garden of trees, trunks so translucent that she can see the water snaking up their veins. The fruits are red, the red of your eyelids when you close your eyes in the sunlight, and Abu plucks one off a branch.

The red fruit is pock-skinned like a pomelo, and when Abu peels it—her body has regrown itself, and her thumbs have been replaced by screwdriver heads, which she uses to break the skin of the fruit—there is a mushroom inside its core, white and the texture of pith. The mushrooms proliferate like freckles at her feet, growing as soon as the sun touches the soil. Kneeling, Abu digs up the mushrooms with her bare hands, but they hatch faster than she can uproot them, and soon they are growing out of her pores, her nostrils, plugging even her throat, and then she is awake, gasping, her mouth full of spongy doorknobs, and I am beside her, kneading her chest with my hands.

In the kitchen, our client Tian Ayi waits for Abu's waking. Abu rises from the sofa and walks through the hanging shower curtain she uses to divide the kitchen from the dream room. The dream room is empty except for the sofa. No shrines, no TV, no interfering signals, no surveillance from any gods. In the kitchen, Abu sits down across from Tian Ayi, who is worrying her earlobe between her two fingers, rolling her pearl earring back and forth. *Your daughter,* Abu says, and Tian Ayi lets go of her earring, looks down into her tea as if there are fish frolicking on the surface of it, as if she is hungry to hook it out with her tongue. She licks the air for our words, tastes her own smoke. *Your daughter has been reincarnated into mushrooms,* Abu says. *She wants to be eaten by you. That is her request. She wants to live inside your body again, to grow in the dark of what loves her.*

Abu beckons me toward the table, and I hand her a square of butcher paper from the roll we keep by the door. She writes on both sides: instructions on how to consume a daughter mushroom without severing the thread of your soul and allowing it to flee you.

Directions:
- Obtain gloves (no latex or rubber—made of a kind of skin, if possible).
- Pick mushrooms only at night and only when the moon is bloodshot. If the moon's veins are all intact and invisible, wait.
- Boil mushrooms in a pot of pet piss. The piss must be from a domesticated animal that has never hunted for its food. Any species will do. The animal must be named a human name.
- Sun-dry mushrooms on your driveway. Dry until they are shriveled to about the size of your nipples.
- Eat in the presence of a photo or portrait of your daughter. Envision that your daughter is embedded inside the mushroom, cuddled in a bloodless embrace. Avoid thoughts of: your childhood, your marriage (past or present), mosquitoes or other insects, men.

When Tian Ayi leaves, her hands running circles around each other like mice, Abu shuts and locks the door and says she cannot sleep any more today. When she sleeps, it's always brief, even at night when she sleeps for nobody. In her dream room, which is now back to being our living room, we sit together and watch the walls. Abu always says that if we watch for long enough, our shadows will get restless and leave our bodies, walking across the walls without us, folding themselves into the shape of other families.

When I dream, it's of Rainie winding a red thread around and around her wrist, and in the center of my chest is a tug, the end of her thread woven through the loom of my ribs. She tugs. I follow the feeling, waiting for her fist to close around me. But as I'm reeled in, nearing and nearing her, I see that her hands are blades, that she is lifting them both at once, that if I don't wake up before I arrive at her wrists, I will be snipped loose from her forever.

Rainie Rears Against Red Thread
and Unwillingly Attends a Q&A
with the Strays

At night, Rainie woke to Anita whipping her kitchen window with a length of red thread. Cocking her head at the sound, she got up from the bottom bunk and crawled to the door, swinging it open. Anita lingered outside in the dark, holding an insecticide candle in one hand and a box of matches in the other, a stray red thread clenched between her teeth. *Yours is thinning,* Anita said, and Rainie touched her throat in response. In minutes, Rainie's red thread will have dissolved.

It disappears only sometimes, Rainie said. She knew it was because her mother weakened its presence, snipping it while she was asleep. *Red thread is fatal,* her mother said. *You don't know how many little girls die of strangulation in their sleep.* Rainie asked her mother, *How many?* but didn't receive a response. She suspected her mother harbored some personal grudge against red thread and wondered if she similarly hated the veins beneath her skin, but she decided not to ask. By the next morning, she knew, the thread would regrow itself, heal back into a loop. It was regenerative somehow, and Rainie suspected it was Anita's particular way of knotting, the flightiness of her fingers, that imbued the string with some living properties. Rainie didn't like the way it teethed into her skin, how the red thread turned soggy with her sweat, and she was tempted to snip it off herself whenever it grew back. But she remembered what Anita said, how it was the vein of a promise that would loop their lives together, and though she didn't believe it all the way, she knew that Anita's alternative methods of marking her would involve permanent injury, severe bleeding, and scarring.

Hurry, Anita said, *I think the dogs are nocturnal.* She lit the insecticide candle, and the flame was only the size of a pinky-tip, so weak and wavering it looked like a snip of water. *That's not enough light,* Rainie said, *and dogs are not nocturnal. That's cats, and some species of birds, and raccoons.* But Anita ignored her and tugged her out of the door. *Hurry up,* she said, punctuating the air with her finger, *while the light lasts!* Rainie pointed back at her and said, *You have an entire box of matches. And there are more candles in our garage. Also a flashlight. Why not just use a flashlight? Or the flood lamp your abu keeps because she read about how we're going to be underwater in twenty years and prays she'll be dead by then?*

Shut up, Anita said, and Rainie followed, the thread around her neck clasping her like a set of fingers, her blood tiding toward Anita. She wondered if somehow the threads were magnetized, or had once been braided together and then separated, or if she was just using it as an excuse to follow. To test this, she willed her feet to stutter on the pavement, trying to figure out if it was the thread that moved her first, if her legs were the first responders.

Stop bucking against me, Anita said, and Rainie touched her thinning thread, which was dissolving by the second into the dark. Ahead, Anita walked very slowly to prevent the flame from being extinguished, and Rainie laughed and said it would be easier to just walk in the dark. *This is an adventure,* Anita said, and continued to tiptoe toward the lot and the sycamore. *And this is our map,* Anita added, tossing something white and flimsy to her. Rainie opened it in her hands, unfolding its pleats before realizing it was a McDonald's napkin with the drawing of a dog-headed woman on it. *What's this?* Rainie asked, and Anita said it was a dream she once had, about a series of motherly dog-headed women (or was it woman-headed dogs?) with full teats and rivers tied in their hair like ribbons.

Don't you see them, Anita asked her, *clumped together under the sycamore tree, about to go inside to sleep? The dogs that call themselves widows? The ones that gossip and narrate everything like we're not there?*

But Rainie shook her head. *Dogs don't speak,* Rainie said, looking at Anita's heels as they slipped out of her shoes every time she took a step. She was always wearing hand-me-downs from her cousins that were shipped to her in boxes, and Rainie wanted to slot her hand into that space between heel and shoe, wanted to feel the friction of her feet.

That's because you're not fluent in feces like I am, Anita said, and Rainie continued behind her, counting the sidewalk slabs, dozens before their destination. The apartment buildings above them had a few lit windows, and the sound of faraway traffic on the highway hummed dark as blood. Anita's breathing was louder than the cars, but she refused to listen to Rainie talk about possible asthma and the importance of "in through the nose, out through the mouth." *We're here*, Anita said. They arrived at the lot, the hole at the bottom of the fence wider since they were last here, rounder and smoother at the edges. Anita said that sometimes she came and sanded down the edges of the fence to make it easier for the dogs to go in and out, but it was really just so she could have an easy entrance.

Ahead of them, the strays were awake, their eyes bright and scattered. They were silver at night and bonier too, standing so still that Rainie wondered if their legs breached the asphalt and went down forever, all the way to the core of the world.

They've been teaching me to read, Anita said, dripping wax onto the sidewalk and screwing the base of the candle into the tender puddle. *One of them shat on my feet, and I understood it as ink. I smudged my soles in it and walked up and down the sidewalk, see?* She gestured down at the sidewalk, but Rainie couldn't see any stains on the concrete, any legible footprints. *But I don't think I spelled anything*, Anita said. With the flame below her, only Anita's legs were lit, symmetrical to the legs of the dogs in the lot, and Rainie suddenly felt that they had been plotting something together or that Anita herself was an impostor.

Rainie stepped back from the fence, slanting toward the sycamore. In the dark, she couldn't see the whites of Anita's eyes, only the reflection of the flame in her pupils, yellow and feral. She stepped back again, and this time Anita stepped forward, plunging into the dark with her, taking Rainie by the elbow. *We don't have to go in*, Anita said. *Let's just stand by the fence and see what they spell.*

They're staring, Rainie said, plucking at the absent string around her neck, missing its orbit around her pulse. It had made her feel safe, encircled, and she wished it would grow back faster. *They want us to stare too,* Anita said, *or maybe they don't really have eyes. They see with the sky.*

Rainie was not comforted by this, but she said nothing, remembering what her mother once said about how girls should have ears but not mouths if they wanted to survive. *Ears and not mouths,* Rainie said to herself. *I have ears but no mouths. There's no need to speak.* She stepped forward, pressing her shoulder against Anita's, comforted by the solidity of Anita's bones. They stood in front of the fence. The strays continued to stare, bleaching the night that surrounded them so that they looked like a pocket of daytime.

Open the napkin, Anita said, and Rainie looked down, startled, as Anita wriggled the soggy napkin out of her fist and began to unfurl it. She unfolded the napkin, the pen drawing of the dog-headed woman now beheaded, its face dribbling onto the sidewalk, pooling blue ink. On the backside was a list of questions.

The dogs blinked together, like TV screens shutting off all at once, and Rainie jerked her head back. *I have some things I want to ask them,* Anita said, then abruptly added, *You know, for research, for our game. You can ask too.* But Rainie shook her head, looking at the dogs again, convinced that as long as she looked at them, they would stay still and not fling themselves through the fence.

Anita pressed the napkin to the fence and traced its shredded margins. *Do you hear that?* Anita whispered. *The sycamore.* Rainie stared through the holes of the fence, willed her eyes to wet themselves so that she wouldn't have to blink. *No,* she said, *is it saying something?* All she could hear was the rustle of bark flaking away, the shedding song it always made. *Yes,* Anita said, *the dogpack is speaking to us, and the tree is the echo.*

Rainie stepped closer to the trunk, and carved into its bark was the inscription: *The following account is authored by a pack of dogs. Please be warned that their sense of chronology is impacted by short-term memory and frequent switching between predator/prey mentality.*

A very responsible tree, Anita said. *Maybe it doesn't want to get sued if we find out none of it is true.*

Trees can't get sued, Rainie said. *That would be inhumane.*

Exactly, inhuman, Anita said.

What? Rainie said, but Anita had already begun to recite from her list, which was labeled: *The Testimony of the Dogs.*

Q: Where did you originate?

[The dogs assembled themselves into a curved row of teeth, lowering their heads to speak.]

A: We bitches born buttering up mountains, mending our mothers into one, nipping the teats clean off their chests, funded by blood and what we love. We bitches born from the bladder and named by a woman whose hair is cut weekly to weave through the breaches of trees. Nets to catch rain, fish the clouds down. Our hair diamonded dark, dark you only know before you're born after you're buried. A legend of the first woman we hunted with: She chops off her left breast, and the fat is ringed like a tree. Every part of us wood. We would be women in our next lives except we don't want. Our first language is grape, sweet thumbs of rain, the sky we teeth-stretched taut as skin. Our hind legs lumber, splinter as we run them away. Summers we burn the fields to forever them. From ash we are honest. Our lungs hung as lanterns. The sky scalded white and we run the mountains raw. Yesterday an ache lemoned our legs. To hunt we go with women and the men they set on leashes. Deer turding the trails and we follow the soft lanterns of the bladders inside them. We follow them to the bone and bite their necks into nets. We drag the air from their bellies. Out their soilholes, a water we aren't allowed to drink. When we drink it is never from palms. Thirst is a bell that rings in our blood. We lick the river that chases us like a tongue and pronounces our fur like salt like mirror. We never swim we swing tendons of water between our teeth like a hide dried and sold to the men named ghosts. Those men are not our men. Those men kill the dark inside their bodies. They are bright as the mirrors they bring on their backs and everything they want is onion-bright inside them glowing with what they say is god but what is. They open their lungs to the light. We saw them practicing on our dead. They flip the body inside out, pour it out like salt, call it preserve. They want to know what inside a body is responsible for hunger. They jar us before birth. They don't know hunger is located outside the body. They say it is holy to know a body as blood knows it, from the inside out. We can forage them apart and name them to the sky. Once they smoked a woman down from the mountains and cut open her belly full of fish and planetary. We knew she swam in the river without her skin like us we know our species is sold our family a fudge of mountains and sundown the deer steal their shadows from us. We know to run inside the shadows of women. They lend us the shadows we gown in. We eat our women when they die. Their spears make the shape in the air of our lineage. We are air to everything. The mountain when we run hunches flat so we can fast.

Q: Who hunts you?

[The dogs flip onto their backs, their bellies slick and hairless.]

A: The day the ghostmen come for our deer there is a noose in the sea widening and a neck in the clouds. They stone us to death with resin rain. Our women are shadowmakers lifted by trees their feet in fraternity with feathers. The ghostmen want the mountain. They come in companies of colors, all blood. We offer to make them more skin and shade to go with it. They come with dogs faster than us, dogs the size of seeds, dogseed shot inside deerbodies. They know how to birth holes into anything, even trees. What they practice their wounds on is water. Water sewing itself a sister mouth.

Q: Who?

[The dogs stand up and dip their heads one at a time, slipping themselves under the dirt, wearing the asphalt like a glossy blanket. It ripples up in sheets, a torn sea.]

A: Up the mountain in twenties we sever the deer from their shadows and the ghostmen below begin burning the trees we braided from rain. Burning up the mountain toward us they are silver gilded in sweat and the seed they spit into our bodies cannot be born into anything. We backward into our bodies and scatter like tossed pepper. Bright our women flock down from the trees armed as bees and tongue-sting. One with a net of knives one with a burning sockful of shit one with a spear we know can speak one with a language made of mirrors when she says her name they hear their own they squint like consonants. We have our teeth. When they dig into the mountain their feet shit-deep we teethe their anklebones bitter as grapeseed we suck their bones in our mouths expressive as pebbles and spit to pay back the soil. These ghostmen do not pray when they can prey. Do not walk when they can welt. Every step a stampede. Our legs and lungs shatter air into salt our teeth tearing light into lettuce.

Once we saw our women wearing fires. To greet the ghostmen they must first be fertile as fists. They must impersonate smoke and sell out the sky. We know fire can future us. We must treat our own blood as camouflage. On fire our women bound down mountains through the ghostmen camps and better their bones into ash. In our teeth we carry torches and sinews of light for the clouds to chew alive. We know the breast of everything, the peak where a river ruins its hem, drags a sky through the mud. Deer are down since the ghostmen come: The skins they flog and wear as we wear thirst. We are native to night. Ways to set a river on fire so men cannot cross it: Oil the river's skin. Clot every vein the sea uses to assault the soil with salt. The moon is marine and swims up to give our dark a depth. At night from the mountainbreast we look down at the ghostmen cleaving trees and sleeping inside them. They only know how to chisel perches and not to look down where their feet are fending off the roots. We alone know the difference between wind windowing open our mouths and a hole fathering hurt. We hear the difference between our women holing reeds and whistling through the knots of their fists and how salt punctures the thin scrotal skin of ships. We know how to be the shape of spears spawning dawnblood. We run bellydown to the ground, swallow to the soil, roots recently deceased.

Q: How old are you? In dog years, Rainie clarified, since that would be most logical.

   [The dogs turn sideways and latch on to one another's tails, gnawing them into red rope, linking themselves into a fence. Their bones weaponize, sliding out of them like spears.]

A: Some of us are old enough to remember when the ghostmen first borrowed our deer and returned only the bones and none of the skin. They want the outsides of us, something to hem, to tailor a border around the waist of us worlds. When the fish are finished giving birth from their mouths and the sea is newly mammal, sleeved in fur, it is the season of hunting ghostmen it is the season of grunting holes into the ground and running in the dark beneath their feet, running parallel to their eyes. We find a fish one day after the ghostmen in the night swim through shadows and hook our women onto trees. They dangle as fish and we lick their heels into stones for the river, our mouths full of minced tongue, salt-dissolved teeth. We learn to climb by eyeing the monkeys who begin to torture off their own tails biting them off at the bone chafing them against trunks or swallowing them and choking on their knots. Some are burying themselves in the dirt they divvy into dead they bury their babies first and zip them into the earth clean as rebirth. We don't have tails to climb or hands like our women so we teethe into the trunks and lug we canine our way high and nip the nooses loose as snakes they slither away. Our women they evaporate. Some startle awake and crow and wince into wings. Some we drag down the mountain onto the sand we swallow before we walk into the sea to weigh down our bellies and become whales. We gnaw open our women and load the boats of their bellies with stones and water them until they sink and their faces float to the surface later. Just the faces faces with the depth of the dirt the monkeys bury themselves in. We paw the tips of their tails jabbing out of the ground like weeds the poisonous kind we tug them out again and furnish our mouths with good meat. Since the ghostmen have come for skins everything lays flayed even the trees with roots bending into knees are bone now and bleached of leaves. We look down at our legs and they are split logs and we are bald around our memories. We run now splintering and the ghostmen crown the mountains with their mouths. Someday we know they will walk in the sky and rebrand all blue a crown and blunder down the moon. They whistle to us with ropes in their hands to mint our necks and we open the deer to live inside them. The deer now are born without skin they glisten with goldfat and each vein in their flank parallels a river we once sank with our dead.

Q: What do you hunt?

[The dogs spit out their teeth like handfuls of seed. They open their mouths, rims of pink. They shy away from the fence, and between their legs, their tails whittle into grass blades. They swivel their long snouts from side to side, searching for a place to hide.]

A: The day all the women are stones in the sea we decide to hire back our hunger. We know how to hunt ghosts like we know melons. We nose through the smoke and sniff out their sleep their sleep that sags full of milk and brine. They know how to manufacture it and say we never spoke say we never wore skin say we never sold it to them say we never cored the sleep from them one night at the hinge of the mountain where the shadow rests its head and at the foot of the flood we ran down a rockslide of rubies colliding with their bodies and the night began to wet itself. Rain entered them where we invented entrances. At the throat and belly. We carried away the trunk of the body in triumph. The rain puckered the sky into a scar and we mostly that night died. Some of us thrown later into the river to remember and some of us shot full of seeds and matured into melons and some of us tell the story and bark it into a tree.

Q: How do you give birth?

[The dogs flop onto their sides one at a time.]

A: The story is the story is we were born with ears broad as canopies as the rain. We were born with antlers like the deer until we showed them to the women who wield them as spears and secure their hearts to trees with thorns. Once we gave birth to women who inherited our ears our fear of direct sunlight our fur our mouths our hunger our have. Women born from dogs, they tug your teats into tails. Shirk seen things and originate scent. They say if you help or harm a dog in this life, feed it or beat it, it will reincarnate and return in your next one the women say this dog will heel you, be your demon or your savior,

depends. Depends on if you've listened to the lung of a mountain as it mudslides into your mouth. Depends on if you've ever
loved a ghost or been related to one voluntarily or not it sews
you to its grief depends on if you believe us when we say we ran
underground like unborn rivers we were first to know breath
we were first to shit this soil the fragrance of the fields is our
own is each tree a tail we need to run circular to hunt you are
all our young we ate alive to expedite them into the next life are
you saved now have you found the women to run alongside has
the future flinched again into the past have you furred have
you furied have you burdened the air with your falling have you
slept in the center of a mountain safe as an eggyolk gold and
unstitching into light like salt concedes to spit you are loaned to
the lifetime between gone and grieved.

This time it is Rainie who steps forward to ask a question, trying to ignore Anita, trying not to fall forward on her knees and
beg:

*Q: Why do I have to leave at the end of summer? Why does my mother
say we have to move? She claims it's to take over my aunt's tailoring business in a different city, but I see another reason inside her mouth, hidden in
her throat. Why can't I stay here? With Anita? With you?*

*[A single dog drifts away from the rest of the pack to stand before
Rainie, its spine showing through its fur like an archipelago of bone. The
dog is redfurred, and it speaks in the tone of a widow.]*

A: The reason your mother wishes to sever you from your
pack is because she fears the red thread around your throat.
   Once, when she was a girl, her brother, Swallow, pur-

chased three puppies. They were half woman and half mountaindog, with narrow snouts and teeth long enough to till earth. One of the half-dog/half-woman puppies had a thumbprint of red fur on its forehead, a sign of tamer blood twining through it. When the red-marked dog fought and killed the rooster, Swallow said he had to kill it, since once a half dog/half woman tasted live meat, it would try to murder anything.

The remaining two puppies were identical, bone-blue and running along the road quiet as shadows, and Swallow differentiated between them by smearing his cigarette butt against the hind leg of one of them, raising a scar like a pearl. He had to tell them apart, he said, because he was going to train them to fight. Half-dog/half-woman puppies were bred particularly to fight or to hunt, depending on their sense of smell and the length of their teeth. Their species was catered for grief.

When the two dogs grew to the height of your mother's knees, Swallow constructed a pen out of reeds and called her to come watch; today was the birth of their fate: Today he would fight the dogs. *Whose dogs will they fight?* your mother asked, and Swallow shook his head, saying, *They'll fight each other. We'll keep the one who wins.*

Your mother, Buggy, didn't want to watch. *Those dog-women hunted with us for centuries*, she said, *and they have human faces. Do you want to cease the light from their eyes? Is this how we pay them for their loyalty, their love?* But Swallow said there was no such thing as loyalty. The half dog/half women were hungry, had been starved inside cages that Swallow constructed from wire, and now inside the pen, they snarled at each other, mud mounting their fur as they crouched. Buggy saw the glisten of a pearl scar on one of their legs. She promised to call it Pearl if it won.

Pearl shot forward first, leaping onto the opposite dog, teeth tunneling into its throat, blood pasting itself to the grass.

Pearl won and was roped back into the wire cage, and the other puppy was buried. Everything was decided.

The night before Pearl's next fight, your mother left the house and walked to the dog in its silver basket. It jerked away as soon as it could smell her. She stood back from it, then walked slowly forward until she could see its face, its fur the same density as the dark. She imagined passing her hand through the dog's body.

The dog's eyelids peeled back, revealing rinds of white around its pupils, and it was then that your mother decided the half dog/half woman wouldn't die. It barked at her and she saw its teeth, crooked like a child's and growing in, and she knew it would lose if she didn't save it. She ran back into the house and fetched a red thread unraveled from her mother's dress. Around the trunk of the narrowest tree, she tied a knot, and then she tied the other end of the red thread to her brother's foot while he slept.

In the morning, when she woke, the room was empty and her brother was absent. There was no trace of the string she'd used to tether him to the banana tree, only the snake of a bloodstain that led to the doorway. Outside, your mother ran toward the dog cage, and there was Swallow standing and shouting at the dog: *You will win today, you will win.* She called for her brother, looked at his face to see if it had been rearranged, if his skin had been swapped for banana peel. He ran to her and lifted her by the waist, laughing. *You saved us,* he said. *I got my wish from the banana ghost last night. I wished for my dog-woman to win.*

Your mother smiled and crouched in the mud, trying to

level herself with Pearl, and though she began to laugh too, she thought of what her own mother said, that men were too weak and would never let their ghosts go, not even after they promised to. She glanced to the tree and saw the red thread still belted and knotted around the trunk.

When I see this dog win, I'll do what the ghost wants, he said. *I'll let her go once she grants me my fortune.* Nodding, your mother turned away from the banana tree, the dog, the day, her doubt. She knew, the moment she'd tied the knot around Swallow's ankle, there was a chance the banana ghost would kill him, a chance he would not let her go. But that was his decision, Buggy thought, to let her go or not. As long as he did, as long as he snipped the ghost free when his wish was granted, he would be safe, and the dog would too. And yet, all night, she repeated to herself: *For the life of a dog, for the life of a dog.* For the life of a dog, she'd tied her brother's to a ghost.

Your mother did not watch the fight that night, but she saw blood backfired onto a rock the next day. And she saw Pearl in the wire cage, pristine. *Where's the money?* she asked Swallow, and he said he'd hidden it. *Tell me,* she said, but he shook his head and said, *I've put it somewhere completely safe.*

Every morning after the dog proved itself divine, your mother checked the trunk of the banana tree for the red knot, and every day it was still there. Swallow was starting to tread into perilous territory. When a banana ghost was bound to you, knotted to your bed, it was at your mercy. In exchange for granting you a wish, the banana ghost asked to be set free, for the thread to be severed. But every morning, the red thread remained around the trunk of the tree, meaning that her brother had gotten greedy and still had not let the ghost free, even after she'd granted him his wish. Buggy knew how this story concluded. When you do not uphold your end of the bargain, the banana ghost pursues revenge. But who was she to issue warnings, your mother thought, when she had made the knot in the first place? When she was the one who bound the ghost to her brother?

Your mother reminded Swallow that the banana ghost had given them a victory and now needed to be freed. In the dark, he turned his face to her, his face flipping like a coin, unsettled from any expression for more than a second.

You didn't see her, he said. *You didn't see what she looked like.* Your mother thought he meant she was beautiful and that he wanted to marry her, but he didn't mean that kind of beauty. You would have understood it better, would have known what he meant: When Anita tells you, *I will strike you in the face with my stone,* when her fingers tighten the knot around your neck until you can't breathe, knuckles skimming the bottom of her chin, you understand that beauty is the absence of mercy.

They found Swallow under the banana tree. The red thread around its trunk was frayed, disbanded by days of rain, and Swallow held the thread in his fist while he dreamed himself dead. After he was cremated, your mother freed Pearl from her basket and taught her how to speak human words.

Pearl was her mother. It was an irrational thought, but Buggy knew stories about women born from dogs, women who were now all dead, and she recognized Pearl's eyes. She saw that color in the foam of the river, in her grandmother's blond teeth, and years later when she gave birth to you, she saw that dog's eyes screwed into your sockets, pupils with only the thinnest haloes of light.

Years later, your mother no longer looks at herself in mirrors, instead focusing on her mouth or her shoulders or something behind her: She has grown into her brother's face and wonders if this is part of the banana ghost's punishment, that she will always watch herself with her brother's eyes, that her hands shake whenever they knot or unknot anything.

The reason, you ask? The reason why your mother plots to move you away? She has many reasons, but this one becomes her tongue: She saw that Anita girl (yes, the one beside you, the one with even more questions) with a spool of red yarn. She saw the red thread around your necks, knotting you to vengeful ghosts. She knew that Swallow had followed her somehow, reeled in by that red, and that while fleeing her own face was impossible—resemblance could not be erased—she could swerve the thread of your fate by severing you from Anita.

At night, she stood over your bed, as she once stood over her brother's. She looked down at your red collar and wondered if she had been the one to knot it. She shut her eyes, but in the dark of her own imagining, the red thread around your neck rendered itself into rope, river-thick, dragging her into a past unpaid for.

[*Having concluded its answer, the red-faced dog retreats into the pack.*]

Wow, Anita says.

Rainie is silent. She touches her bare throat, mourning the thread that was once knotted there. She misses it like a major artery, and yet now she knows the danger of binding yourself to someone with no mercy.

The dogs' voices arrive to Rainie and Anita differently, though only Rainie realizes this: To Anita, the dogs sing through the holes in their teeth, threading the air through the instruments of their bones. And Rainie hears it simultaneously through Anita's mind and simultaneously through her own. *They sound like singing, so soft,* Anita says, but Rainie covers her ears with her palms and says, *They sound sharp, so sharp.*

The dogs line up and slip through the hole in the fence, retreating single file into the trunk of the sycamore. Only Anita sees this. Rainie continues to clamp her ears shut, closing her eyes to the unbearable brightness of night. They walk home together, Anita leading Rainie, Rainie refusing to open her eyes.

When Rainie is home, she circles her hands around her throat, mimicking the weight of red thread. She wishes that her mother, though well-meaning and full of warning, had not preyed upon her most important vein.

When she's gnawing at sleep like a bone, trying to keep her mind light as foam, Rainie wakes to the sound of Anita tapping at the window. She knows it's Anita and not a tired branch because Anita's tapping contains no discernible rhythm, no consistency. It sounds like a sparrow spasming against the glass. Before anyone else wakes, Rainie scurries over and presses her lips to the glass, muttering at her own reflection, assuming that Anita is behind her face.

In response to Rainie's shushing and gesturing, which translates into, *Please remember, the general populace is asleep,* Anita nods and resumes facing the pane, carving this question into the window's condensation, her words whitening in the moonlight:

Are you really going to leave? Wow this window is sweaty

Rainie goes outside and stands beside Anita on the pavement, cupping her hand over Anita's mouth, tracing on the window:

U write too big   Window too small   Write smaller
for room for me

If you leave me you leave the dogs the dead the tree the
fossils I named like the stork bone the spork bone

                write smaller

Why leave

Mama says red thread is dangerous   will choke me

Statistically you are more likely to be strangled by
human hands [unintelligible smear] and my abu says I
can summon in dreams so I will summon you you cannot
leave

Conserve letters   say u not you   y not why

You conserve letters you're writing over me

No

Why   Y   Why

I don't know I have to follow my family   I have to
u heard the dogs, didn't u? Mama is afraid of the thread
on my neck

Follow me

Cant

I will wait for u　　　and every name you go by

Bye good night I have to sleep

No　　　Don't go yet　　　please　　　　　dog　　　Rainie
wait　　　Okay　　　　　Dream me?

Anita Recounts Strange Occurrences in the Week Before Rainie Leaves Her Destined Love, and Dreams Fail to Manifest an Appropriate Stone

Aweek before Rainie's leaving, my question still quarrels with her window. The glass is veined where our words weighed. My Υ Υ Υ Υ Υ scarring the glass, resulting in damages that make Rainie's mother sigh and say she'll never get the deposit back. The plan is to delay Rainie by wounding her permanently.

I pray for lengthening nights, more time, and as soon as I do, a dog-headed woman resumes visiting our dreams. Abu says it's because the fortune teller was wrong. We woke up one day with our pots full of dog urine, and Abu said this meant our duplex was not once an ox jaw, it was actually a dog pound, shut down later for cruelty. The floors in the kitchen are still concrete, hosed down every morning by Vivian and me, and we can still smell the rug of blood left behind by their deaths. Abu said that dogs were killed on this floor in all kinds of ways: Injections of mercury. Given gas. Rolled through a patty machine. Rainie said those stories are just to scare me.

Abu told me that if I ever lose anything, I just have to go to sleep and dream back the memories I've littered behind me. She says sometimes you wake up with what you've lost embedded inside your fist or around your wrist. One time she lost her wristwatch, the Seiko she bought at the outlet mall, and so she went to sleep with her wrist folded beneath her. When she woke, the wristwatch was in her mouth, metallic and heavy and choking her, and there were pearls scattered at her feet. I decide to do the same: I will dream up the stone I need. The one I promised to lob at Rainie's face, scarring her brow so that she will always remember me. The scar will unite us again someday, and no matter how her face changes, I will always be able to recognize the seam on her forehead. Like the boy in the story who unveils his bride and is astonished by the mark that mars her otherwise-flawless face, I will pledge myself to her imperfections. And like the girl in the story, her blood will be betrothed to mine.

I clench my fists in my sleep, but when I wake up, they have not been replaced by boulders. In light of my failure, I decide to go harass Rainie. I wait in her doorway with the fossil I found most recently, a spork like a stork's foot, and I lob it at Rainie's head as soon as she answers.

You're going to kill me if you keep doing that, Rainie says.

I'll do it lightly, I say. *I only need you to scar. I only need to put it in writing that we will reunite.* But plastic doesn't touch deep enough.

After hearing this, Rainie decides it's easier to play dead, so she lies on her back in the doorway. Only the thread around her neck is alive, regrown in the night, thickening at the knot. I bend over her, my snout nearing her throat, and when Rainie swallows, I know what she's thinking: that it's better not to play dead when rabid dogs chase you, it's better to stand your ground and layer your shadow across it like cement. Running or playing dead only triggers its desire to feast or chase, and so Rainie jerks awake, her forehead colliding with my mouth, knocking one of my front teeth into a door hinge.

I laugh and tip my head back, the tooth swinging with a rusted sound. *I'm not dead,* Rainie says, *I'm not.*

Of course not, I say, *or else I'd see you like the strays, sheltered in the sycamore tree at night.* A conglomeration of ghosts. When Rainie says that we also seek shelter under the sycamore, and we're not ghosts, I tell her: *Maybe we're all dead, or they're the ones alive.*

That night, Rainie's mother bent over her bed and snipped the thread clean, freeing her daughter once and for all. Then she balled up the thread and incinerated it in a tin cough-drop dish, though the burning produced no ash or smoke, no evidence at all. At her throat, Rainie still felt the clot of extra blood, the slow and heavy beat of it, and the dogs on her roof confirmed this, running to its rhythm.

Anita Encounters a Dog of Dubious Origin, and Rainie Enters a Viscous Slumber

I try again to summon the stone by sleeping all day while Abu and Vivian are away, but in all my dreams there is no stone in my hands: Instead, I carry a briefcase full of squirrel bones, and I have to pluck my way through all of them, sorting the bones by size, and Abu's wristwatch is in my mouth, ticking, and I know if I run out of time, the house will return to an ox jaw or a dog pound, and Rainie and I will be euthanized, our forearms hooked up to jugs of pesticide in the garage. My dreams usually lack tactility, dissolving before I can delve in fully, so at least this is progress. Soon I will own a stone coated in shards of glass, a planet made of pulverized dreams.

In the evening, I wait by Rainie's window, and she bounds up to the glass, mouthing, *What do you want?* and I say, *Don't forget, I am still going to find a stone, a big one, to strike you with before you leave,* and I notice that her neck is bare. Where the red thread used to be, there is now a purple-blue line. *Traitor,* I want to say, but instead I watch Rainie return to playing on a fake piano. She plays on a foam keyboard so that she can practice her scales even without sound, can memorize the patterns and imagine what they might echo like. I used to watch her through the window as she practiced, making a note with my mouth each time she pressed a foam key, alternating between shrieking and whistling and moaning like Vivian when she's on the toilet. I tap my forehead against Rainie's window until she mouths, *Stop it, you'll crack it,* but I say I'll keep drumming until she concedes to see me, because Abu always says my head is harder than the pit of a mountain, that she should drill a hole in it to let the light in and all the birds out.

Even though Rainie isn't wearing her collar, I say, *Let's be dogs, one last time,* and I don't tell her about the dog-headed woman in my dreams and how Abu told me it could be a warning. Rainie doesn't believe in them anyway, and she tells me she has a new definition for dreams. Dreams are like straws: You suck the day through them, sip it into your mind, and when you're done you discard it.

We walk to the abandoned lot together. I scan for a stone to scar Rainie, but all I can see are bits of cinder block and gravel and what I think is a bullet casing but what Rainie says is a little girl's whistle. In the sea-shifting shadows of the lot, the dogpack sleeps belly-up in the heat, too tired to climb into the sycamore trunk. Their tails are knotted into rescue rope, and I say, *See, even dogs believe in knots, why did you cut yours off?*

Rainie leans against the sycamore, flakes of bark in her hair like dandruff, not answering. She watches the dogs with me, the little ones rolled into apples, loitering against the bellies of the big ones.

All the dogs have fogged eyes, some of them with no eyes at all, the sockets filled with moss or mold or white-capped mushrooms. They condense into a sea and then spray apart when I rattle the fence and hiss at them. Rainie says, *Stop, you're scaring them*, but I'm just trying to speak. We used to share a language with the dogs, Abu says. They used to hunt with us. Now the only thing we share is teeth and an ability to dream.

While the pack lolls about, the red-furred dog stands in the center of the lot, gnawing what I think is a squirrel skull and what Rainie says is a plum pit. Today only its neck is scabbed with red fur, its face and beard bleached white. Its tail is red-orange, a lit wick that disappears when it's whipped.

Look, I say, *it's that scabby dog who attacked my feces!* I press my face to the fence—Rainie yanks at the hem of my shirt and says, *Not too close, you'll get tetanus*—and purse my lips at it, spit. The red dog's paws wear boots of dried drool, and saliva sheathes each of its teeth, weaving into its beard and drying metallic. We both speak a language that's liquid. *Hey*, I say to the dog, *it's me. Last time we really met, you saw the backside of me, not the front. Don't you recognize your relatives? Did you end up eating my poop? I hope it was nutritious.*

I dilate my mouth from *o* to *O*, prodding the air with my tongue. *Recognize me now?* I say.

That's enough, Rainie says. *It will think you're being sarcastic. Take it back.*

The red dog raises its head, spits out the skull, and nods at me twice, which Rainie says was not really communication but an attempt to rid itself of three fleas riding its forehead. But I say, *No, it remembers me. Look how it turns its head from side to side and scans every bone inside me; look how its red fur rhymes with the thread around my neck, the one I still bear because I am devoted, descended from dog feces, the only one currently concerned with braiding together our fates.*

Shh, Rainie says. *You're agitating.*

The red dog's right ear, which flops against its head, is crafted from baloney. It is blown erect by the breath of a neighboring dog, whose tail sweeps dust into our mouths. It cups the words I whisper through the fence: *Someday let's meet skin to skin, or at least tell me how you installed your red thread permanently, turned it into anatomy. Turned it into fur.* I shake the fence and whistle at the red one, its head cocked. It opens its mouth. From behind the fence, I can see only one row of teeth ringing the top of its jaw, no bottom teeth at all. I snap my own mouth in sympathy. Its gums must bleed perpetually, reddening the hem of its dreams. *You're the one who knows me,* I whisper, while the dog juices the moon in its jaw and says nothing. Rainie presses her palm against my mouth and says, *Those dogs need to sleep.* The salt of her sweat scours the cuts on my lips.

But the scabby dog bucks its head again. When it swings its head from side to side, I see it is not empty. In its mouth is a white stone, gagged up or foraged from the sky, a white stone with pocks of black and silver, steaming like an egg. I rattle the fence again, calling to the dog, *Come, bring me that stone, there's a face I need to strike open with it,* but the dog disappears into a tire, curling inside. Rainie is not watching the dog but my face. She says, *I don't scar, not even the time my brothers got mad at me and threw me at the TV and it broke and a piece of glass got stuck in my neck.* She traces a spot on the side of her neck. I lean forward and lick it.

Everyone scars, I tell her, and whistle at the tire where the dog hides.

I ask Rainie if she trusts me, and she nods, though the bareness of her neck says otherwise, and there's a look on her face like when she prods the roadkill with a chopstick, crushing the lattice of a possum spine, watching to see what will eventually circle to eat it. *Okay,* I say, *if you trust me, listen: I'm going to scar us both, not just you. We're going to be identical, the same scar on your face on my face, okay?*

Turning away from her, I punch the fence with my fist and the red dog leaps out of the tire, pacing toward me, the white stone still fitted in its jaw. I thread my hand through the fence and hum at the dog, asking it to drop the stone in my palm, even though I know Abu would say not to stick my hand through fences like that, that when she was growing up on an island of stray dogs there was a boy she knew, a cousin, who stuck his hand through a hole in a fence on a dare, but on the other side was a white-bearded dog, and the dog not only bit off his hand but ate it too. The dog stops a few feet away from me, the stone shimmering with sweat, and I say to Rainie, *It knows of me, it knows me, and that stone is one of our bones. We have to get that stone back.* It belongs inside us, a real fossil, an organ that just needs to be reheated.

You go stick your hand through the fence, I tell Rainie, *so it knows you too. So it knows that knowing me means knowing you. Receive the gift it's offering to us, a striking stone, a summoning one.*

Slow, slow, and Rainie does it, pushing her fist through the chain-link fence before unfolding her fingers one by one, and the dog watches on its haunches, the stone wet-looking, no edge to it, not a stone good for striking but for swallowing.

Before I can withdraw my original thoughts, before I can

tell Rainie it's not the right kind of rock, no serrated edges for scarring, it's all wrong, wrong, the dog leaps forward, fluorescent teeth, throat an electric green, the stone falling out of the orbit of its mouth, its jaw coming to crown Rainie's wrist. Her whole hand disappears inside the dog, and the sound that comes out of her is scattered far as birds, so that the whole neighborhood can hear some piece of it, the delay of her shout arriving later that night in the form of rain, the streets stained.

I grip Rainie's waist and yank her away from the fence, and her hand slips out of the dog's mouth like a fish, slimed in spit but intact, except now there's a dog's tooth adorning the center of her inner wrist like a pearl. Rainie goes slack and heavy in my arms, and I have to drag her home by the ankles, slow, and by the time I'm back at the duplex it's night and her back is a railroad of scrapes. Rainie's mother comes running out of the front unit, a needle between her teeth, asking where we've been, and I look for the shape of Abu behind her, but there's no one there but a shadow, not even a useful one with muscles. No one has been looking for me.

I tell Rainie's mother we were attacked by a dog, but she can see no wound on me, only Rainie asleep. We lift her together into the dim living room and sprawl Rainie on the sofa, holding her by the ankles and the fists while she writhes, eyes shut but mouth open, fog rolling out of her throat. *Where is she bitten?* Rainie's mother asks.

I lift up her right wrist, turning it over to show her the tooth bejeweling it. No blood, just an expertly set and centered gem on her inner wrist, the enamel yellowing and rot-speckled, which actually gives it good dimension, a carnivorous glamour. Rainie's mother clamps her wrist between her knees and brushes her thumb over the tooth, saying, *This can't be removed—look how deep it is in her,* and she's right, it looks almost pretty, set so centrally. Rainie flinches when we touch the dog-tooth, her mouth opening wide enough that I see all her teeth, loose and flickering like light switches. *Go home,* Rainie's mother tells me, but I spend all night on the floor next to the sofa, sleeping curled like those dogs in the lot, raising my head when the moonlight munches through the curtains and bites at her cheeks. Beside me, Rainie's mother prays and sprays Rainie's wrist with alcohol, but she still doesn't wake.

By morning, Rainie's entire arm is translucent, her skin filled with shower-steam air, thick and cottony, but she isn't dead, and she's stopped sweating through her shirts and her mouth is now shut, no longer wide open and panting. *What do we do?* I ask her mother. *She's disappearing.* But Rainie's mother is not worried and says we just have to wait, though I am tired of waiting for things to leave me, Rainie included, and so that morning I shovel my thumbnail into the meat above Rainie's eyebrow, impressing a half-moon that fills with blood. I whisper to her neck: *I don't have a stone, but I have my hands. Now you're scarred. Now you can't leave me. You could never leave me.* Rainie rolls over in her sleep, her eyeballs bulging through the lids, and in the afternoon when it's hot, I lick leaves and stick them cool to her skin.

Everyone still talks about it. We, the dogs in the sycamore tree, punctuate the story by clapping together our leaves: Rainie was unconscious for two weeks, a relatively brief sleep, at least relatively. She was asleep with a dogbite darning her wrist, wearing a tooth she still can't remove, and guess who was responsible but that other girl, Anita, who called the dog to attack Rainie because she couldn't bear to be left. That girl is a real dog, even rolls around in the mud like one, and did you see what Rainie's mother did to ensure her daughter's awakening, promising three dozen frozen steaks to the god of dogs if Rainie got better, and now how is she going to buy all those steaks? Is she going to kill herself a cow? And rumor is, Anita wasn't afraid after the first few days of Rainie's inexplicable sleep; in fact, she licked the foam from Rainie's mouth, scooping it into her palms and lathering her face with it. Rainie's mother told her to go wash her face, that she could get rabies that way, but Anita wanted whatever sleep was shrouding Rainie. Anita waited for all those days, sitting vigil in Rainie's shadow, red thread between her teeth and embroidering her neck, nibbling extra holes in Rainie's earlobes so that she could thread her with these words: *I will not leave. I will wait. If you don't wake up, I'll tunnel through your sleep and meet you in the dark of your eye sockets. I will curl up beneath your eyelids.*

Loyal as a dog, loyal as lice, Anita stayed awake beside the sofa, curled at its feet, thieving in late at night when Rainie's mother was not there to keep watch. Rainie pedaled her feet through the air, flipped herself faceup and facedown, and spoke in her sleep to a series of dogs, saying, *Calm, calm, come, bring me the entrails, the head.*

When she woke at last, after two weeks of sleep, Rainie claimed she remembered none of the dreams, but Anita knew they were dog dreams, and dogs have a better memory than women. *You'll remember,* Anita said, *and when you do, you have to promise to give me a portion of your dreams. You have to promise not to leave me out.* A part of her was jealous that Rainie had dreamed so deeply for two weeks straight, while she had never strayed further than a single night. *Were you ever lost?* she asked Rainie. *Did you ever dream so deeply that you found the underside of the island, the other side of the world? Can I come with you next time? Why don't we fall asleep, side by side, and wander away together? Will you promise to never leave me behind? For two weeks, you stranded me awake while you were adventuring in your dreams. How could you?*

Rainie shook her head and said she didn't remember wandering away from her body. The two-week dream buried itself deep in Rainie's mind, hardening into a seed. Rainie insisted that nothing was growing, that she recalled nothing about her two weeks of unconsciousness, only that her wrist kept itching, a tooth throbbing on its surface.

The Dream that Rainie Forgot (and Will Someday Soon Remember)

For a while there was a rumor that the city was sinking. One day the city would retract like the talons of an animal and the mountains would migrate over it and the sky would settle on top like new skin and the city would forever be a blister and no one would be around to pop it. But there were many rumors like that, packs of rumors roaming the streets and mugging people of their secrets and lies, and to believe them meant you were participating in the crime. Besides, local officials compensated for the rumors of a sinking city by pouring layers of concrete over the original silt before building things on top of it. The city was concerned with being seen. The city was named so many times in so many different languages by various countries that had occupied it, and because there would be political consequences in choosing one name over the others, the city decided to eradicate all names, both individual and collective. Silence was a sport, with teams competing in a relay where members took turns being silent—no writing allowed, no preserved language of any kind—for as long as possible before passing it on to the next person, a game that could span generations, as some women could be silent for their entire lives before handing it off as inheritance. The men lacked patience.

In the summers, silence thickened into a pelt and everybody wore it. Sea-fog crouched over the city and grew fingers, stealing the city's buildings like a ghost restocking its bones. The summer was looking for another city to host it, looking for a beast with an infinite appetite for heat. Mudslides swiped away highways, and only the mountains that used their trees as stilts remained upright.

That summer, the dogs decided they would no longer live in the mountains, where the rain was hotter and more acidic than the blood inside them and burned bald patches into their pelts. Most became city strays, eating ends of littered sausages, eating roadkill, eating rats, eating one another, drinking oil gathered in gutters, drinking blistered rain, licking opals of sweat off each other's rump. In the city, residents assimilated to the dogs' appetites, the new cleanness of the streets, the bare bones of roadkill like spilled pearls, but several problems persisted: The dogs were loud and left slicks of sweat on the street. They barked to one another at night and howled when they were hit. To weed the city of public dog feces, some residents hunted the streets at night for dogs knotted in sleep, vulnerable in their dreams.

But the dogs bred faster than they were weeded. Furthermore, when drivers attempted to run them over in the street, they discovered that the dogs' blood was solid. The dogs could erect their blood into walls and crush oncoming traffic. Their blood could be unspooled from their bodies as lengths of thread, unknotted and whole, and so long as they still possessed teeth, they could reel their blood back into their burst torsos, resurrecting fully. Some residents capitalized on this novelty by selling red-thread jewelry to tourists, braided necklaces and beaded bracelets and knotted tiaras, advertising them as relics of longevity, though the dogs often mistook these red-thread trinkets for chew toys and leapt onto vendors' tables and blankets, gnawing so much of the merchandise that it no longer became profitable to make souvenirs of their blood.

By the end of summer, during the last assault of rain, the streets became beaded with dogs, and the barking drove certain residents to build basements and live underground until the dogs could be solved the way the city solved its name. In August, all the dogs were pregnant, bellies dragging on the street, some wider than doorways. It was then that the residents realized all the dogs were capable of carrying. There were rumors that the dogs had lapped up the raindrops, hard and silver like batteries, and that their pregnancies were actually just bloating and soon they'd explode. The rain was also responsible for the rumors that women everywhere were going bald as their elbows, birthing daughters with tadpole toes, growing puddles instead of mouths.

The dogs were glossy as citrus, and the water in their bellies swung and soured, pickling whatever was inside them. In the fall, when the rain ended but the heat did not, all the dogs simultaneously swam onto their sides, panting on the pavement, splayed and iridescent as oysters. They pushed all day, all night too, and the howling was so loud and so lasting that everyone in the city safety-pinned their ears shut or clamped their fists to the sides of their heads or, in desperation, cut off their ears entirely, though that only served to tunnel the sound more directly into their skulls.

On the second night of moaning, when the dogs were writhing on the street, some on all fours, haunches humming, some having bitten off their own tongues, the ribbons of pink flopping down the street like mackerel, the dogs gave birth to human babies. Hairless and wrapped in pouches of skin that felt like silk but were seamed. The dogs stood up as a pack, stood in the street proud as teeth, and then they ran back toward the mountains, slipping in the mud mixed with blood. Some stayed in the city, but those were the ones that were dying, their babies lodged inside them, the ones that were incinerated in the crematorium and thanked for the silence of their smoke.

The babies bit out of their skin-sacks and crawled onto their street, many already saying their names, relieving the residents of having to decide for them. Some were transported by bus to empty lots, but most were adopted, fetched from the pavement, more out of a desire to clean the city than to care for them, but many were loved.

When the babies grow into women, no one tells them that they are born from dogs, but they know the rumors and they wring it into some version of the truth, some version in which the dogs are tall as buildings and the sky strokes their backs. But they have never seen the dogs that birthed them, because most have disappeared, and the ones that have been crossbred with other species are mostly silent. Some of the women born from dogs are betrayed by the length of their tongues or the triangular shape of their ears or the fur that shadows their spines or their love of belly rubs and touches behind the ears. Some of them dream of hunting or being hunted. Every night is the depth of a bite. Many carry their dreams as an external organ, a hinged piece of meat in the shape of a dog's heart. Some buy slabs of raw meat and teethe them secretly in bed, or use them as pillows, or warm them between their thighs, reenacting their births.

For generations, ever since the first time they looked into rain puddles and saw dogs lapping the underside of that water, they were taught that sons are born and daughters are bred. Sons are alive and daughters are given life, conditionally. Before their own daughters are born, they are told: *If you have a daughter, don't worry, that's a good thing, despite what most people say. At least you'll have someone to take care of you when you're old. They're not totally worthless.*

You will want to respond: *But she hasn't even been born yet! I haven't even wiped the shit from her ass or shown her how to eat fish with bones! And you've indebted her to me? When she hasn't even gotten the chance to grow a single bone of her own? You've separated her from her life already, before I've gotten the chance to stitch it to the inside of her skin? Should I dismantle her now and give her out in pieces, divvying up her liver and bartering her bladder? Would that satisfy you? If instead of opening her mouth for milk, she grew udders for you to juice?* Being bred means you are expected to serve a purpose, a specific usage, even before you are named or held or happened. You display certain desirable traits, are funneled into a particular future. You have been summoned to feed others before you are fed. Remember and remember: You were bred to prioritize other lives. In contemporary language, you are an insurance policy.

On the other hand, a son is a possibility. Who and what will he be? Those questions are not asked of the women-born-from-dogs, nor of their daughters-born-from-women-born-from-dogs. Those daughters grow up sympathetic to mutts, unidentifiable dogs that are unique and yet look like every other stray. Ordinary dogs with ordinary wants, except that each is irreplicable, each contains illegible blood. An unknowable lineage, a red thread so knotted and tangled it's impossible to unspool it from their bodies without severing it in several places.

Some of the women-born-from-dogs emigrate, with or without their daughters, leaving the island for various mainlands. They tell stories of roaming the city at night with other girls, of their tendency to eat furniture, the irresistibility of a table leg, wood gleaming like bone, and how some of them never learned to walk on two legs, or how some of them don't like to wear things around their necks and others love the feeling of being encircled, only going outside if someone leads them, of knots living inside them, their sensitive snouts revealing what the city has always been, a colony of cows or a desert or a bay, and the people in their countries call it a symptom, probably from an exploded nuclear plant or insecticides glossing their local vegetables, pollution from factories or smoke from razed cane fields, the pitfalls of drinking out of plastic bottles, all that smog from taxis, the beaches where the sea solidified around your feet, where whales beached and exploded, where people ate all kinds of wild things, anything with wings, but that was not why the women-born-from-dogs told stories about themselves. They were not looking for a diagnosis, they were not looking for blame, they were trying to ask something, do I belong to you, do you recognize me, do you remember us, do you deserve us. Did you turn away when we moaned out of our mothers, and why? What about their pain was strange? What is the difference between being found and being foreign? What were we raised to be if not forgotten?

In the mountains, the dogs maintain their silence, turning away nightly from an interrogation of stars, mouths of light. Only on certain nights, nights that know only how to rope, how to tighten around you and deliver you blue, do the dogs finally raise their heads, still dragging their blood behind them, and howl. Behind, trails of their blood lift and sash the trees, tinseling everything. They howl and howl, though there is no one they want to speak to. The sound doubles back into their mouths, pleated with pleading: *Give us back our daughters. We abandoned them only because we thought they'd return to us on their own. We prayed to bear them dead, and even now we mourn that they live without missing us, live without a language for the women they've lost, live so far that when they die, we will not be allowed to eat their bodies.*

Anita Delivers a Fossilized Apology

This is my account of Rainie's two-week sleep and its immediate aftermath.

The dogpack gathers outside my window, chorusing: *Your story's accuracy may be slightly distorted by your jealousy of her dreams and the pain of being left behind in the conscious world!*

I ignore their protests. After all, they're not even anatomically accurate. Dogs don't have human mouths and human tongues. So here goes:

The first night Rainie sleeps, I water her dreaming body. I treat her needs tenderly. Because she drinks nothing, it's important to moisturize the surface of her body. I bring Abu's sponges, the ones she yells at me for leaving in the sink—she says they'll grow mold, and I say they'll get to swim down the drain anytime and ride to the sea—and I bring the towel Vivian says is for faces only, not for scrubbing ass cracks in the shower, and I bring my bedsheet, heavy with last night's sweat, and I wring it all over Rainie's face and torso. Then I cover Rainie with the strangled bedsheet so that mushrooms will grow more easily out of all her surfaces. The more shadows I layer over her, the more habitats I will sustain.

I know I'm making a difference, because her mustache hair grows an instant two millimeters and her nostrils dilate in her sleep, ready to be plugged with seeds, and the soil beneath her skin is damp and moldable. After Rainie's face is watered, I bring a length of thread to tie around her pinky finger. Since red thread has become endangered in my household, I had to forage it from the hem of Vivian's skirt, the new plaid one she wears to her after-school shelving job at the library, except she steals pages out of books and hoards them in her pillow so she can read in her sleep.

The red thread I knot around Rainie's finger was severed by my own molars, so I pray it clenches to her second knuckle with the strength of my jaw. The thread will bind her soul to its socket. Abu says it's important to tether dreamers to their bodies. It's easy to wander off without a fishline or someone to reel you in, someone to wait. I know that Rainie isn't like me: She wants to return to her body. She doesn't accept the possibility of getting lost, of straying. She would resist exploring, instead of enjoying the deviation from her body.

Rainie sleeps faceup on the sofa, and beneath my sheet, her slack arms are arranged like carrots on a cutting board. For some reason, Rainie's mother didn't let me clean her, still chases me away when she sees me kneeling by the sofa, my head bobbing up like a buoy. She throws the rag at me, yanks me out by the earlobes, duct-tapes the windows.

The thirteenth night, I crawl in through the open window. Rainie's mother is in the kitchen, filling a bowl with water she will either dribble into Rainie's mouth or inject into her belly directly, so she isn't watching. I walk on my elbows and knees, look down at Rainie. The sweat-soaked sheet I used to moisturize Rainie has been stripped from her, and someone—most likely her mother, which I try not to fault her for—has changed her into pajamas with pink and white stripes. I want to tell Rainie's mother it's important not to change her appearance, in case her spirit gets confused about which body to return to, but I'm supposed to be outside.

The only water receptacle I have now is my mouth, so I rise on my knees and bend over her lips, which have been slathered in some kind of substance to prevent cracking or flaking. This is unwisely water-resistant. They don't know how to care for the dreaming, I realize: Their care is only calcifying her. There is a bruise surrounding the dogtooth, protecting it like a moat. Blood stagnates beneath her skin, sleeving her purple up to the elbow, and someone has tried to ice away the soreness. I can feel the tooth throbbing at the back of my own jaw, scattering my thoughts. To thaw her, I hover my mouth over her exposed wrist, tucked next to her side, the tooth shuddering up and down with her breath, pulsing at the roots. A tooth requires saliva the way a fish requires a river or sea or lake, and I am here to home it. My spit thickens into thread and hangs out of my mouth, the tip of it touching Rainie's wrist-tooth. That's when I feel fingers clasped around my ears. I'm in the air, my legs kicking, and Rainie's mother pants as she lifts me.

Get out of here, she says. *Use your own legs, or I'll lock you out like a dog. Don't disturb someone who's resting.* But even as she sets me down on the carpet and I walk toward the door, the thread of my spit lengthens, pulled like a strand of molten sugar, tethering my jaw to Rainie's wrist. Rainie's mother runs to the kitchen and hacks at the spit-thread with her cleaver, but it tautens and thrums a high note, a struck chord. Her blade bounces off the glittering string again and again, and as I back away, her eyes ride the spit-thread between us, gliding back and forth between Rainie's sleeping body and my awake one, scanning for the thinnest part of the thread to sever, and I know she must have tried to slaughter the thread I tied around Rainie's swollen pinky, except it must have been too tight to snip it without cutting Rainie too, and that is what I intended, to embed the red in her, to make separation possible only through bleeding.

Keep going, Rainie's mother says, standing beside her daughter, her cleaver still raised, aimed at nothing. *Take another step, another.* The incredible tensile strength of my spit is something I will have to tell Rainie about when she wakes. We should test the dogs' saliva too. I will remember to tell her. I suture the distance between us, and even when the door shuts, the thread only bends, shimmering in the air like a heat wave, my words sliding down its length like beads. I import my words directly from my mouth to her wrist: *I will come find you.*

In your dreams, look for me in the mouth of everything. I'll look for you, too. We are tethered by thread, and you can always return to me through it, or I can return to you. You don't have to walk it like a tightrope or play it like the string of an instrument. Just follow it with a single finger. You'll never lose it, even if it's narrow as a hair. Believe me. Believe it's the spine of everything you touch.

———

When Rainie wakes, I'm not beside her or underneath her or sprinkling her with spit (someday she'll thank me for her skin's water-gloss, especially in our unusually dry climate). She wakes alone, and while she cannot find me, I'm back at the lot where the red dog ran at us, and the stone is there, white and round and speckled. I bring it home to boil and disinfect. It bobs on the surface of the water, broad as a skull, and I wait for it to hatch something. Finally I give up and slosh the water onto the driveway, the stone tucked between my knees, and before Rainie and the rest of the Tsais leave our street, I loan her the stone. I tell her I've been planning to strike her with it, but because it's smooth, she can keep it instead as a surrogate head, something to hollow out and use as her skull someday if she ever needs it. I can tell her mother doesn't want Rainie to keep it, but Rainie takes it from me anyway, rolling it into the trunk of her brother's Subaru, all their belongings tied to the top of the car. I imagine them gone down the street, the car with a hitch in one wheel so that it gallops instead of gliding.

I spend the night in her half of the duplex before she leaves. As an apology gift, I bring her my pineapple cake tin full of fossils, tucking it into my pants before entering.

Rainie is sitting upright on the sofa. I hear her brothers in the kitchen, shuffling cards, her mother at the sink, water hissing. The duplex is empty when I enter it, not even a lightbulb screwed into the ceiling, but the sofa is still there, its bald cushions bearing Rainie. The sofa floats two inches above the carpet like an island. Her neck is bare, and I resist the urge to knot my fingers around it, especially since she was so recently unconscious and still looks exhausted. *Cover your toes when you sleep,* I want to tell her, *because anything that breaches the borders of the bed can enter your dreams.*

Nibbling on her pinky nail, Rainie looks up at me and says they can't get the sofa to stop floating, so they aren't taking it. There's a policy in their new building about furniture, which must be bolted down at all times or be subject to gravity. She cups her hands, and I look up for the rain she's summoning before realizing she's asking for her gift. I kneel in front of the sofa and offer her the cake tin on flat palms, sitting the way dogs do, and she looks at me without taking it. The neck of her Tweety Bird T-shirt is brown with sweat, and I can feel her heat so bittersweet against my skin and under my tongue. I lift my hand and press it to her forehead, feeling for a fever, but Rainie flinches away. *What is it?* she asks, pointing at the pineapple cake tin I've set in her lap. *I already have the stone,* she says. *It's so heavy that one of our tires burst when we loaded it in.*

This is more important, I tell her, so she pops open the tin. The mirrored lining of the lid shines on her face. I wonder if her wrist is heavy, if she considers the tooth her own. Reaching inside the tin, Rainie plucks out a glowing green gem. *Is this a jelly bean?* she asks, her voice so quiet now I wonder if she's wading back into sleep. *That's the kidney of a man-eating lizard,* I say. *It's one of our fossils.* Rainie drops the kidney back into the tin, ringing the bottom like a bell, and then she lifts the lid and says I should keep these for myself. *It's basically garbage,* she says.

I snatch the lid from her and sit down next to her on the sofa, brushing my wrist against her toothed one. She flinches again. *No,* I tell her, *I've collected all the organs for you, see? The hair of a man-faced fish. The tongue of a stray dog, spotted like a rotting banana peel. The belly of a butterfly, thimble-thick and inside out. The five-chambered heart of a woman.*

That's the plastic that holds a six-pack, Rainie says about my heart, balling it in her fist, warping the iridescent skin. She sifts through the tin with her fingers, her nails scraping the bottom, and then she pries the lid from my hands and clicks it back on. Her hands are trembling when she gives the tin back to me, when she says her mother told her to pack light. *She means pack the sun,* I say, *and a star or two. And also take the lightbulbs at your own pace.*

Rainie laughs and nudges the tin with her knuckles, turning her face away, and I can tell by the width of the sky in her window that it's starting to become night and Rainie will have to drive away soon. I can also tell the time by Rainie's eyes, because she blinks a lot when it's starting to get dark. *It's to train my eyes to adjust to the dark quicker,* she says. *I expose myself to little nights along the way.*

I will miss us in the garage, I tell her, *when we kept our mouths open and drank from the ceiling. The strays will follow you because you've taken their tooth.* Rainie twists away from me when I say this, her thumb pressed to the tooth on her wrist, and I know she doesn't want to hear it.

We should be buried together, I tell Rainie. *That way we can surface together.* This is the line I've been saving, the one I was supposed to say when I presented her with the fossils, but I'd forgotten to say it, and Rainie ignores me. Her nails tap the lid of the cake tin. *Open your mouth,* I tell Rainie, and she blinks at me. She says she hasn't brushed her teeth in a couple of weeks, having been in a coma, but I tell her to just do it. I lift her chin and look in, pushing my forefinger down the corridor of her throat, parsing through the dark, and beneath me, Rainie gasps and gags, her arms flailing against the sofa, her teeth guillotining my finger.

When I wrestle my finger back out, Rainie hacks and asks

me why I did that, why, why why do I. *I was just checking*, I say, *and it's confirmed: You're empty, so you need these organs. They expand in water and in the dark, just swallow.* When I grip the tin, I realize that my finger is bleeding, missing a triangle of skin. Rainie startles, taking my hand. She sets it down on the sofa and then sits on it. When I laugh, she looks at me and says, *I just need to apply pressure to stop the bleeding, and I'm heavier than you.*

No, I say, wriggling my fingers beneath her weight. *You're empty, you need to refill.* Rainie says, *Fine. If I take the fossils, will you promise not to choke me again?* I point at the thread around my neck with my free hand, saying I can't promise, but I smile because now she's wounded me back. Now there will be a scar on my finger where her tooth nicked me, matching the one on her forehead. The place above her eyebrow where I pressed my fingernail in deep, matching the depth of her sleep. Our scars are a map back to each other.

Rainie's mother stands in the doorway of the kitchen and looks at both of us, my hand beneath Rainie, Rainie shaking off her sweat like a wet dog, the tin of fossils between us. *Go home,* she tells me, *and take your blood with you!* I stand up and press my hand to my chest, looking down at Rainie. She smiles, a wire of blood wrapped around her front tooth. *The sooner you go, the sooner you come back,* I tell her. *That's what my abu always says. So hurry up and leave.*

I leave her half of the duplex and feel her watching me. She waits for me to look back at her, but I repeat what Abu says—*the sooner you leave, the sooner you return, leave, return, leave, return, leave*—until all I can hear is Abu calling for me from the kitchen, her finger hooked around my neck thread, tugging me home.

In the morning, I look in through the dust-furred window in their door and see only the floating sofa, the smudge of my blood on the rightmost cushion. I knock on the windows with my fists. I wait for the sofa to thud back to the ground, weighed down by Rainie on top of it.

Behind me, Abu and Vivian are rustling through the white bags of trash the Tsais left behind, their hands wading through layer after layer. *Not even recyclables,* Abu says, her hands sheathed in rubber gloves. Abu says the best part of people moving out is getting to be nosy and harvesting their belongings. Vivian says she and Mr. McDonald's once found a good TV in the trash and even a collection of emerald rings, which may have been dyed glass but in the moment, in their palms, were definitely real. As they bend and burrow their hands into the smallest bag, the one they didn't even bother to knot again, I see a familiar brightness, a fragment of light. I walk up behind Abu and the bag shimmies open, revealing what glows at the bottom of it: my pineapple cake tin, the green paint flaked away, the gold beneath too bright to be real.

Empty, I say, *it's empty,* but Abu reaches in and lifts it, saying, *Aha, this can be recycled.* Then she shakes it a few times and says, *Wait, there's still something inside.* I hear my fossils fling themselves around, their dull rattle like a memory of rain, and I wonder if Rainie can hear it too, however far away, the bones she forgot to take. I forgot to ask: *Am I the reason you're leaving?* But I don't want to hear the answer, don't want to be complicit in our distance.

Clasping my hands around the tin, I tug it away from Abu. The sun microwaves the metal until it steams, vibrating with pressure, hot condensation collecting on my face and on the lid. I hear my fossils transforming inside the tin: The kidney leaping to land in my palm, the heart dividing its five chambers into ten, the belly reassembling, condensing into a gem.

Correspondence Between Our Organs

An Introductory Letter Full of Skeletons

Dear Rainie:

I do believe that at her core (which is the gnawed heart of a pear, mostly meatless) your mother does care for living things. Once, I saw her feed the strays in the lot with good meat. An entire slice of Wagyu beef. Even I wouldn't have done that. What did they do to deserve those beautiful sheets of meat with windows of fat? But I was standing behind the sycamore and I spied her wadding up the beef and pressing it through the fence hole. The red dog got it, the one who is always the closest—while the other dogs

dangle their balls and lick their asses in the far corner
of the lot, this one is always right beside us. It's waiting for me. Just like I'm waiting for you. Your mother
claims I belong outside the house, but she loves those
strays, I think, deep inside. But very deep, like bowel-
deep, inaccessible to most things. Not anywhere near
the surface where she knows. So deep that she can't
dig it all out of her and show it to everyone. I saw an
oxtail waving in the mouth of one of those dogs and
knew it was your mother who gave them bones.

Speaking of bones, Winny is a newborn who
lacks transparency. She doesn't tell us when she's
hungry. She was gestated for about as long as a dog,
and it shows. She plays all day. She's a liar already
and was designed for thievery, her fingers the lon-
gest part of her, adult in their slimness while the
rest of her body resembles a glossy roast ham in
Costco ads, and already she's plucking things, bobby
pins from our hair, the nonworking phone from the
wall, and one time even Abu's Seiko watch, which
she unstrapped while feigning sleep in Abu's arms,
soaking the watch in her mouth and sucking off its
silver paint until Abu woke and unraveled it from
her throat. Later, in recalling this incident, Abu
would interpret this act of thievery as an early sign
of Winny's irreverence for chronology, her refusal
to confine time to lines, wicks or otherwise, and by
suckling on the watch and feeling its tick against her
tongue, she was attempting to derail our family from
today and return us to our first doghood. Is Winny
an act of sabotage, or is she just trying to remember

us? Does she have any bones of her own, or does she steal them out of our bodies when we sleep, which is why we are starting to become floppy, our meat mudsliding from room to room, our gelatinous arms jiggling her to sleep?

Now that I've said some nice and generous things about your ancestry (and further tickled you with news), I hope you will continue to correspond with me. If you want to know what happens next in the fate of your family and this narrator, write back.

The History of Our Tongues

Dear Rainie:

You haven't written back, which I think is more my fault than yours. I should have ended on more of a cliffhanger. I hope this will be a bit more enticing.

I do feel bad that I was a bad influence on you, according to most living things, mostly your mother. I don't think anything I ever did qualifies as an apology, but this is the closest I can come to it: a burp. Do you remember the time we were sitting at my dining table and you were eating with us and you burped? And how I took credit for it so that Abu would slap my arm instead of yours? And you told me later it was unfair because your brothers burped all the time and no one slapped their arms, and no one would slap their arms for as long as they lived? And I thought you were telling me that their arms would outlive them, would grapple with their graves and turn into rabid corpse-arms climbing out their own ashes, and I was momentarily impressed by your brothers, especially the older one, who had a lot of boogers that never ripened and fell out of his nose. Do you agree now that I was a good friend for owning that burp? Not everyone is willing to adopt their friend's belly gas. And why is gas different in a girl? Maybe since we're girls, our gas is poisonous and if it's ever released from either end, it'll shrivel everyone like a slug? I enjoy being in the presence of your gases. Being loved by the air that was inside you. On the other hand, you insult me often. You say that my tongue is weirdly purple and so I should learn to speak without showing it to anyone. But my tongue is historical and should be preserved in its current state. In my family, we have a history of finding our tongues in unknown orifices, such as inside other people's urns, inside eye sockets, and inside the moon's dimples. Our tongues precede us, probing themselves into available spaces, and we can only trail after their slime, trying to keep up.

On one of those many mornings before you abandoned me, I woke up with my tongue slugging out of my mouth, desperate to escape the fence of my teeth. The red thread tied around my neck fattened into an entrail, slick and oily-sheened. I grasped the entrail with both hands and yanked, and it released my neck like a snake before slackening into thread again. After I reknotted it and told Abu about the sudden strangulation, she sighed and said for the thirty-fourth time that I'd better bury it somewhere.

She said that our history was the history of dismemberment, a history of emptied torsos, and that a long time ago, when the underside of the island was the topside, missionaries came to the island and attempted to convert us. I thought Abu meant conversion as in the kind you do with currency, exchanging our bones for another species', our tongues for eels and our feet for fish and our limbs for lakes, but Abu said no, it was about what you believed in, what you did with your dead. I told Abu I believed in dogs, the stray ones in the empty lot that were a frothing sea, that ran in a pack so tightly woven they could carry the sky on their backs without letting any light leak through. I also believed in red thread and ropes of all species, including rainbows in the kitchen sink that acted as a bridge between the living and the dead.

Abu said my affinity for rope was because, long ago, we stored our bones inside new dog bodies and formed a pack and ran down the mountain and swarmed the missionaries and dismembered them. We opened their torsos with our teeth, and our heads transformed into women's heads. With our canines, we snipped out the entrails and stomach and bladder and spleen and lastly the tongue. According to later records, we carried the organs away in our human mouths, bounding away on dog legs, leaving only the empty, mutilated trunks behind. I asked Abu what we did with the organs in our mouths, and she said some of us swallowed and others of us carried them for a long time in the hammock of our tongues. Back then, our tongues could grow and retract to any

length we wanted, depending on how long we'd de-
ferred our hunger. Some of us had been hungry for
many generations and therefore had tongues as long
as bloodlines, tongues that could lasso mountains
and yank them to their knees, while others of us had
tongues as blunt as thumbs or as narrow as needles.

Abu said that those of us who cradled the organs on our tongues eventually gave birth from the
mouth, and that these babies rode everywhere on the
backs of dogs and invented a language that consisted
only of swallowing: swallows that took seconds to
unfurl, swallows that seemed weighted by a throatful
of stones, swallows that unknotted phlegm, swallows
that required the tongue to flick back like a whip,
swallows that sloshed, dry swallows, half swallows,
swallows that created a total vacuum in the mouth,
allowing teeth to detach and float around in zero
gravity.

The next time I saw you, I licked your entire face
and belly and the place where I once knotted a red
thread, which I suspected was a sun-dried dog entrail, but I still didn't know a word for you, not even
now that you've left. When I told you the story of the
man who was emptied, the dogs with women's heads,
you said you knew a similar story from your mother,
about the Entrail Eater, who unzipped children's bellies with her tongue and slurped out the jelly inside
them. Consequently, their mothers had to stitch them
substitute organs—some of them shaping new livers
out of dog feces, others sewing new stomachs from
fish skins. Others foraged for organs, traversing other

mountains and other forests for carcasses of dogs or men, pecking their bones clean like crows, carrying the organs home in purses around their waists. The mothers built a giant body out of mud to store all their spare organs, in case any of their children were ever emptied. This was the part of the story that the written accounts never recorded, though if they had bothered to follow the dogs with women's heads, they would have seen many of them bury the organs in the soil or pickle them in ponds of seawater, keeping them fresh for generations.

Look, Abu said, scraping at the plaster walls of our house with her nails. Beneath the first layer was flesh. The wall licked her hand and gloved it in slobber. I pressed my hand to the opposite wall and felt it pulse and flex like a belly, and beneath it I could feel the snaking of intestines and the drumbeat of a tongue as the house swallowed and swallowed around us. One day when the plaster collapses like a broken wing and the wood beams rescind into the dirt, the house will finally succeed in digesting us, returning to its first life, lifting our beds like tongues and drooling all over our bones until we glow.

An Appendix on the Appendix

Dear Rainie:

I'm assuming that you're not responding to these letters for a variety of reasons. This variety can include:

- You have returned to your dog-bitten state of slumber. If that is the case, know that I've been trying to break into your dreams. (At night, if you see a fist through the ceiling, that's just me knocking. Don't be alarmed. I'm trying to dream my way back to you. Keep your sleep thin and porous, and I should be able to join you under the sheet of it. I go to sleep with my ponytail or two of my braids gripped in my fist so I'll have a tether to hold on to, a self to come back to. But I'd let go if it means reaching you.)
- You have become a dog and prefer other means of communication.
- You have become a tree and prefer productive silence.
- You have become your mother and have to give birth to yourself first, so that you exist for me to correspond with.

Any other reasons are unacceptable.

Here is also a list of things I will do to you if you don't respond:
- Bite you.
- To do the above, I have to actually be in your presence, which I will achieve after I've found you in my sleep and have learned to traverse your dreams.
- After biting you, I will obtain red thread and knot it around your neck and shellac the knot so that it will be undoable.
- I will sic the strays on you, even though they

don't listen, and they would rather hump you
than disembowel you. Besides, I'm not trying to
get you disemboweled. You need your bowels to
respond.

In the meantime, while I wait and you continue
not to care, I enclose my appendix, which I might
have to get removed soon, because Abu says we have
a history of ripening appendices that have to be
plucked from the body. Abu also says I can't actually
fit an organ into a letter envelope, because three-
dimensional objects don't behave two-dimensionally,
so instead, I enclose another definition.

The definition of an appendix is information
that might burden the reader or be too distracting or
inappropriate for the main text. It must also include
content that is "easily presented in print format."
Here, I present my grandmother's appendix, which
cannot be printed but can be reproduced orally,
through story:

Once when Abu was a girl, her mother called
her daughters in from the fields, demanding a mirror: Her appendix had burst and she was going to
perform immediate surgery on herself (she had a
good grasp of anatomy, both human and ghost,
because her grandmother had dismembered missionaries). However, Abu and her sisters were so frantic
and mindless with worry that they were unable to
locate a functional mirror—the nearest surfaces were
made of skin, dirt, tin, and wood—and so they ran
to one of several local rivers and attempted to pry off

its surface. Back then, Abu said, all the rivers were
protesting the government and had rebelled by turning themselves into lids. Nothing could move them,
not even when the local men grew out their nails and
gathered on the riverbank and attempted to pry off
the river-lids. Abu and her sisters wedged their nails
between the river-lid and the bank, but they only
succeeded in uprooting their fingernails from their
beds and spraying significant blood. Abu suggested
that they carve out a piece of the river-lid and carry
it away on their backs, but the river-lid was made of
a material too rigid to break off.

It was my first aunt who suggested they attempt
to melt the river-lid by farting, that the heat and
gas inside their bodies could dissolve anything, and
seeing no harm in this suggestion, the six sisters
scattered across the surface of the river and farted
with an enormous amount of concentration, emit-
ting precise beams of heat. The river shuddered
beneath them and began to liquefy, causing all six
sisters to scuttle back to the bank, as they did not
know how to swim. When they had safely stumbled
to land, they turned and saw the river transform
from solid to liquid. In fact, the river had been
fooling around with them and could have done this
at any time, but it was amused by their theatrical
efforts to thaw it.

The sisters rolled up a thin sheet of river and ran
to their mother's house, unfurling the water across
the ceiling so that their mother could lie on her back
and perform appendix surgery. Prior to unzipping

her skin, my grandmother emptied herself of blood to prevent misplacing any of it, siphoning it into a dozen covered buckets for temporary storage.

Consequently, after these events, Abu and her sisters sparked an annual ritual in which young girls ran to the river and squatted in the mud, hovering above the surface and farting with as much force as they had stored—often swallowing mouthfuls of air in preparation—and counting with their fingers how many rings ricocheted in the water and how many fish had been summoned to the scent.

The Hsia Family Tampers
with the Red Thread of Fate, and
Anita Gives Cunnilingus to a Tree,
Not Unwilling

Though Abu officially exiled all forms of red thread from our household, unwinding her last red-threaded bobbin and incinerating its full length, I unravel a spool of dental floss and slit the meat of my finger on Abu's cleaver and dye the floss with my blood, sun-drying it into a shade of red that reminds me of the dog that bit Rainie.

Tonight, I sleep with the red floss threaded through my fist and try to dream my body beside Rainie's. My snout buried in her backside.

When I wake up, Vivian is beating me with her pillow, telling me to stop farting in my sleep, I am an animal, disgusting, and *If you keep farting I'll plug up your ass with the largest carrot I can rip out of the side-yard soil, my god*. Because I miss Rainie, who would not have woken me, I go back to sleep with the red floss in my fist, thinking of how to summon her, how to find her in my sleep. I want to wander away in a dream that stretches longer than two weeks, want to stray all the way to the tombstones of her teeth, to the doorway of her death. I want to wake inside Rainie's body instead.

If Rainie was able to dream for two weeks and still return to the world, then why can't I leave myself behind for a while? I hope at least that Rainie will be beside me when I awaken from my dreams, crouching over my body as she tends to my thirst, just as I tended to hers. When she fell asleep for two weeks, I stood vigil by her side, ensuring that she would return to me. I wanted to be the first thing she saw when she woke. Maybe, to summon her to my side, I only need to wander away for a while. I only need her to come back and reel me in, to save me from straying.

On the count of three, I open my fist, imagine a red thread slipping out of my fingers, a balloon string floating high into the atmosphere. I set free my body's tether and wade forward with my eyes closed, burrowing deeper into my dream. When I open my eyes, I am next to the sycamore, submerged in sleep, its roots flapping loose, the tree tall with a vertical slit down the length of it.

Beside me, the lot is dotted with dogs. Though the fence is usually mottled with rust and bird shit, tonight it is liquid, a purple pane of water that distorts the dogs behind it, bloating their tongues big as ships, blurring their bodies into a single tentacled being. The only dog that is clarified by a filter of water is the red-bearded one, who tonight is red-rumped. Its proportions are distorted, its paws broad as rain puddles. When it opens its mouth to bark at me, I see its missing tooth, a hole in the top row. A seed could be slipped into that socket to grow a new one, I think, but I can't find a seed on the sidewalk. Howling now, the red dog laps at the fence made of water, trying to drink it. It wants to reach me. It pushes its nose through the water, breaching the surface like a fin, pointing at the sycamore. *Listen.*

The street is flooded, the moon bobbing on its surface like a skinned apple, speckled with black dirt, and when I approach the tree, I see that its trunk is thumbed open, a slit in it that pulses open and shut. I know from the smell of the slit: It produces sap, salty as the back of Rainie's neck after a day of being dogs. I tug myself out of the water of the street, clinging to the trunk of the tree, and tuck my tongue under the sea, into the slit at the center of the trunk. Behind me, the red dog sets its jaw and whistles to me through the hole of its missing tooth. Its hiss slips into the trunk. The dog is guiding me in, so I flick my tongue deeper into that dark, nudging it, coaxing the sponge inside to harden and hive. The trunk closes then, the slit healing around the hilt of my tongue, and I am sewn mouth-first against its bark, hot and sensitive like the skin of a thigh. The tree says, *Hold me,* so I knot my arms around it, clutching my wrists, pressing myself so hard against it, my hipbones hack at the wood.

Look up, the tree says, and though I can't move my face, fused to the trunk and sheened in sap, I roll my eyes upward, buoy them toward the branches, and see that perched among the mirrored leaves is a woman.

She makes a language of the leaves, sitting on the bough as if it's a swing and rattling the branches with her hands to make the leaves chime together. The woman blurs, wearing something other than skin, hair like a field on fire. Her eyes are a dog's. She is naked, her chest grained like wood. I blink at the woman, attempting to clarify her, to delineate her from the tree, but the woman climbs onto the branch and continues to ascend, waving her foot in a way that charms me. *Wait for me,* I want to say, but my tongue is stitched to the trunk, pinned full of splinters. I breathe through the trunk of the tree, its marrow spongy and light, and when I inhale through my nose, the trunk swells in symmetry.

With my hands clasped, my arms twined around the trunk, I realize that it is too late to find a way back to my sleeping body. My fist no longer remembers its fragile thread, so slender and rootless. It craves only the solidity of this tree, its rooted monstrosity. The water in the street sidles up to me, surrounding me like a dogpack, nipping at my thighs. *Good dog,* I pray, as the water rises to my thighs. I hum to the woman in the tree, asking her to lift me into the branches, to rescue me. The sycamore thickens, bursting out of my arms, but I still try desperately to contain it in my embrace. My left shoulder is jostled from its socket, and I wonder if people have bones in their dreams. The trunk expands like dough and absorbs me, folding me into its body, the wood rippling with fat, and as I disappear inside the trunk, I imagine all my pores expanding. A million holes to string with red thread, each one leading me home.

My veins braid into the trunk. The branches turn hefty as meat, broadcasting my blood through its leaves. Leaves rust and fall like coins to the concrete. The sky fills with my cry. Jets of silver light. I am a tree's feast.

In the morning, Abu finds me stiff and satin-skinned, each of my veins replaced with red thread, no blood running through me.

An Abbreviated List of All
the Ways the Hsia Family Attempts
to Revive Anita

Together, Abu and Vivian rattle me, picking up each of my limbs like a different instrument they don't know how to play, and when Vivian asks if I'm dead, if my organs are now balls of wool, Abu slaps her and says, *Where is it, the red thread, the one she must have been holding, did it slip from her fist, did she try to dream without it? Did she let go on purpose? Who or what was she trying to follow?*

They open all the windows in the house to fill me with light, coax me back into the body. *Her blood's out*, Abu says. *She's full of thread.* Abu slits the pad of my forefinger with the blade of a scissor and pulls out a thread of my blood, tugging and tugging until it's as long as the hallway, then curses and says,

It's too much. She knots the thread close to my finger, clots the blood, trims the length. The thread is wet, which means it's recent, which means I am not too lost in my dream that I can't be reeled back with a fishline. Vivian slings me onto the sofa, trying to wake me with her fists, the flat of her hand, a bag of frozen dumplings smacked against my cheek, a pinky soaked in boiling water, an entire handful of salt poured into my mouth, then sugar, then oil, no swallow. Abu visits a bait-and-tackle store, purchasing a spool of fishing line, transparent and thicker than any thread. She bends a paper clip into a hook and ties it to one end, then lowers the line into my mouth while Vivian props it open. The wire hook wades into my belly. Abu waits for a tug on the other end. She and Vivian sit beside my mattress, the two of them like that the entire day, fishing inside me, waiting for me to wake, thrashing.

At the end of the day, when Vivian is asleep beside my thread-stuffed body, when Abu is leaned over me, still cursing, saying I am too selfish to dream, dreaming should always be on behalf of someone else, dreaming should be performed for the dead only, she feels a tug at the end of her line. Jerking awake, Vivian watches as Abu unreels the hook from me, lifting it out of my mouth, and snagged on the end of the paper-clip hook is a lank petal—*No, a peel,* Vivian says, a rind of some kind, silk on one side and velvet flesh on the other. Vivian licks it with the tip of her tongue: *A banana peel,* she says, *so sweet so sweet,* and Abu leans back against the bedroom wall, kneels. *I know,* Abu says to the ceiling, though all that lives there is a stain in the shape of a fist, opening its fingers every morning. *I know what kind of ghost this is,* she says.

Abu preserves the banana rind in a jar until it shrivels. *A banana ghost must have kidnapped her,* Abu says, but she says this with doubt, knowing her daughter and her daughter's desires, her willingness to be taken, to trade her life for a tree's. She knows the city should have severed that sycamore long ago, that it must be in violation of some kind of code, but when she calls, the city informs her that the tree has indeed been cut down many times for interfering with power lines but that it grew back at the startling rate of a few days, and so they have decided to deal with it the way they dealt with most things, by ignoring it.

To take a girl back from a dream, Abu says, *we must tug on her ears and her arms and her ankles.* After two hours of tugging, Abu says instead: *We must terrify her. We must stage an attack on her body so that her spirit will be forced to return just to rescue it.* Vivian and Abu arm themselves with forks and tiptoe down the hallway, sticking to their shadows, and then they leap through the doorway, pretending to stab me in the belly or hack off my head, but I don't return to my body, and their weapons embed in the sofa.

Another strategy, Abu says, *is to persuade her back to waking. Convince her home. We do this by reminding her of all the pleasures of corporeal life.* Abu opens and shuts my jaw like a puppet's, miming the motion of chewing. *Tickle her,* Abu tells Vivian, *make her laugh,* but not even a tissue paper dragged across the sole of my foot can rally a sound from me. Abu and Vivian sugar my lips, urge me to lick, but my mouth mimics a suture. Another way, Abu explains, is to decorate me brightly so that my soul knows where to land when it's ready, and so they paint me like a runway, a dashed white line down the center of my body, peppercorns sprinkled on my cheeks like glitter, the soles of my feet painted silver.

When they have exhausted Abu's various methods, verbal threats, and physical intimidations, such as wedging my hand in the door crack and threatening to slam the door shut unless my soul comes back right now, as well as other known strategies such as praying, politely asking, and singing familiar songs, they sleep for the first time in three days. Vivian on my left side and Abu on my right, my body silent as a tree between them, and I want to return if just to say I'm safe, that I'm not worried about my body if I know they will watch over it, that the banana ghost will not hurt me, I know her face and I will branch toward her, I will reach for the rust-red streak in her long black hair, I will chime my leaves in greeting, I know her face as my own, I see the symmetry between us, my fear of heights and her fear of the ground, her beckoning from the branches and my burial inside the trunk, and inside her lungs I am freed from forgetting, and I remember the face of the woman in the branches. The woman who uprooted me.

Anita Meets the First of Her Many Mothers, and the Sycamore Tree Provides a Spiritual Dwelling

Inside the trunk of the tree, I squirrel deep into the dark. In the branches above me, the banana ghost is swinging her legs, picking at a knot in the branch like a loosening scab. She wears my face. I remember Rainie's mother, who knotted her brother to a banana ghost like this one, and I know I should be afraid. *First mother of many,* I say, *will you let me go? I won't ask you for anything, not even the lottery numbers. I never once made a knot around your trunk or drove needles into your marrow. I didn't once try to trap you inside me.* But the banana ghost perches and hums, and the marrow of the trunk swells like bread and burrows into my mouth, and I can no longer speak nor breathe nor remember any name. I try to remember everything Abu told me about dreaming, how if there's a light switch anywhere in your dream, on a wall or the ceiling or embedded in the bottom of your foot like a splinter, you must flick it. If the lights don't work, you're dreaming, and this is when you need to bash your head against a doorframe or drown your head in the sink or run in place until the aching makes you wake. But we had power outages often because of the sycamore's interference, and the lights didn't turn on even when I was awake, and so I always injured myself for nothing.

I asked Abu, *If our lights don't work anywhere, in our sleep or in the day, what's the difference between dreaming and being awake?* But Abu sees the dead in her dreams, sweeping their desires into dung piles, and she says that's the difference. The dead can choose to appear in dreams. I wonder if this means the woman who gave birth to me is dead, if that is why I see her now, perched in my branches like a god of truth. She is a banana dangling from a ceiling, a lightbulb riddled with rot, darkening the room instead of brightening it. Nurturing mushrooms and spawning shadows.

Inside the trunk of the tree, my heart sponges up excess rain, my veins replace their blood with red thread. Am I dead, I think, or just alive outside my body? I know, in this moment of wondering, that I was born to wander away from my original form, that I was meant to let go of myself. To dream without the walls of a skull. I dream of my first mother, the woman wearing a belt of pearls, leaves overlapping into a dress. Circling the tree is a pack of dogs, and from the sound of their voices I know they are mountaindogs like the kind in old stories, not an officially registered species and therefore not known by anybody, rescued from boys who feed them balls of meat with glass shards embedded inside them, just to watch them shit blood, rescued from thirst, from flooding gutters, and when they run they remember the give of mud, dragging the body of a deer for miles, up the mountain, stealing velvet off the antlers, dressing inside it, remembering the story of the girl who drags herself out of a deer carcass, following the hunter home, becoming his wife. The dogs tell me: *It is better to be asleep, the moon swinging for you only, do you hear it, do you think where you live is called a city, you have never seen one then, a city is a fist, it exists to beat you, that's what your mothers knew, both of them, the first who left you behind, don't you know who she is didn't we send her to you the red dog with the stone in its mouth stolen did she try to bite you did Rainie run away that's a good girl a good girl she was once your mother.*

Inside the trunk of the tree are shelves—no, bunks—with stone-mattressed beds, layers and layers of women sleeping suspended between one another.

Circling the trunk are the dogs, who bring me lists of things with their teeth, abbreviated here: a factory filled with aquariums, a baby on a bottom bunk—Abu's memories. Then other colors, brought to me in the jaw of dogs: a sea-hemmed city, beached whales that exploded, rains of meat, a highway on stilts, elevated above a field, you, the one who sleeps on the lowest bunk, I see you standing in the field with your hair hazed into two braids. Back then you despised the taste of bananas, the quickness with which they rotted in the dark of your house, and you hated good news, announcements of marriages and graduations and gratitude, because it meant that a neighbor would arrive with a basket of bananas, a gift, and you and your mother and your siblings would have to eat them all, black spots of rot orbiting, and your mother would say, *Don't complain about receiving something, my god, I give you something sweet and you spit.*

You are sick of bananas, spineless, smashed against the street, the starch cottoning the back of your throat. You chew everything compulsively, including your hair and knuckles. You require something in your mouth at all times, a fact that many men try to take advantage of. You have a twin who is called prettier, though you have the same face, the same birthmarks on the back of your neck that your brothers used as targets when you were younger, making catapults out of wood and leather, asking you two to run in the field like deer while they tried to hunt you, stone you exactly where you were stained. She is called pretty because she possessed something you could only skim the surface of with your fingers, a kind of smokiness, the way she filled a room so completely, all the presence of a fire.

Your twin marries a man from the city and the two of you live with him, and he likes you better: Your sister is his wife, but you are his knife. He carries you close, takes you on the gondola that climbs the sky, that lowers you onto a mountain where a teahouse stands at the very tip, where you and the man split the dark into sips. This man was descended from duck farmers, from the same northern region as you, but now the only duck he'll touch is the kind hanging in the restaurants, glazed and plum-dipped, and though he claims he has never touched a live duck, never slit its carotid artery to bleed it out, leaving only the meat, he has hands that wring the sheets when he sleeps, the motion of unscrewing a neckbone: He can disguise those hands only in the day.

In the city, everyone is a searchlight. The dogs stray across the streets, sprawl in the middle of swamps. The sun schedules its suicide every evening, smashing into the street, and in the hills that no longer grow trees, houses sprout like teeth. You do not recognize these dogs, deboned, afraid in the day and mean at night, nothing to hunt but themselves. In the apartment compound, concrete floors and no curtains, thumbs of light prying at your eyes, you and your sister on both sides of the man. One of you is pregnant, brittle-boned, and it is your sister who is sick out the square window, raining onto the people below. She is sick out the window because it is dramatic, and she wants to make a statement.

Your twin takes a job at a garment factory. At home, she enjoys cutting swaths of newspaper for her own patterns to be traced on, and at night she falls asleep thinking she's still holding a pair of scissors, so that she can dream of returning his touch with a blade to his balls. While she works, the man visits restaurants and tries to convince them to buy his family's ducks, promising that by the end of the month their customers will double, triple, he will grant them a week of ducks for free, because their meat is different, rich and flavorful as rust, because the ducks are starved and it makes them forage on their own, and their flesh is flavored with everything they find. While they are out, you stay in the apartment and paste over the concrete walls with sheets of newspaper.

You wish you were the pregnant one, the sister in possession of something, the one who inherited her mother's bracelet, a band of red-and-gold thread with a pattern of mountains stitched in seed pearl. When she's asleep, you unknot it from your sister's wrist, slung across the man's sweat-glazed belly, and wear it around your own wrist, lifting it to the window, imagining it around your sister's wrist as she plucks the feathers off the duck: bone juxtaposed with golden thread.

You never thought of wanting a child, but it would be something to occupy your body so that you could vacate it.

You dream of holding your baby like a balloon, its umbilical cord looped around your wrist, the baby floating above your head. Waking, you want to be the day's anchor.

You wonder if the man knows the difference between you and your sister, your missing molar, the scar where a rooster spurred you, or if sometimes he turns to her in the night thinking she is you, silent because he has forgotten both your names. If the child is born live, would you be its mother or its shadow?

When your sister's baby arrives at night, a baby like a plucked hen, the purple of drained blood, you move into the pearl-factory dormitory. When you slept between your sister and her husband, your breasts filled with milk, and the baby could not differentiate you from its own mother. Babies and men, you thought, they really are the same species. Needy. When the stains darken the front of your shirt, you scoop water from the tanks and dash it across your chest, attempting to camouflage it. You are not capable of care: You repeat this to yourself, hoisting the knife again, wedging it between the lips of the oyster.

At night you sleep on the bottom bunk of the dormitory, beneath two other women. The woman on the very top steers her head into the ceiling every morning, spitting each curse word like a bead, rolling them beneath the bed.

The woman in the middle bunk, the one directly above you—she wet her mattress once but wouldn't admit it, claiming that what splattered on your forehead that night was rain, though you are two layers removed from the ceiling, and it hadn't rained at all that night—is your kin. You know because she avoids looking at you, swerving in the hallways or in the shared bathroom. Your face is so familiar to her that she fears it, foreshadowing ghosts.

You do not know what part of the factory she works in, but her hands are small and hollow-boned like a bird, and you hear her slapping mosquitoes and flies against the wall in her sleep. She must be a stringer, the ones who thread the pearls into labyrinthine necklaces or wire the pearls into brooches. You hear her hands all night, humming electric in the air, sometimes between her legs, her tongue paddling toward some word it has lost.

Unlike the other women, who lean against the wall in the hallway, who smoke out the window, who steal necklaces and are rapidly fired, who steal oysters and eat them raw in bed, swallowing the pearl or spitting it at the wall, who cry into their pillows, who hump the pillows, who write letters to the south, who marry quickly and say, don't worry, someday a man will invent you too, the middle-bunk woman never loved a pearl, never cared about working in the proximity of beauty. She looks like the kind of woman who dreams for utility, does nothing without purpose. She hangs her sheets out the window to dry but never bothers to clean her mattress, the one with a yellow stain, and every night you smell her above you, the sour-sweet of her release, her fingers poking holes into the day like a doily.

One day in the factory, your knife buries itself in your palm, and the bossman says, *Go home, don't bleed on the goods.* Your hand swathed thick as a child, cradled to your chest. That night is the first night the middle-bunk woman speaks to you—she always talks up to the top-bunk woman, never talks down to you, not even the night she pissed on you—and she asks, *How deep?* You wonder if maybe she is speaking in her sleep, some erotic dream, though you know she dreams only to hear stories and wield them later as weapons. But she is asking you how deep is the cut, and in the dark you unwrap your hand, which you raise above your head until your arm aches. The wound is blanched and glowing, split skin overlapping. *I know how to stitch*, she speaks to you, lowering her voice on the end of a fishline, dangling it above your lips. *Okay*, you say, and she climbs her way down to you, her feet appearing first, pulsing like raw oyster flesh.

She kneels beside your bunk and reaches for your hand, which you give over easily. Her breath banding around your wrist, suppressing your pulse. Already it feels like the wound has migrated somewhere else, and her hands will have to roam you to find it. She looks at the slit in your palm, deep and hissing, and with her other hand she plucks a hair from her head. Her elbows are the sharpest you've ever seen, spear tips, her whole body a direction.

A needle emerges in the dark between you. You are propped up now, on your average elbows, and she is threading her hair through the needle. *Our hair*, you want to say, *is so strong it can drag an anchor up from the water*, but that's just a myth. The needle threads through the flaps of your skin, shutting the wound in your palm like an eyelid, and at the end, when she makes a knot and bites off the excess hair, you pretend you were looking at your hand the whole time and not watching her, kneeling in front of you, head bowed, the closest thing to surrender you've ever seen her pretend.

The next morning, the hair rivers through your palm, thick as a splinter, thicker than when she first stitched it, and with a red sheen that looks like blood running through it. You wonder if it is possible for a strand of hair to carry blood like a vein, and you almost ask her, except the middle-bunk woman still does not look at you. Only at night, in the bathroom with only one drain, the floor slanted so that all water flees to it, you squat on the tiles and pour buckets of water over yourself, your once-a-week bath. Behind you, the middle-bunk woman approaches in the dim, offers to wash your hair. *Don't get that hand wet,* she says. So you lift your hand away from your body as she slips the rest of the water over your head like a hood, twists your hair and wrings it, scrubs your back with the balding washcloth.

Your hand stitched with her hair: It glows in the bathroom, the thread shrinking, worming into your meat. When the supervisor tells you to work the showcase room for a few days before returning to the floor, there are rumors you got the job through unseemly means. They say this because you are silent in the dorms every night. A mouth unoccupied by speech must be full of a man. You look to the middle-bunk woman to contradict this, to say that you are injured and your hand is stitched with hair. Somewhere in your palm, a nerve has been severed, and you can't feel the center of your inner wrist. It feels like a dog has grown its tooth there. The middle-bunk woman says nothing about you or the rumors, and when you walk the hallways instead of sleeping, because the hair in your hand is flame-hot and singeing your skin, she doesn't get out of bed and follow you. She doesn't bend over your palm and tug out the hair with her teeth. When your hand begins to smell of smoke, you run to the bathroom and plunge your hand into the pots of water stored under the sink. There will be a typhoon tomorrow, and for days there will be no running water or electricity and you will all drink and bathe from those buckets, the water now wriggling with your blood.

While you walk the hallways, you think maybe the middle-bunk woman likes that you are a rumor and she is the one who sleeps above you, floating between the floor and the ceiling, never jamming her head against the plaster like the top-bunk woman or stepping on insects in the morning like you. She is suspended between your two bodies, untouched by anything, and one night you kick both feet against her mattress, aiming your heels into her lower back. She wakes and rolls over but says nothing. *The hair,* you say. *I can't get it out of my palm. It's healed, but I can't pull it out.* It's the simplest kind of stitch, but her hair makes it complicated, the knot tightening on its own.

She descends from her bunk, kneels again beside your bed, and in this dark you see that inside her left eye floats a fleck of silver, like litter on a river, and you want to pluck it out of her sight. *Let me see,* she says, and you give her your hand. She nestles it on her lap and cranes her neck over it, traces her hair spidering through your palm, and before you can ask her to unstitch it, she kisses you once on the wrist, in the place where you're numb, and the nerve comes unplugged. *It will come out on its own,* she says, before ascending, and all night you look up at the backside of her mattress, moldy and yellow with sweat, a mushroom sprouting from one of its seams. Even when she lifts her head, the wet of her lips crowning your wrists, she doesn't look directly at you. You want to say, *I could have told the truth, cut the rumors at the root. But I want you to defend me or accuse me. Speak of me. I want to occupy your imagination. I want to show off the hair stitched into me, a red thread throbbing. Take ownership,* you want to say, *of the wound or the suture, either one, as long as you say my name, as long as you look at me tonight.*

There's a pay phone outside the dormitory that the girls line up for, and every month you call your sister, the baby in the background, nestling its noise between you. The month of your injury, she says—*please come home—our husband misses you—*

come take the baby—I want to visit our mother—I want to go back to that beach—you know the one where you accidentally swallowed the sun and had a weeklong fever—come take the baby—our husband won't even notice I'm not myself—you can be mother for a whole—I'll go back to our mother and tell her how we're doing—I'll bring her the shoes I bought for her—the baby—I stand on the street and watch the women pass—I copy the number of pleats in their skirts—trace the pattern onto newspaper— come—the baby—it wants—

Your sister says she wants to go home. In the language you split with her, the word for *home* is said by two people, the first person saying the first syllable and the receiver saying the second, a collaborative vocabulary. This is the language of the underside, where you were both born, and it has long gone extinct on the topside. The girls at the factory talk often of the underside, how no one must care about pearls down there. Pearls lack mystery for those born in the sea. You try to remember whether pearls were important on the underside, but you no longer remember what it was like to breathe water.

You are complicit in your sister's theater—she says to take the bus back to her apartment, to meet her outside so she can teach you to wrap your body around the baby's, and *then you will walk up the six flights of stairs and replace me in the kitchen, and he will never know the difference, sister, I swear, just remember not to speak any of our underside language, not even to the radio or to a dog, because he knows I never do that, we have a radio now, did I tell you, it was junked but he fixed it, too bad all we get are speeches, all day long, speeches, don't you miss our mother, god, I never want to sew anything ever again, trace another pattern, even though I look good in all these pleats, I swear, I'm as hunched as a knuckle now, you wouldn't recognize me, or maybe only you would.*

You go to your sister, switch places with her. You carry the baby up the stairs. You cook and wipe the windows, hide your injured hand, the only thing that might pause him—*when did you cut yourself?*—but he doesn't look at your hands, nothing below the mouth. You sleep on your sister's side of the bed. The baby knows and doesn't recognize you, crying all night even when you ball a handkerchief in its mouth, even when you turn the baby upside down, because that's the way to hypnotize a chicken, tucking its body upside down under one arm. But the baby only cries harder, and the stitches in your palm loosen and undo, a scarf of your blood trailing on the floor.

In the morning, when the man is gone to visit restaurants and offer them samples of his family's ducks, you go back to the dorm with the baby strapped to you. Inside the dorm, the women are still asleep, but soon they'll wake, and the fan will be so full of fly carcasses that its blades are too bogged down to whip new air into the room. Soon they will line up for the bathroom and talk about the new color of oyster they're breeding in the tanks, pink in some lights and gold in others. When you mount the cement stairs of the dorm, the baby goes sullen as a stone and burrows into your arms. You wonder if the baby knows it is in the presence of weapons, women who do not confuse flesh with the precious.

Level with your head is the middle bunk and the woman who sleeps on it. In your arms, the baby is quiet as a color, and you wonder if this is the kind of daughter the woman dreams of birthing, if in her dreams she is laboring, reaching down between her legs and finding a coiled wire, pulling out an electric fan from inside her. When she plugs the baby into the wall, it will deliver cool air to the room. There is nothing of your sister's face in this baby, nothing but the threshed hair on her head, strands so thick the outer layer shucks away to reveal a core of silver wire underneath. This is the kind of daughter the middle-bunk woman would love, look at, say the name of, feed handfuls of pearls to, teaching her how to round syllables and string them into the jewelry of sentences.

You lay the baby on your bottom bunk. Before you leave the dorm, you pluck a strand of hair from the baby's head. It is the length of your palm. You will save the hair, coiled, at the bottom of your sewing kit, the one you brought with you to the dorm even though there was nothing to sew but the sheets to your skin. The hair was for a sequel wound, and you knew there would be a time when you'd need to sew another life closed.

The middle-bunk woman was right: The hair in your palm did dissolve after months, ducking into your blood. By then you are gone from the city and its dogs. This version of the story where the middle-bunk woman—FeiFei—tells her daughter, years later, about how she rescued a baby from the bunk beneath her: You have never contradicted it.

I don't know which story is the true one, but you tell me from the branches of the tree that it no longer matters. You speak through the mouths of the dogs ringing the trunk, and when I ask if Abu/FeiFei saved me or stole me, if she cared for me or captured me, maybe you would say they were the same. The woman who gave birth to me, the sister who imperson-ated her, the woman who took me from the bunk—three women, each bound to the other by a red thread, which I un-reel now in my dreams. In the branches of the tree I kneel inside, you swing your feet and say that you plucked a hair from FeiFei's head one night while she was asleep. In case you ever needed to sew up another cut. I ask if I can see it. I lost the thread I'd been holding in my fist and have no way to find my body. Would she lend it to me, that hair, so that I can find my way back?

But you don't hand me anything, so I bob in the dark, calling for Rainie, and for the woman who raised me, the one who stands on the driveway with an electric flyswatter, having been traumatized by insects in her dorm room, and says, *Look how much I love you, I let you choose which bunk to sleep in, I brought you here to this day, look at the way the sun tracks its blood down my palm and behind the mountains, follow it, and I'll still be there, my daughter.* Abu's story and yours: Which is real? Am I given or left? I ask the dogs, knocking my knuckles against the inside of the trunk, but they don't answer. They paw at the bark, trying to unbury me from the trunk, but I have already decided I prefer the marrow of trees, prefer to be a bloodless body, no lineage spearing through me.

What Happens While Anita Is Asleep
(Having Wandered from Her Body)

I. What Abu and Vivian do: Worry () Worry () Worry. Anita's silence silkens into many pearls, released in blank spit-bubbles: (). Stringing the air for many days.

II. Vivian and Abu sit by her bedside and take turns plucking hairs from her head, one at a time, in a method they found on the internet: *pluck each hair off the sleeping scalp and tie the strands end to end, into a glossed rope, then tie the foot of the bed to any doorknob in the house, a tightrope for the dreaming to return to their original bodies.* However, after approximately one hundred hairs each, Anita's scalp begins to bleed continuously, and they must wrap her scalp in six towels and swear to each other not to pluck another hair for as long as they have hands.

III. Rainie does not know. At night, in another city, she sleeps with the white stone in her bed, the stone that Anita coaxed out of the dog's mouth. *I will strike you with a stone and scar you. We will meet again.* Rainie hears a voice wrung from this stone when she cuddles it to sleep, but it is lower than Anita's voice, and she wonders if there is a banana tree on the premises of her new apartment building. She remembers her neighbor, a man, standing in the hallway one evening, peeling a banana with only his thumbnail and saying, *You know, back in the old days my brother used to tell me, don't beat the bird so much, it'll shed its wings and fall onto the ground between your legs, but I always did, and that's why my little bird looks like this now, deflated, but it used to fly. Do you want to revive it?* And Rainie runs back into her own doorway and hefts the white stone into her hands—it's the size of two fists, the texture of nicked teeth. She thinks of throwing it through the neighbor's window. There is one night she sits on the stone for hours, believing it might hatch, that Anita has manufactured some kind of miracle, but though it hums with her heat, there is nothing inside knitting its wings from lies.

IV. One summer, the summer before Rainie left, Anita's belly swelled, raising her shirtfront like a mast, and all the rest of the girls in the neighborhood shook their heads at her and said, She's shipwrecked. Every night that summer, Anita sat on the toilet for an hour and emitted water, her belly big as a ball gown, and when Abu took her to the neighbor with shaded glasses and a drawn-on beard, he said, *It's probably a tapeworm.* He held his forefingers four inches apart and said, *Based on your weight loss and the appetite of the worm, I'd say it's this long. And what's she wearing around her neck?* He examined her red thread as if it were a new parasitic species, shining his flashlight at it, tugging it away from the skin and asking her if it

hurt to be separated from it. *No*, Anita said, and the man nodded. He said, *You know, if you wear knots on your body like this,*
worms will fill your belly. He gave her a soup in a plastic bag, and
she drank it at home. Every day after that, when Anita shat in
the toilet, Abu reached inside the bowl with a chopstick and
stirred the water for signs of a white worm, glimmering four
inches long. The girls in the neighborhood spread a rumor
that Anita was pregnant and Rainie was the father, Mr. Dyke
and Mrs. Lezzie. Finally, in July, the worm reared its head,
wriggling around in the bowl like a spasming string of light,
and Abu fished it out and sealed it into a plastic bag. The man
examined it, then sealed the worm into a plastic water bottle.
Anita carried the worm back to the duplex, glowing inside the
bottle, white like the flesh of banana, and showed Rainie
when she was home. They swirled the bottle around, rubbed
it like a lamp, watched the worm circle itself, floating, waiting
for it to explode. *Remember*, Anita said, *when we thought babies were*
made when men took hammers to women's bellies? And we said it had to
be true because their belly-skins were buttoned back together, and we could
still see the seams, the empty button hole? At their throats, the red
threads reared like worms, alive and wet, burrowing into their
necks.

V. In the years Anita went missing from her body, Rainie
kept the stone beside her bed, even after her mother said there
was moss growing on it and it was starting to smell. Rainie
refused to donate it back to the dirt. With her long sleeves, she
hid the dog's tooth embedded in her wrist, set like a pearl, unable to dig it out with the tips of scissors or her own incisors.
Years later there was a woman she slept with, a coworker at
the pawnshop where she was in charge of evaluating gem-
stones, divining lineages in the cracks of a thing, the seams

inside a diamond or the mottled fog in a ruby, searching for a clarity and transparency that not even light could achieve. This woman brushed the dogtooth with her thumb and asked if Rainie feared it might be cancerous. It looked like a kind of mole, except bright instead of dark. If its shape mutated, she should consult a doctor. No, Rainie said, she'd never wondered. She thought of the tapeworm knotted in the bottle of formaldehyde, how long she'd loved it and envied it. A tapeworm ate everything inside you, the way a ghost ate everything you left for it, offered it. Anita was an altar for worms. At night, Rainie wondered if Anita still kept the worm and the bottle, if the dogs still tilled the dirt in the sycamore lot. Beside her, the woman suckled her wrist and nibbled at the dogtooth. Rainie bucked her head, barking out, and the woman laughed. *Little puppy,* she said. She taught Rainie how to bite a pearl to test its reality, how to shine silver with a special cloth, how to touch a hip where it's ticklish: grasp it like a handlebar, ride the dark.

VI. Anita dreams. She speaks to the banana ghost and begs for a thread, for a fishhook, anything with hold. *Take me back to my body,* she says, crouched in the tree. *I have drifted away for long enough. I have communed with ghosts. Now show me to the sky.* The neighbors visit her unresponsive body, laid out on a mattress in the driveway like a state funeral, the mattress dressed in Saran Wrap so that urine slides right off it. They crown her brow with kisses, dahlia stems, and coins rubbed faceless by their thumbs. They burn incense, pray in churches and temples, feed their ghosts and their dogs, tell their daughters not to be dogs or else they'll end up like this, asleep, lost without their bodies in some tongued dream. Vivian and Abu tend to her body as if it's a tree, though it grows much faster than anything they've seeded or weeded in the side yard: They trim her hair, bathe her by lowering her into the water together in a cage they built from chicken wire, repeating her name, *Anita, Anita, Anita,* as if to remind her that she was once given one, though she no longer responds the way she used to, shrugging in her sleep as if to say, *I'd rather not.*

Once in a while she has a nightmare and Vivian holds her mouth open, and later, Vivian's daughter, Winny, does this too when she grows hands of her own, preventing Anita from biting off her tongue. Though Anita doesn't speak in her sleep, she laughs, especially when Vivian tells her stories of Mr. McDonald's, how he learned to hump from watching stray dogs and his mother caught him doing all the door-knobs in the house and chased him out with a meat tender-izer. *Dogs,* Vivian says, *all of them,* but Anita stops laughing and her tongue unknots, slouching out of her mouth.

Dogs, Anita repeats, and it is the only word she will say in a decade.

Rainie Tsai Discovers that Dendrology Is Not Dentistry, and a Branch Is Returned to Her, in Living Condition

During the decade in which Anita slept, liver spots appeared on the backs of Rainie's hands. She placed pennies on top of them, gilding each spot, and fell asleep with the coins cooling the backs of her hands. Her mother, Buggy, worried about whether the spots were cancerous or latent signs of decay or predictors of dementia, but everyone said they were just cosmetic, a mottling that happened naturally, except no other part of Rainie's body appeared to be aging at the same pace. The dogtooth in her wrist, too, was just another form of ornamentation, and Rainie began to wonder if she'd one day become a chandelier, a decorative body with dazzling enamel.

When she was nineteen, Rainie was let go from her job as a receptionist at a dental office. The phrase *let go* dangled in her throat for weeks afterward. There was no longer a set time to wake up, a set time to leave the house and get paid and come back, and she felt that some essential tether to herself had been snipped. Her mother encouraged her to find another job quickly, but Rainie entered a limbo. It was like her limbs had let go of her body. It was uncannily similar to the sleep she'd once been submerged in for two weeks, where the world was an illusion, and if she only refused to participate in its engine, she would wake and be saved. But this time the sleep must be permanent, because the sensation of floating continued. She imagined swinging from the highest branch of a sycamore tree, letting go to land on the pavement below, where dogs would gnaw her meat and bury her bones. At least being eaten would return her to her body.

In the week before she was let go, Rainie had been called incompetent for canceling appointments without being asked to, though she contested this. Rainie distinctly remembered receiving phone calls from patients requesting cancellations, and their inability to remember those phone calls must be a sign of deep conspiracy. Most likely, some of them were ghosts or calling her in their sleep. Hadn't Anita's mother once said that sleep-talking was a common ailment, leftover language from our days of speaking to the dead and to dogs?

Rainie was told by the senior receptionist, who shared a desk with her, that she had to learn to separate her selves. *What do you mean?* Rainie asked. She imagined herself slit in half with one of the many slender and sharp-tipped tools the dentists used. Once, someone had walked confidently into the waiting room, which contained a TV and a game console that didn't work, and the friction of the woman's feet against the gray carpet created a static shock that managed to turn the TV on to a channel about dog breeds. The woman, panting steam, hooked a finger into the side of her mouth and yanked her lip out of the way. *Look,* the woman said, gnawing on her own finger as she spoke. *Look at this shit.* Rainie leaned forward over the desk and looked but couldn't see anything but her blistered gums. *Look,* she said again, and with the woman's mouth wide open, Rainie saw it: At the back of the woman's mouth, on the lower right-hand side, was a single white mushroom growing from her gums. It smelled sour, like pickled cabbage.

Rainie leaned back, remembering all her mother's warnings about rabies, and the tooth embedded in her wrist began to itch. She always wore long sleeves to disguise it, or a piece of statement jewelry that distracted from her tooth accessory. Though she tried not to itch it in public, she scratched it through her sleeve until the skin bled. Now it was practically humming, growing a millimeter farther out of her skin, and Rainie could not bear its irritation. The tooth propelled her hand like a magnet, and before she realized what she was doing, she had reached out and jabbed her finger into the woman's parted lips, grazing her front teeth. The woman jerked away, bringing her hand to her face, and Rainie retracted her hand quickly, pushing down on her wrist-tooth until the pain blotted out her embarrassment. *I'm sorry,* she wanted to say, *but the tooth on my wrist wants to belong in your mouth. A rootless tooth cannot help where it wanders.* But she could not say it. In the brief silence that followed, they stared at each other in the fluorescent light, the woman shielding her mouth as if she was about to vomit. Rainie lowered her head and mumbled, *Sorry, sorry, sorry.*

It turned out that the woman had developed an infection after her wisdom-teeth surgery, and a pocket of pus had formed in the wounded socket. It had to be popped and disinfected, and one of the assistants later told Rainie that she'd seen flesh get sucked out of the socket and into the milky tube. *A chunk of flesh,* she said, holding out the tip of her pinky. *You wouldn't think there could be so much meat in a socket that small, but it came out. Like a little animal.*

Rainie was thinking about the little slime animal sucked out of a mouth and through a tube when the senior receptionist said again, *You have to separate your selves. Your work self from your personal self.*

Weren't all selves personal, by definition? Rainie wanted to ask this but said nothing. She only nodded and said the senior receptionist was right. The next week, the dentist asked to see her privately. He led her to one of the private rooms, and for a second she wondered if she had an appointment with him, if he was going to ask her to bare her teeth. Instead, he told her that they were going to have two full-time receptionists rather than many part-time receptionists and that her two coworkers had already agreed to take on her hours. Rainie nodded, avoiding the glare of the dentist's glasses, deciding to look instead at the translucent white tube used for sucking up spit and toothpaste-foam from a patient's mouth, envisioning a ball of meat no bigger than her fingertip. She imagined it was the exact size of the flesh displaced from her wrist by a dog's tooth.

Later, she would wish that she'd been the one to quit. But in reality, she thought, it was Anita who was the type to revolt against the narrative of her incompetence. It was Anita who refused to taper her temper. Rainie would split all her selves if she needed to. When her mother heard about the loss of her job, she only said to Rainie that it would be good for her: After all, the proximity to so many sickened teeth, infected and rotting and aching and throbbing, was bound to have ailed her wrist-tooth eventually. The tooth in her wrist was mostly dormant, only occasionally sore when exposed to sudden changes in temperature, but it would eventually gain ideas from her workplace. It would learn to gather plaque as stubborn as tile grout, or it would learn to impact its roots or dry out its socket, or it would tell her it wanted to be straightened, even though it was the only tooth in her wrist and had no neighbors to align with.

So Rainie spent the rest of the summer helping her middle brother assemble a new anatomy for his car. *It's a JDM,* he said, patting its side. *Japanese Domestic Market. Or, as I like to call it, Japanese Dream Machine.* Rainie tried not to splatter its hood with laughter.

In the middle of that summer of car parts, Rainie's brother said she should get out every once in a while, so she took the bus to the beach alone, prodding at the dogtooth petrified in her wrist, remembering the time her mother had driven them to the beach and Rainie fell asleep, her head resting on her oldest brother's shoulder. When she woke and turned her head to the window: water. They were driving along the spine of a cliff, and the sea arrived as suddenly as a bone poking through meat, spittle hitting the passenger window. There was no railing along the cliff-road, nothing to buckle the car to the ground, and so Rainie screamed when her mother drifted over to the left, laughing and saying, *If I wanted to, I could drive us into the sea right now; we could live at the bottom if we wanted to.* Rainie asked her mother what was at the bottom of the ocean. *Dogs,* her mother said. *Dogs with human eyes.* That was what made the water clench and release like a muscle: dogs running beneath the surface, trying to get home, trying to climb ashore. That was why the waves beat themselves against land.

On the bus to the beach, Rainie met the dendrologist. The dendrologist got off at her stop, at one of the smaller beaches with stone caves, images battered into the surface of the rock by waves, silhouettes like dancing women. The woman introduced herself as a dendrologist. *A dentist?* Rainie said, trying to remain open-minded. She had only recently fled the authority of dentists.

The woman was older than her, vaguely somewhere between her age and her mother's, and there were silver strands shadowing the black in her hair. But the strands were white only near the roots: Near the tips, Rainie realized, they were the color of rust, dried blood. It was strange that select strands of her hair were half white and half red, as if they really had oxidized into that shade. She'd seen that exact color of hair before only on a dog.

The dendrologist's jeans were white at the knee, a symptom of praying or constant kneeling. She had a long face like a snout, her ears jutting from her head. Her teeth were elongated and sinking into the butter of her lower lip. She moved as unselfconsciously as a dog, so beautifully unburdened. Rainie resisted the urge to stroke the dendrologist's forehead with one finger, to scratch behind the woman's ear.

The dendrologist said, *No, not a dentist, a dendrologist. I study trees.*

Rainie laughed.

A tree doctor, she said. *I didn't think those were real. Do you know about sycamores? I used to think they were named that because they were all sick. I thought they would collapse and die.*

The dendrologist laughed at this. *Yes, I know those trees,* she said. *But what kind of sycamore? There are many.*

The kind that is filled with dogs, Rainie wanted to say. *Where dog-women enter at night to sleep and gossip, insisting they are our mothers. What do you call a tree like that?*

But Rainie did not speak this aloud. Instead, she studied the dendrologist, who wore a ring on each finger, bands of silver, and Rainie wondered if she was collecting rings like a tree, stacking them to mark time, memories. If Rainie grew rings inside her bones, she knew what they would mark: every year since she'd moved away from Anita. Though Rainie never tried to find Anita again, partly out of an ancestral fear. She remembered what Anita had said: She would scar Rainie to see her again. But in the end, the scar on her forehead had faded, which meant Anita hadn't meant it, and the story of the thread was just a story, frayed, and years of telling had torn it. When she thought of Anita, it was the same way she thought about first seeing the sea, her terror: the white foam like floating bones, nothing between the car and gravity. She'd opened the door, and if she'd leaned on it just a little, she would have fallen into the mouths of human-eyed dogs.

Rainie looked at the beach, the litter fluttering like flocks of birds, the seagull cracking a clam against a rock, meat pearling in its throat. The sand was empty except for a man sunning himself on the rocks, lying naked on an island of stone, unmoved by the birds shitting above him. *But there aren't any trees here,* Rainie said, and the dendrologist spun the ring on her thumb. The dendrologist nudged her glasses to the top of her head. She squinted at Rainie and smiled, one of her teeth nicking her lower lip. *No, but there are trees in the hills. Have you seen them?* Rainie laughed and looked up at the stone cliffs staggering above them. *Are you asking me if I've seen a tree? I've seen a tree.*

The dendrologist walked ahead of her, toward the sea, and Rainie realized that the woman had been barefoot this entire time. Rainie herself never took off her shoes outside, especially not at the beach, even if her shoes were filled with sand and her socks were weighed with pebbles. Her mother always told her not to walk barefoot anywhere, because she could someday step on a needle and get a disease and turn purple and die, and besides, it was uncivilized.

The dendrologist walked bare-soled all the way to the water, the back of her shirt soaked, and Rainie followed. They stood ankle-deep in the sand as the water skittered up to their feet and then shied. *What do you do to the trees once you find them?* Rainie said. She felt the heat of the dendrologist's shoulder, the expansive scent of her sweat. *I study the understory,* the dendrologist said, turning her head to look at Rainie. *Let me show you.*

You're not a dentist or a dendrologist, Rainie said, *you're a dog.* The dendrologist smiled, and her canines were gold—not real gold, Rainie believed, but some kind of calcified light. Her tongue slopped forward, squirming out of her mouth, and Rainie observed it was an atypically long tongue, the kind that might be used for lapping loose waters, dredging shallow seas, or flinging you a pink lifeline.

I can't swim, Rainie told the dendrologist, then shook her head to negate what she'd said. She didn't want to tell the dendrologist this. She didn't want to admit her wariness of water, how she still preferred to see the sea from above, from the distance of a cliff, and imagine it was run by dogs.

That day, the dendrologist walked her up the pedestrian trail—still barefoot, even in the soil filled with stones and shit—and Rainie followed. Anita always said Rainie was good at this, following, heeling. *Let's be sisters,* said a voice in the soil. *Bite your finger open and press it to mine. Let's touch bloods, together our reds.*

Along the trail, trees wilted beneath the weight of fog. *The understory,* the dendrologist said, her glasses throwing their glint across Rainie's face, *is here.* She kneeled on the side of the trail, grasping Rainie's wrist and pressing her hand against a sapling, its roots aboveground like uncoiled rope, its bark a bastardized version of skin, pored and hairless but with risen seams, patches of bark sewn together by lines of ants. *Seedlings, saplings, shrubbery. Low things, knee-level. The understory.*

Rainie followed the fake dendrologist off the path. Though the dendrologist was barefoot, she didn't seem to notice the stones and twigs sharp as fish-bones. Behind her, Rainie winced as the shrub leaves hooked into her knees. She could only see the outlines of trees like beheaded bodies. *Without the understory,* the dendrologist was saying, *the entire forest collapses.* Rainie didn't think this was true: It would just be like removing ornamentation, like taking the furniture out of a house. In the center of her inner wrist, her tooth ached and itched.

The fog lowered itself, flattened into a milk-colored field. They were in a clearing, and Rainie's knees and calves cringed with cuts. Trees applauded their branches, though there was no wind, and their red-flaked bark reminded Rainie of the pork jerky her aunts sent from the island, pounds of it, strips you could use as whips. *You have to bleed the pig out to get meat like this,* her mother had said, and Rainie squinted to look at the dendrologist, who was now on her hands and knees, nuzzling the ground with her whole face like a rooting pig.

This is a sycamore, she said, lifting her dirt-smeared face and pointing directly in front of her. *It doesn't belong here,* she said, and Rainie stepped forward, pressing her palm to its flaky trunk. It was only as tall as her. It looked nothing like she remembered it, the sycamore Anita used to kiss with her fists, the one only she could hear.

These are often found in very polluted parts of the world, the dendrologist said, *because the bark peels often, shedding what has touched it.* Rainie replied, *Like my eczema,* and the dendrologist laughed and said, *No, not at all, I'm saying it can absorb great impact. Good wood for butcher blocks. Good wood to wound.*

Look, the dendrologist said, standing up and turning away. The sycamore was swathed in fog, blurring. Rainie stared at the back of the dendrologist's bare neck: There was a nipple studding the back of it. Rainie wanted suddenly to push her to the dirt, kneel down, and suckle from it. Rainie had heard of floating nipples, ones that bloomed open on hips, on the backs of hands, on the tops of heads, but she'd never seen one. The dendrologist lifted her head from the leaf-laced dirt and said, *See all the seedlings,* indicating a row of green sprouts around her knees. *What I love about the understory,* the dendrologist said, *is that it's patient. It waits for something above it, a part of the canopy, to die and gape open. Then it grows up into the space left behind.* Rainie said that sounded like predation, not patience. Like it was waiting for the death of what lived above it. *Don't sound so sinister,* the dendrologist said, bending again to sniff the ground. *It's just succession.* Rainie reached out, flicking the nipple on the back of the woman's neck.

She flinched, standing up and grasping Rainie's hands by the wrists. *I want you to stay in touch with me,* she told Rainie, *so I can show you what I'm studying.* But Rainie said, *I don't know what you mean by studying.* Still, the dendrologist kneeled in the soil again and brushed the sprouts with the back of her hand. She said, *I don't kill trees, if that's what you're asking. It's possible to take samples of the marrow and sap without permanent damage.* Marrow, Rainie repeated to herself, marrow, marrow, as in bone. She thought of the sycamore and the dogs that circled it. *If a tree has marrow, then it must have blood,* Rainie said, *because that's the job of marrow, making blood.* The dendrologist looked up at her, the lenses of her glasses like two licked pennies. *Well,* she said, *I didn't mean that kind of marrow.* But why not, Rainie thought, and said, *I knew a tree growing up. I mean, I knew this girl.* The girl lived in the same duplex that she moved into. The first time she met the girl was on the street, when Rainie was observing two dead possums in a gutter, and the girl saw her looking and said, *They must have died together like this, at the same time.* Rainie asked the girl, *Why is that?* and she said, *Because if one of them had died first, the other would have eaten it.* Was that really true? Rainie still didn't know, but she had believed the girl instantly. She had thanked the girl for her brutality.

The dendrologist said that this girl—Anita—sounded disturbed. *But isn't it just as unnatural to speak to trees?* Rainie asked. *Don't you wonder what is buried beneath all this green?* The dendrologist stood up. *I'm going to the real mountains this week,* the dendrologist said, stepping closer, the lenses of her glasses etched with scratches that spelled something. *I know what you're thinking,* the dendrologist said, plucking a leaf off Rainie's cheek, leaving the lace of its veins on her face. *You think camping is just a way of disappearing into the woods, never to be seen again,* she said.

But Rainie went. The dendrologist picked her up in an SUV the color of a fly's teal eyes, and Rainie's mother watched from the window, her hands submerged in the sink. *Be careful of trees*, her mother said. *They have arms for a reason.* The dendrologist packed a tent, silver blankets, sleeping bags, pouches of water—but they didn't need the tent, the dendrologist said, because they were staying in a cabin.

There was a row of cabins the size of storage shacks, plywood with chicken-wire windows, and in front of each cabin was a metal box, latched and locked. *It's a bear box*, the dendrologist explained, *for putting food or other fragrant materials inside.* The only things Rainie knew how to pack were fragrant: pork jerky from her mother, bags of dehydrated seafood, powdered flavoring packets. She was taught to fear hunger more than bears. With embarrassment, Rainie emptied the entirety of her duct-taped backpack into the bear box. There was nothing she'd brought besides her clothing, Rainie realized, that was safe to sleep with.

The dendrologist took Rainie by the hand, her palm cold and unlined, and tugged her toward a metallic basin she'd brought and filled with water. There was a bathroom somewhere in the dark, waiting to be carved up by their flashlight beams, but she told Rainie to wash her face and brush her teeth using the water in the round metallic basin, which was ankle-deep. Rainie obeyed, scrubbing her teeth with her finger, gulping water from her palms, but when she turned to spit out the mouthful of foam onto the stones of the campground, the dendrologist said no, spit back into the basin. Rainie obeyed, and even in the dim—only the dendrologist's flashlight, which dangled in a holster outside the cabin, produced any local light—she saw the white froth of her spit and speckles of the watercress she'd eaten earlier. Then, to her horror, Rainie watched the dendrologist kneel in front of the same basin and proceed to wash her face and brush her teeth using the same water, without refilling it with whatever fresh source she'd located.

Rainie grasped the dendrologist's shoulder and tried to pull her back from the mouth-murky water, which the dendrologist was now swishing from cheek to cheek, but her body didn't budge. She could only watch as the dendrologist pivoted, smiling at her. This time, though, her smile was a seam, her cheeks caving in to stone, her lips receding into her mouth like fingers into a fist. Rainie took a step back, but the dendrologist beckoned her. When she shifted forward, she looked into the basin and saw that at the bottom of it was a fish, frying in its own light. Not a fish, she realized, but a set of teeth with gold canines flashing like fins, their brightness slitting the sullied water, parting it like hair.

You wear dentures? Rainie asked, but the dendrologist just continued to smile. Her mouth sucked inward like a sleeve turning itself inside out, and she was no longer familiar. It was an act of intimacy, Rainie thought, to see each other before sleep. And yet she felt that they had both slipped into other skins. Become other animals. The water bubbled up in the basin, as if the set of teeth at the bottom were trying to breathe, swimming for the surface.

That night they slept in the same sleeping bag, feigning a need for body heat, but it was summer and their skin cleaved, their thighs honeyed together. Unable to sleep, Rainie wondered whether the teeth were surviving in their basin outside, if they might develop toothache, if the dendrologist was capable of feeling toothache, even without any roots. Maybe they should have put the teeth in the bear box—whatever lived in your mouth must qualify as fragrant. Rainie remembered another story Anita told her when she'd first moved in: how the duplex was haunted by a perverted ghost that would undress them and leave their clothes at the foot of the bed. They'd wake up stuck, skin to skin. It never happened, but Rainie wished it had.

In the dark, Rainie woke with her face pressed against the dendrologist's chest, a hot seam of liquid stitching its way down her leg. She raised herself onto her elbows, squirming out of the silver sleeping bag, afraid she had wet herself. But the dendrologist whispered, *It's me, it's me, sorry, sorry.* The dendrologist rose in the dark and stepped out of her underwear. Her skin was barcoded by moonlight that slid in through the square window. Bare like that, the dendrologist opened the door of the cabin and walked out onto the pebbled ground, the wet underwear slung around her wrist like a bracelet. Rainie heard the bear box rattle open and shut. When the dendrologist returned, she told Rainie, *The bears would've smelled it.*

And what? Rainie wanted to say. *What would the bears do if they smelled it?* For the rest of the night, she waited for the bear to appear in the doorway, for the roof to be peeled away. In the morning, Rainie felt the dendrologist press against her, sticky and sweet and bare.

That day, the dendrologist introduced her to trees along a trail, fog accumulating like a layer of fat. To Rainie, all the trees looked the same, like trees, and halfway back to the cabin she asked, *Are there sycamores here?* She described the one she grew up with. The dendrologist shook her head. That night, while the dendrologist was leaned over a log, striking flint against a stone—though later they'd use her torch for the campfire—Rainie unlocked the bear box and looked inside. There were granola bars, the jerky, pouches of instant stew, but no underwear, no scent of anything, and Rainie wondered if a bear had eaten it or if the dendrologist had taken it somewhere and buried it or washed it in secret, ashamed, except the dendrologist didn't seem capable of feeling shame—she was only curious.

Later, when the dendrologist was driving back, the mountains looking like a movie set, as if the peaks would topple if she touched them, Rainie asked what she'd done with the wet underwear. Not turning her head, the dendrologist said, *I don't know what you're talking about.* Rainie wondered if she'd imagined it, the dendrologist standing up, the glow of her pubic hair, the underwear lassoed around her wrist like the ring of an alien planet. How much she wanted to rejoin that orbit.

In front of Rainie's apartment building, the dendrologist idled the car and said, *Thank you for coming with me.* Rainie turned her head, and the dendrologist's mouth pressed against hers so briefly that Rainie didn't have time to react. Her heat greased Rainie's lips, remaining there for many days. *I have a gift for you,* she said to Rainie. *Turn off your eyes.* Rainie startled. It was what Anita used to say to her: *Turn off your eyes* instead of *shut them.*

When she turned on her eyes again, Rainie's hands were wrapped around a branch, long as her forearm and flaking. It was a sycamore branch, white and forked in the middle, forming a shallow *Y,* the bark littering her lap. *Where did you get this?* Rainie asked. The dendrologist smiled and said, *You know, what's unusual about sycamores is that their roots are mostly aboveground.* Rainie said she knew. That's why the dead and the dogs liked to stand beneath them, because they could wrap the roots around their feet and remember their dreams.

When she arrived home, Rainie placed the sycamore branch next to her mattress and slept with one palm pressed against the knuckle at its center. Her mother told her to get rid of it, that there could be insects beneath the bark or that its color would attract bad luck, but Rainie kept it anyway. It retained the heat of a forearm. She trained her jaw to widen around it so that she could embrace the branch with her teeth.

Two nights after she brought it home, Rainie woke up with the branch between her legs, grinding against her, sawing at her. It reminded her of a story her mother once told her: In her childhood, her mother had woken up to a banana tree growing in the center of her bed, her legs parted around its trunk.

On the fourth morning, Rainie woke with the branch raised in her hands like a flag, and swinging at the end of it was the fabric of the dendrologist's underwear, mildewed and wet, smelling of pickled fruit. Rainie sat up, plucking the curled fabric off the branch's tip, and resisted the urge to ball it under her pillow. She felt like an animal dragging its prey into the trees to feed alone.

That was when Rainie's mother said the branch had to be broken at the knuckle and thrown away. What would appear on it next? A flock of predatory birds? Would a power line wrap around it? But the branch was familiar to her, its hinge like a friendly elbow. *Do you remember,* Rainie asked her mother, and then stopped. She'd wanted to ask if her mother remembered that old duplex, that sycamore where the dogs appeared.

Of course I remember that old sycamore tree, Rainie's mother said, guessing the shape of her daughter's distress. She'd once seen her dead brother's face embedded in its trunk, but when she reached out to stroke it, he burst into brittle leaves.

Rainie asked what happened to the girl in the back of the duplex, but she already knew what her mother would say: She stayed. *That family,* her mother said, *you know they'll never go any-where. The fact that they ever left their hometown is already a miracle. Families like that, they die where they're born.* Rainie asked if it wasn't better to die where you were born, where you could always be found. But her mother said she wanted to die like a tree in a wildfire, upward. And Anita once wanted to die like a stray dog, remembered by nobody.

Her mother didn't remember the address of the old du-plex, but Rainie found it on the library computer by searching two streets she remembered, both named after flowers, though the irony was that no flowers grew there because of the drought. Clicking on street view, she found the tree, leafless and dying but still upright, crowned in a haze that she wasn't sure was fog or smoke or evaporated breast milk. She zoomed in on the tree, which blurred and then focused, sometimes showing itself naked and sometimes dressing itself in a pix-elated gown. It decided on daring. The image cleared, and now Rainie could see its bare trunk, patches of white bark flayed away to reveal the skin beneath. Beyond it were blurred dogs, one of them leaping, suspended in the air with its tongue kiting above.

Rainie tried to rotate the image, but she could only see the street-facing side of the tree, and as she dragged her cursor up the flaking trunk, she noticed that there was a birthmark on the upper part of its trunk, a disc of black that had dimension, a hole or an open sore, sponged with rot. A branch had been severed there, she realized. In her bedroom, Rainie lifted the branch and looked at its flat side, sawed from the trunk. It was purple-black like a bruise, soft when she rested her thumb against it. The knuckle in the center of the branch, too, was beginning to soften and stink. This branch must be the sycamore's severed limb, and the dendrologist had been a dog after all, bringing the branch to her like a prize, summoning her home.

Rainie slept with the branch in her arms. She wanted to sew it back to its home. In the morning, she told her mother she was going to the duplex, that there was something she needed to return to the tree, something she hadn't meant to take. It was like a game of fetch: She had learned to clamp the branch in her jaws, and now she had to run back to her owner.

Her mother sat down at the kitchen table, spread a sheet of newspaper, and skinned an apple with a serrated knife. *I hope it's that branch you're taking with you,* she told Rainie. *It's starting to smell. Be careful.* Rainie noticed it then, the singed-meat smell of the limb, and so she bundled the softening bough in three sheets of the *World Journal* and agreed.

She wasn't sure if the tree would recognize her—no thread around her neck, no scabs on her knees, no startle in her skin—but she knew Anita would adopt the branch. Anita adopted all kinds of things: possum skeletons silvering in the heat, pine cones with chipped teeth, leaves lanced with holes. She called them all bones. Shedding its papery bark, the branch flexed like an arm, bending at the knuckle so that its fingers pointed out the doorway, herding Rainie home.

The Hsia Family Receives a Long-Loved Visitor, and Rainie Witnesses the Slow Rotting of Her Fated Love

The branch sat in Rainie's lap, twitching and flaking white bark at her feet. She secured the branch under her arm as she got off at the only stop she recognized. Rainie had boarded the bus at the stop outside her apartment building, falling asleep in the back, and when she woke, it was evening. She was in another city.

She stepped onto the sidewalk, which appeared to be sinking into the buttery tar of the blacktop. Rainie walked farther along until she saw the familiar empty lot, which now contained several abandoned shopping carts and discarded vacuum cleaners, the cords coiled like snakes. The sycamore still leaned over the chain-link fence, feigning fascination with its own shadow. Its branches bowed downward, and only two leaves remained, flapping like ears. The tree was dying, Rainie realized. When she stopped beneath it—it was not much taller than she was—she circled the trunk to look for the black socket where her branch was severed. It was forehead-level, perfectly circular, emanating the stench of rot. A crow landed on one of the dead branches and lowered it. Rainie turned away from the tree, prancing over its rope-thin roots, and remembered what the dendrologist/dog said. All of its arteries were dredged to the surface, unable to hide any of itself.

The duplex squatted low, its front door slightly crooked. In the driveway was a pothole that Anita once filled with still water, breeding mosquitoes to unleash on Rainie's brothers. Rainie wondered if Anita would still remember the girl she promised to scar and see again. Maybe Anita had been right, then: Every meeting required blood. Every separation was of the flesh. Rainie rubbed the dogtooth embedded in her right wrist, rolling it like a bead, shivering as it sank deeper into her.

With the branch in her left hand, Rainie opened the wood gate to the side yard and knocked on the back door of the duplex. She waited. The door's wood was so damp it absorbed the sound of her fist. At her feet, the welcome mat was razed like a field of crops, golden and smoky, hemmed with red thread. When she looked up from it, Anita's mother was standing in the doorway. The same always-damp hands, the same smile, slow and full of effort, dredged to the surface. *My sky,* Anita's mother said, *a little doggie's shown up on our doorstep. Vivian, come see.* Rainie smiled and offered the branch with both hands, worried that holding it in one hand like a hilt might appear threatening. But Anita's mother ignored the branch and told Rainie to *come in, come in, Vivian, look, it's Rainie, don't you remember, she's got such a round face now, that's good, you've eaten well, and your moles have all shifted, also good, the one on your nose means you're coming into wealth, Vivian, come here.*

The house was dim and pulsing like a ripe plum, and Rainie wondered why the curtains weren't open and why the lights weren't on, why the carpet was callused with brown and white mushrooms. In the kitchen, Vivian was sitting on the linoleum with a child in her lap, facing the refrigerator. Rainie thought at first that the child was a dog, those glossy and stately hunting dogs in European paintings, with her head pricked up, alert, listening for a soft something, but the girl introduced herself as Winny. The last time Rainie had seen Winny, her ears were floppy like a puppy's, folding themselves so that she couldn't hear anything unless you held them open. Now she was ten, her hair long to her hips. Vivian stood up, urging Winny to walk ahead of her. When Rainie first heard Anita talk about the potential name Winny, she'd asked, *Like a horse? Whinny?* Anita had said, *No, like a winner. Winny. She'll never lose anything.*

Vivian was shorter than her now, at the level of her nose, and Rainie looked down in surprise. As always, Vivian was alien. Her eyes in the dim were yellow and yearning. Her mouth was an alcove for the sun and the moon to sleep in. Rainie had always suspected that Vivian was essential to this earth. The first time she saw Vivian was through a window, only her face and shoulders visible. Rainie had immediately averted her eyes, frightened into submission. She knew she would die if she saw Vivian in her entirety, like a deity revealing their true and fatal form.

What did you bring us? Vivian asked with authority, as if she'd been expecting Rainie all that evening. Vivian had decided to dispose of the decade between Rainie's departure and return. She waved her hand in the air, dismissing years of absence. Rainie responded a few moments too late: *Vivian-how-are-you, here is what I brought you.* This time she offered the bone-branch like a bouquet, and it was Winny who reached forward and plucked it quickly from her hands. *You should put this back,* Winny said. *The tree didn't take any of your arms.* Vivian laughed and said, *Winny, go watch the weather or something—you know that's her favorite channel, the weather? We tried to get her to watch cartoons or even the news, but she likes the weather. She likes the woman who says it. She likes the picture of clouds. She doesn't know it's all green screen and thinks the woman is standing in the middle of a hurricane or is hovering in the sky, just standing there on a cloud like a god from the stories.* Rainie laughed, though she was worried about what Winny was doing on the sofa in the living room. She bent the branch in her lap, testing its tendons.

How's your mother? Your brothers? Anita's mother asked, inviting her to sit at the dining table in the kitchen, a foldout card table with a white dish of peanuts, another of peaches, and a sleeve of crackers. *Eat something.* It was clear to Rainie that Anita no longer lived here, and Rainie was strangely relieved by this. Anita had left, gotten a car or a job or gone to college or somewhere else, and this meant at least one of them had abandoned their vow to be dogs. Rainie felt released from responsibility, knowing Anita hadn't truly waited for her. It was no longer Rainie's bargain to uphold, now that Anita had left home. Who had abandoned whom?

My mother and brothers? They're living, Rainie said, then realized the vagueness of this. *I mean, they're more than alive,* she said, then stopped. *I mean, how is Anita doing?* Vivian touched a peanut to her tongue and swallowed, looking down at her hands.

Pickling, she said. Rainie cocked her head, wondering if she'd misheard. In the darkness of the room, the silhouettes of the two women blurred into each other, so that sitting side by side they looked like they sprouted from the same shadow. Their posture was slumped, tired. Anita's mother looked at Rainie and said, *More precise than* pickling, *she's asleep right now.* Rainie startled, leaning back in the wooden chair, and said, *She's here? I can wait.* On the sofa, Winny sighed and turned on the Weather Channel, her face bluing with the light of an artificial sky, and said, *She's been asleep for years, so if you want to wait, you should have brought something to entertain yourself. Besides this branch. It's getting kind of soft—should we refrigerate it?*

Vivian stood up from the table and swiped Winny off the sofa, grasping her by the armpits and tugging her like a corpse down the dark hallway that led to the bedroom. *What does that mean?* Rainie asked. She tried to laugh and dispel Winny's words, wanting to ask if this was something Winny had learned to repeat from TV. *Asleep for years.* But Anita's mother was silent, and Rainie could not meet her eyes. At last Rainie stood up, not knowing where to go, asking if she could turn on the lights. *We keep it dark in here,* Anita's mother said, with no apology in her voice, *so that she can find her way back to her body. Too many competing lights would make it hard for her to find it. We want her to be the brightest.* Rainie jerked toward the door, wondering if maybe Anita's mother was sick, sick the way her grandmother had been, taping the mouths of faucets because she believed they were speaking to her, filling a sock with pennies in order to beat intruders to death. Maybe it was good that Winny had confiscated the branch from the rest of her family.

But Anita's mother linked an arm through Rainie's, pulling her toward the hallway. *You want to see her, don't you, my doglike daughter?* Rainie choked, and Anita's mother interpreted her cough as confirmation. *Come, come,* she said, and Rainie followed her along the hallway, the carpet crowded with mushrooms small and black, buttons down the back of a dress. There hadn't been a carpet in this hallway before, just a floor that could be wiped down, and Rainie wondered if the mushrooms were planted on purpose, glowing a black road for her feet to follow.

Rainie widened her eyes in the dark and bowed her head to enter the bedroom. The floor receded to concrete, cool beneath Rainie's stocking feet, and the walls of the room were humming, reminding her of the time she saw honey slinking out of an outlet and her mother had to call the landlord, who called the exterminator, who extracted a whole hive from the wall. Rainie couldn't believe that so much could be living there without her knowing. Inside the bedroom, the walls were butchered into bark, the paint flaking and snowing to the floor. Vivian and Winny were kneeling, scraping at something with a toothbrush. It was Anita, lying slack on the mattress, her eyelids glowing like mushroom caps. *We have to clean the insect eggs from the corners of her eyes and her ears,* Vivian said, not raising her head. She was scouring Anita's eyelids, telling Winny not to scrape too hard or else she'd burst the eyeballs underneath.

Anita lay with the stillness of an embalmed saint—legs straight, arms branched by her sides. But even in the dim, even laid out like that in her red-and-white polka-dot pajamas, which Rainie had often dreamed were blinking nocturnal eyes, there was a sense of movement beneath her skin, her heart a hive yearning to release its light, to pour out its blood like bees. Ants sewed themselves to the mattress, stitching across Anita's neck, a dark necklace that clasped and knotted on its own. Rainie kneeled between Vivian and Winny, hovering her hand, stroking the back of Anita's knuckles with her thumb. The bones rolled like beads, not tethered to anything, and Rainie gasped. Winny smiled and said, *Don't worry, we displaced a few of her bones too. We touched her face, and her cheekbone moved all the way down to her jaw like a continent, and for a while she looked like a jigsaw piece, except not fitting anything, but the next morning the cheekbone migrated back, so don't worry about that. She'll straighten up tomorrow, we promise.*

Rainie bowed her head. She never thought Winny would grow up with a mouth of her own, a voice so similar to Anita's. In the dark, Anita's pupils were visible through their lids, bright and flitting. Up and down, side to side, her eyes wandered, delighting in their own decay. Her mouth cinched and relaxed as if a string were threaded through her lips, manipulated by someone else. But it was her ears that seemed the least asleep, ears that cocked and swiveled like a dog's, pinning back their lobes when Rainie reached out to pet them. She felt a strange wave of admiration: Anita did not stay still for anything, not even for death. She was slippery with sleep, inhospitable to human touch. Only other creatures could fertilize her dreams: Clusters of oily insect eggs clung to Anita's upper lip, a writhing dew. Without thinking, Rainie reached forward and swiped one off, but Anita's lip indented where she touched it, maintaining the crater of her fingertip. Sweat filled the well and a fly landed in it, drowning.

Anita's nose was sunken into a steaming bowl of mud, a burrow for barn swallows and worms. Her face, torn of its columns and slowly concaving, had relocated all its flesh to her neck. It pulsed and bulged like a tree trunk, and Rainie had a feeling her neck would be the last part of her to rot, growing until it speared through the ceiling of her skull. The ants were her worshippers, creatures who lived off crumbs and corpses, devotees of the dropped and forgotten. They roped her neck and pearled her jaw on their daily pilgrimage, parading into her ear canals. Stringing night through her mind.

The ants around her throat slotted one by one into her skull, and it was then that Rainie saw a red line around her neck, a thread sunk so deep into the skin it looked like a deep-sea trench. Vivian followed her gaze and said, *We tried to snip off her thread collar so she wouldn't choke, or at least relocate it to her hand so she could follow it home like a rope, but then it sank like that. We can't dig it out without hurting her.* It was an artery now, that loop of red, and Rainie raised her hand to her own bare neck, her skin stinging where she touched it. She wondered if this was all a punishment, some kind of nightmare scene that Anita had staged to scare Rainie into remembering her promise. *Wear this thread and we'll find each other forever.* Rainie had left, and now Anita was an anthill, her body evacuated, her skin resewn over boneless inhabitants. All because Rainie had allowed her thread to be severed, unwilling to fight for its survival. Leaning forward, she pressed her forehead into the hard edge of the mattress and said, *Give it to me, Anita, I'll wear it for you. I'll let it tighten around my neck until my head is squeezed off, Anita, let me. I'm sorry I didn't listen. I'm sorry I let it be taken from me. I let you be taken from me.*

Once, when they were little, Anita brought home a moth in its cocoon, its brown casing like a bullet shell, and when they cracked it open, the moth inside wasn't fully developed. It still had the many legs of something crawling, but with the beginnings of wings. It was deciding between sky and soil, between flight and fear. A body bridging, branching into its next life. That was what Anita's body looked like—like that moth they smeared across the pavement after they realized they couldn't place it back inside the past. She didn't look like she was merely resting. She was bunkered inside her body for the purpose of transformation. Anita interpreted sleep as a mutiny against her body, expecting to emerge from it with a name that everyone prayed to. The eggs beading her face, the walls warping like bark—it all shone with proof that Anita was hatching herself holy, decaying into something divine.

How long, Rainie said. She pulled up the collar of her shirt, wanting to hide the bareness of her neck. In Anita's presence it felt somehow obscene not to have any red on her, not to be bound to anything. *Ten years,* Vivian said, *ish.* Rainie calculated: She had left the duplex when she was ten, which meant Anita had cocooned herself not long after. Prior to leaving, she'd been bitten by the red dog and had fallen asleep for two weeks. Anita must have taken it as a challenge. She dug her own deep sleep and buried herself in it for a decade.

As if she knew that Rainie was blaming herself, Vivian said, *It was her fault. She went dreaming with a red thread in her fist and let go of it. She got lost in a dream and hasn't come back yet.* Anita's mother stood in the doorway. *Yet,* she said to them all, *yet. She hasn't appeared in one of my dreams yet, so she's still alive and wandering.*

Do you want to stay? Winny asked, and at first Rainie thought she meant stay in this room with Anita or join her in an unanchored dream. But then Vivian said she could sleep in the other bedroom with them, they had a futon, and at least she had to stay and eat, stay, and Rainie wondered if they'd brought her into this room in order to guilt her, asking her to stay for as long as Anita continued to sleep, a kind of symmetry—*our daughter has drifted, so we will keep another for as long as our own is missing.* Rainie agreed, the tooth in her wrist rattling like a loose screw. It was what she owed Anita.

Rainie looked down at Anita again, wanting to turn away and curtain that face forever, to foreclose this entire day and depart, but she forced herself to pay witness for as long as possible. This was her penance. A slug mounted the bridge of Anita's nose, seeking the torn sleeve of her nostril, its slime like soured moonlight. Rainie reached out to remove it, her hands trembling, but she could not bring herself to touch that alien face. The distance between their bodies felt planetary. She'd once been Anita's accomplice, corroborating her truths and lies, wearing that same collar of red, but now their histories had splintered. Nothing could braid them together again. Rainie wondered if this sleep was caused by her leaving. Because she had culled Anita from her life and waited like the understory of a tree, growing into that vacated space, pruning Anita from her future. Maybe this whole time they'd been apart, some part of her had been waiting to steal Anita's place in the sun, to climb up Anita's spine and spread her own leaves into a canopy, shadowing everything beneath her, gold and gloating. Anita had always been more alive than the sea, the director of their destiny, the skeleton of their stories. Without her, Rainie was untethered, the red thread around her neck snipped to pieces and scattered into ash, and now she wondered if she'd been only a parasite, clinging to Anita's host body. When she left, she'd disturbed some ecosystem within Anita. In the dim room where Anita decayed, Rainie shifted away so that her shadow no longer soiled Anita's body. Then she reached out and touched Anita's cheeks, her jawbone, the pulse of her left wrist, feeling the knot of her blood, the warmth of her bunched-up breath, hoping she was to blame. As long as it was her fault, she could fix it.

Rainie decided she had to stay, had to stand guard. Anita's shadow, which had hardened from years of not being properly walked or otherwise exercised, could not be allowed to solidify and house her forever. Rainie would play a dog again and pay her debt, be the loyal creature that watches over its owner, the breed she'd failed to be. After watching Anita dream for another hour, Rainie fell asleep in the other room with Vivian and Winny, mistaking the drone of three electrical fans for the sound of clouds vacuuming birds out of the sky.

In the morning, light entered the room, and Rainie woke without remembering what dreams she'd hunted down like deer, which dreams she'd made bleed. The room was empty, the futons on either side of her already vacated, and in the kitchen was the sound of something sizzling. Rainie walked down the hallway, pausing at Anita's doorway. It felt wrong to enter the room by herself, like entering a temple without any reason to worship, there only to gawk at gods, but she wanted confirmation that Anita was alive. A satellite body, powered by proximity to other bodies.

Lost in her sleep, wandered away in a dream. There was a song about it, but Rainie didn't remember where she'd heard it. Maybe it was the dogs who'd authored it. Anita was still laid out on the mattress, but the smell of the room was different, almost singed. As she neared Anita's body, the walls let down their paint, strips of it unfurling onto the floor. If this was the kindling, Anita was the pyre. But when Rainie kneeled beside the mattress, Anita's face was no longer buoyant and full of movement. A shadow slid over her body like a shroud. Blood fermented beneath her skin, waiting to become a bruise, and the smell of rot lingered in the air.

Rainie called for Vivian, who called for Anita's mother, who walked in with an air of calm authority. Vivian said it was time to flip her over and check for bedsores, for feces, for the fog inside her, but Anita's mother appeared unaware of the smell and said instead, *Decay. I knew when you touched her, she would dew like this. We tried pickling her when the rot first set in. We filled the bathtub with vinegar and put a lid on her. Made of shrink wrap. But she didn't pickle. The rot continued. We even went all the way to the sea to fetch real seawater. Bucketsful to pour over her, to soak her mattress. Salt is a preservative. But she still keeps unshaping.*

Vivian reached for Rainie's hands, flipping them over. *Look at these spots,* Vivian said, tracing the penny-colored stains on Rainie's skin. *It's touching you too.* Rainie stared at her own hands, wanting to ask how fast the rot was entering her, but Vivian turned away. Anita's mother surveyed the decay. In her right hand was the sycamore branch, slim as a wrist squeezed bloodless.

Why did you bring this? Anita's mother asked her, looking down at the branch.

I thought you might know how to reattach it, Rainie said, but she wasn't sure that the sycamore could be saved. That Anita could be. *I wasn't the one who chopped it off,* Rainie said, this time to Vivian, though Vivian was not listening to either of them and was instead toweling Anita's forehead with lemon juice, which could prevent an apple slice from yellowing.

This is what we were afraid of, Vivian said, *that she was going to rot away entirely. But then you came and accelerated it. You. Where did you touch her?* Rainie shook her head and tapped the dogtooth embedded in her wrist, half-expecting it to be soft with rot, loosening from her. Where Rainie had touched Anita's hand the night before, there were now swarms of ants, tunneling toward her bone. Rainie turned away in shame. *God, god,* Vivian said, *she'll have no body by tomorrow. Get the tape, the bleach, help me kill these damn things.* But Anita's mother told them there wasn't a way to kill those ants, wasn't a way to salvage anything from them. *How can you say this,* Vivian said. *She'll disappear.*

Anita's mother whipped the branch through the air, broke it against the wall. *You don't know,* she said. *This is a beginning.*

Vivian crouched, plucking up the two pieces of the branch. *We can tape it together,* Vivian said, *or glue it, or I don't know. We can do something.* Rainie said, *It's just a branch,* and Anita's mother laughed with her head lowered. *It's more than that. It's the elbow of that sycamore. You wouldn't know,* she told Rainie. *If you'd been mothered my way, you'd know. I can recognize anything by its bones, can identify a daughter by a strand of her hair, a tree by whatever bird trusts its branches. I once lived beside a swamp, and there were limbs in the water, stewing, and my sisters and I always looked for a full body, a cadaver we could sell to a medical school in the city, but there were only ever pieces of men, intestines, jawbone, bladder full of coins.*

Rainie said, *Did you ever find a face in those waters, one of your own dead?*

Shaking her head, Anita's mother said, *You see, we had to find new ways to recognize each other. Not by our outsides. You can't trust the outside of anything.* Anita's mother said to Rainie, *You should know this too: A long time ago, when the dogs lived, men came. We opened their bodies, carried away their organs, the fluted ribs, the bladders already empty. We wanted their wormy parts, their warmest parts. But the men, they weren't like us: They thought that we had stolen something sacred.*

They didn't believe in rearranging the body. But we were inventive, in death especially.

Vivian said, *It's so cruel, to take the body apart like that.* On her lap, Winny sucked on the knuckle of her thumb and said, *Mama, when you dice the meat, you multiply it. You make more of it.* Anita's mother laughed at this, tapped the girl's kneecap. *So smart. Like my daughter. Even in her sleep, she stokes her body, stirs it. I've heard her sing.*

You belong to this history too, Anita's mother was explaining. *You can learn it too, how to recognize a body by looking at its interior first. Show me a kidney and I know its kin. Show me a sycamore branch and I can tell you if it's your grandfather's arm. If my daughter was inside out, asleep on that mattress without any of her skin, her organs arranged like wet gems, would you know her?*

Rainie recoiled from the question. *Yes,* she said, *I would know her by the breadth of her blood.* When Anita cut her palm on the chain-link fence or bit herself in the forearm playing dog, playing dawn, she bled all the way home. Her bleeding was widespread. Once, when she cut herself picking windshield glass off the street, saying she was afraid the dogs would step on it or mistake it for sugar, her blood spread itself thin as steam, a red haze floating in the air for days. *But I don't even know what her other insides are shaped like,* Rainie said, looking down at the table. Vivian said, *Oh, I do. I go to the butcher's all the time with Ayi, and the organ meats are always the cheapest. Have you had breakfast yet?*

Rainie said she had not. She was no longer sure what they were speaking about. She stood up to leave, but the hallway behind her was humid, water droplets turning the air into mirrors: When she went down the hall, she felt like she was walking toward herself. She turned back, unwilling to look at her own reflection, and ended up again in Anita's room. The corner of Anita's left eye was filled with pith, and Rainie reached out to scrape it away. *Don't touch her,* Vivian said. *You'll rot her away faster than these ants can eat her.*

Rainie said that she needed to leave now for real, go home, that her mother and brothers were waiting for her, that she had work to do, her mother having only two hands. Vivian wasn't listening, looking instead at Anita. *If you leave, the ants will eat her anyway. She can't stay lost this long. She's going to disappear.* One summer, Vivian stole a melon off the back of a truck idling behind the supermarket. The melon was more pristine than the moon, and even its skin of scars looked delicate as lace, lash-marks raised. Rainie and Anita and Vivian passed the melon from lap to lap, stroking it, petting its web of scars. They liked the size of it. They liked to roll it gently down the short driveway and catch it before the gutter. They tucked the melon under their shirts and pretended to be pregnant or humped like a camel. Every day they said they would eat it, placing it inside the refrigerator, but every day they found new ways to mother it. Finally the melon rotted, despite their be-lief that their touch had immortalized it, and swarms of fruit flies infested its flesh.

That rot was inside Anita. Rainie had brought it to her, she was sure, and soon she would have no body to return to. Kneeling beside the mattress, Rainie noticed that one of its bottom corners was raised an inch above the ground. She ex-amined Anita, worried for a second that one of Anita's limbs was now floating, no longer weighing the mattress down evenly, but then Vivian said, *Oh, that's just something she buried. Don't go digging around.* But Rainie ignored her, wedging her hand beneath the corner of the mattress, and with her middle finger probed at something hard and metallic fitted into a dug-out crevice. She shimmied it out, trying not to disturb Anita on the mattress. It was a tin, brass and lightweight, and there was a fleck of green paint on its lid that she remembered. Lifting the lid, Rainie saw herself reflected in the foggy bottom. Clanking inside were a series of safety pins, a plastic six-pack collar, balled-up twine, a pea that was somehow still frozen, white buttons, two jelly beans. Rainie remembered: They were fossils, the tin of fossils Anita had given her before she left. Hadn't she taken them with her, along with the stone that struck her? How did Anita still have this, buried beneath her? But then Vivian spoke from behind Rainie: *We found that in your trash after you moved. Anita kept it and wouldn't let us throw it out. She made a home for it under there.* And Rainie remembered. She remembered that she left it. Placing the tin on the floor beside the mattress, she turned to face Vivian and said, *It's nothing, it's nothing.* Vivian nodded, and as Rainie stood up and backed out of the doorway, Vivian knelt to say to Anita, *Don't worry, we won't let you go bad. Come home soon.*

Rainie remembered. The tin full of litter—no, histories—and the trash bag her mother gave her before she moved, telling her to toss out everything that was useless. Her mother telling her to keep the tin at least. Rainie remembered. She brought her hand to her bare neck again. She should have pedestaled that tin in her hands and named each of those bones, should have sat on it like a series of eggs. She should have lifted each fossil to the kitchen light and looked at it with shut eyes, feeling it only with her fingers, and said, *Yes, a kidney, a silver femur, a pea-green brain. Yes, yes, yes, Anita, yes.* But Rainie always refused to look, and now, in the kitchen, she watched Winny eat a braised egg with her hands, her fingertips darkening. *The egg is a stone,* Rainie said, shutting her eyes in the dim kitchen light, *and a stone is a bone.* Rainie was going mad. Like a dog, she thought, giggling. She looked at Winny's face, waiting for Anita's to surface and spread across it. Winny's mouth pursed around the egg, sucking its salt. *I see,* she said to Winny. *I see you now. Stay there, stay there. Wait for me.*

Rainie remembered the shade of that day with the dendrologist. Her tongue stung with recalled salt. The sea, the birds threading in and out of the water, sewing some word in the water that Rainie couldn't read. The clearing, sproutlings, the understory: what waited patiently below, waiting for a gap to grow into. Waiting for a death above it. Rainie decided, in all her madness, that she would build Anita an understory, a body to grow into, a body to replace the one that was decaying. Just like the stories Anita used to tell her, about the Entrail Eater and the mothers who dismembered men and stored substitute organs in the soil, in their own mouths, in jars of seawater. Mothers with the torsos of dogs and the heads of women.

Winny sat on the kitchen floor with the egg in her mouth. In her hands, two pieces of the sycamore branch were going limp. Anita's mother was unwrapping a newspapered package. *This is a kidney,* she said. *I don't think I can preserve it for long. She needs harder organs, sturdier meat.* In her palms, the kidney glowed, purple and pursed, not translucent at all, not what Rainie imagined the inside of the body to look like. Rainie knew what Anita would say if she were here: *You know what a body's made of. You unburied us from this pavement.*

This can be her arms, Rainie said, plucking up the two halves of the sycamore branch. Vivian stared at the limbs. *Whose arms?* she said, but Anita's mother smiled. *I knew you would come back. That thread she was holding. There used to be one around your neck.* Vivian balled the wet newspaper in her fist, kneading it: *What do you mean, what do you mean, what are you two talking about?*

Building a new body, Rainie said. *Another Anita to inherit Anita. I'm the dog with the woman's mouth, performing surgery with my teeth. I'm going to fill her with things she remembers.*

The History of Our Intestines: A Juvenile Attempt at Poetry that I Will Deeply Regret in Coming Years, from Yours Truly (Truly Truly)

Dear Rainie:

When I was a baby
    (and you too!!!!!)
        my shits were the size
           of an adult's—like a banana, she said, holding one
                        up to show me —
           my aunts said!!!!!!! Impressive!!! It was a sign
      my intestines were river-thick
    strong as rope to hang a man.
Come look, come look

Abu said, unwrapping my diaper to show them the size of my
shits—*look*

> *how they're waisted, how they hold*
> > *shape in the water like bigfish*
> *look how her shits float like the dead*
> > *her intestines are strong enough to seatbelt*
> *us   look look*
> *when she's a woman her shits will be the size of an elephant's*
> > *she'll have the memory of a bone*
> > *multiplying when it breaks*
> *her shits will be the size of islands*
> *we're born on   her shits will raft   will field*
> *whole forests will be seeded in her shit-paddies*
> > *her shits will dam floods*
> *her shits will be the width of gardens   every time she shits*
> *a ghost   will gag around it   a sky   will clog*
> *constipation for many centuries   anyway that's why my nickname is elephant*
> *you didn't know that did you??   You don't know me at all*

Rainie Seeks Out New Intestines

Rainie could not fall asleep the night she decided to build Anita's new body. In the morning, there would be a mission, and she had never once had a mission. Missions required a doglike determination, and the only thing still doglike about her was her overactive salivary glands. But as sleep tried to prod its way into her eye sockets, she remembered the time she fell asleep for two weeks and how Anita had waited for her beside the sofa, risking her own hide. Rainie's mother said she'd spanked Anita both inside and outside of the house, but Anita still returned when she could, shriveling in the sofa's shadow, waiting for her beloved to wake.

She kept saying you needed a tether, Rainie's mother had said, *you needed someone to hold on to. She may have been a terrible child, a terrible daughter, but she was a loyal dog, albeit a stinky one. She was*

*practically going to dive into your sleep and wade in after you if you didn't
come out soon.*

Rainie opened her eyes. She was in Winny and Vivian's
room, their two bodies indistinguishable in the dark. Rainie
had insisted on sleeping on the floor last night instead of the
futon. She took it as punishment for all the days Anita had
waited for her on the floor while she slept above. It should be
easy, Rainie thought, deciding to be Anita's tether. It was only
fair. Anita waited for her once, and now Rainie was going to
do the same. And she was going to return the favor with inter-
est, by building a substitute body to replace Anita's rotting
one. A self to come back to. A love to lure her home.

Rainie swallowed, half-expecting to feel the pressure of a
red-thread collar. As she shifted on the floor, trying not to disturb Vivian and Winny beside her, Rainie played with all the
loose threads of her thoughts. Anita always had faith they
would find each other again, but Rainie had never had that
same strength of faith, not once. She'd been willing to participate in Anita's games, wearing their threads, digging up bones.
But she'd thought of her participation as passive. Waiting was
not a passive thing, as she'd once believed. Anita had been
waiting all this time for her, biding her time outside her body,
wandering away in dreams, and Anita was never passive.

At last, Rainie gave up on sleep and stood up. Maybe what
she really feared was joining Anita in her rotting slumber.
Maybe her inability to sleep was just another selfishness.

She stepped into the dark hallway, the carpet so cold it felt
damp against her bare feet. At the end of the hall, to the left,
a fragrant light seeped out under the door. It must be Anita's
mother, holding vigil over Anita's decaying body. Perhaps she
thought exposure to light would trick Anita's body into forget-

ting another day was passing. Another attempt at preservation.

Rainie walked toward the kitchen, the faucet shining like a skeleton. Her only beacon. But when she reached out for it, a voice behind her warned: *The water gets stuck. Sometimes it comes out as rust.*

Turning around, Rainie squinted into the dim and saw Anita's mother standing before her, wearing pajamas with clouds printed on them. Lightning tethered the clouds to the ground, flashes of jagged laughter. Her hands were sheathed in blue surgical gloves, clenched around sheets of crinkled notebook paper.

I meant to give these to you, Anita's mother said, *but they were under the mattress and were all sweaty, so I had to dry them out first. Sorry they're so wrinkled. And that some of the words can't be saved.*

She extended her gloved hands, and Rainie took the translucent sheets of paper, which rubbed together like cricket wings, singing. It was too dark to read them, and they were so water-stained that the blue lines of the paper had flooded out some of the letters, each word about as legible as crushed insects. But she could still read two words in the top left corner: *Dear Rainie.* Her name, somehow, had survived the sweat flood, but nothing else was salvageable. Rainie resisted the urge to run into Anita's bedroom and slap her with these letters, to knot her flaccid and rot-riddled fingers around a pen and puppet her hand across the page, forcing her to rewrite every waterlogged word.

She wrote letters to you, Anita's mother said, *but she said you didn't answer the first few. So she didn't send the rest. She said she didn't have to. She would give them to you in person someday, and you would regret being neglectful. She always wanted to be the world's leading source of guilt. Given that she's currently vacated her body, I'll have to be her substitute.*

Idiot, Rainie said. *I never received her letters.* But as soon as she spoke it aloud, she realized she'd never checked for any correspondence from Anita. It was possible that her mother had received and trashed the letters before Rainie could read them, given how hard she'd tried to sever Rainie's red-thread collar and how much she'd hated the way Anita hovered over Rainie. And yet Rainie's mother had also allowed her to board a bus and return to this neighborhood. She must have thought that Rainie's severance from Anita was complete, their relationship long ago ended. There was no way the ghost of red thread could continue to link them. Rainie might have once believed the same thing. But Anita was an invasive species, and now she lived in Rainie's mind, in her marrow, in the soft of her thigh.

Rainie lowered her head over the letters, rubbing the precious sheets between her fingers, trying to align their ruffled corners. *Sorry, I shouldn't have called her an idiot aloud. I shouldn't speak ill of the sleeping.*

You should say more things aloud. I prefer you at this volume, Anita's mother said. She peeled the gloves off her hands one at a time, flipped them inside out, and then put them back on.

My daughter is indeed an idiot, she said. *I think she was afraid there was a chance you'd never reply, and she'd rather not have risked it. She chickened out, as they say. I never understood that saying. Chickens are extremely brave. They eat rodents and snakes, you know.*

Anita isn't afraid to risk, Rainie said, stepping deeper into the kitchen. The shine of the wet sink might show her a way into these words.

Anita is willing, Rainie said. *That's who she is.*

Anita's mother smiled and scratched her chin, powdering the tip of it, and said Rainie was wrong.

When it came to you, she said, *my daughter was afraid.*

Rainie didn't know whether to believe this. It was unbearable to imagine Anita afraid back then, or afraid now, stranded in her sleep. Rainie prayed she wasn't wading alone.

Oh, she's not alone, Anita's mother said, and Rainie realized she must have spoken her prayer aloud. Maybe she had more faith than she knew.

No one is ever alone in their dreams. You don't have to fear that, Anita's mother said. *Fear the fact that she's rotting more and more rapidly. It seems sleep is a slippery slope into total physical decay. At least for some people I know.*

She laughed, and Rainie wondered how she was laughing while the fog of fear approached every horizon, how she could let it inside herself so casually, opening the door to any weather. The Hsia family experienced fear differently from Rainie, who tried to avoid the feeling as much as possible, since it was a close relative of failure. But this family invited fear as if it were love.

You can't sleep, Anita's mother said. *I don't either. But that's just because I have to be awake when she wakes. She was the same way about you, back when you were asleep. She was always there.*

I remember, Rainie said. *Even though I wasn't conscious. I remember.*

Rainie paused. She could speak forever with Anita's mother, so long as the darkness remained as a buffer.

What if I get lost in my sleep too? Rainie said. *Then I won't even be able to stay awake to wait for Anita.*

Anita's mother shook her head and said, *That won't happen to us. You're like me. I used to sleep in a bunk bed, a middle bunk, just*

*like you. I remember you used to complain about sleeping between broth-
ers. Your sky and your ground were your blood relations. I slept between
women. And while they slept, I could only listen. I failed at sleep for a
long time, another thing that alienated me.*

Here, Anita's mother said. *I don't have red thread, but take this.*

She slipped something out of the sleeve of her storm-
patterned pajamas. It was a silken string she'd peeled off the
spine of a green bean, the exact length of her forefinger. Sticky
and warm, the thread wriggled into Rainie's fist. The tighter
she gripped it, the more it bloated like a throat full of water.

This is the nearest living string, Anita's mother said. *Sorry it's so
short. But hold on to this when you sleep tonight. Hold on to it the way I
hold on to her, my daughter. Even knowing she dissolves in the dark, I hold
her. I hold her. Like this. A string in both fists.* She lifted her hands
and pumped them up and down, milking an invisible creature.

That night, Rainie allowed the dark to eat her headfirst,
joining Anita in the belly of sleep. In her fist was a rivering
heat, the string running through her like blood, filling her
heart to its lid.

In the morning, when Rainie woke again, Vivian was standing
over her, straddling her on the floor. *Let's shower a different way,*
Vivian said. *In the morning, first thing. I see the dogs do it, spraying one
another with a hose they found.*

To save water in the worst year of the drought, Vivian
instructed Rainie to stand inside a basin while showering.
When the water climbed to the rim of the bucket, it was time
for the shower to end. Winny bathed in this water, or else Vivian used it to wash the windows or slop onto the kitchen floor
or spoon-feed the basil plants in the side yard. Water that has

wrapped around a body: It's particularly nutritious, storying the soil, teaching the basil to grow in the shape of girls, all of them swaying with Winny's slouched posture.

In the shower, with her hair slopping down her back, Rainie wondered if hair was an organ. Or were organs only things that belonged inside the body? But skin was a surface, and it was an organ. Maybe organs had to be alive, and hair was dead. She had once been so authoritative in determining what was and wasn't alive. Anita was always trying to prove her wrong, and now that her soul had wandered away, she'd submitted final proof of her other lives.

Begin, Rainie repeated to herself, *begin.* Begin with all the organs she'd eaten, their names: liver, kidney, lung, stomach, intestines, maybe tongue, maybe bladder. Sitting wet in the kitchen, Rainie bowed her head as Anita's mother wrung her hair out, commented on its length. *So long,* she said. Anita always knew how to locate longing. She identified her joys and griefs and assigned them each a region in the body. *I'm hungry in my knees. My ears thirst. I love you in my wrists. I miss you in my ribs. I eat you in my hips.*

But Rainie imagined her interior as empty architecture: nothing tethered inside her, just a floating fist, a grasped wind.

To begin: intestines. Rainie had seen her mother slice pork intestines into rings, boil them until the surface of the water radiated. But she didn't know where to acquire a pig and how to retrieve its intestines. *It doesn't have to be so literal,* Vivian said, hanging Rainie's towel over the back of her chair. She walked barefoot through the kitchen, leaving footprints of sweat. *For her intestines, anything chewy will do. It just has to be non-perishable, since it could be a while before she returns. She needs a body that will endure longer than meat.*

Rainie asked if they couldn't just freeze her, but Vivian shook her head and said freezing did not allow the blood to flow, and blood was Anita's last rope.

That's disturbing, Rainie said, but she was already fantasizing about all forms of rope, all types of hollow tubes. Straws were too stiff to be intestines. Rope would fray. Scarves were too slippery to host knots, any shape. Rubber tubing would work, but she needed elasticity. Sleeves, maybe. Rainie yanked at her own, but sleeves were shapeless without arms inside them. To build Anita a new body, there would need to be structural integrity. But Rainie had never built anything, other than the time she helped her middle brother restore his car. This body was not for her brother to sit in and steer.

On the sofa, Winny chewed on the two halves of the sycamore branch, watching Rainie with animal curiosity. Rainie tried to smile back reassuringly as she left, hair heavy and wet down her back, heading for the abandoned lot. Inside, a few of the dogs shared their sleep with the sycamore tree. Others paced the length of the fence, watching Rainie. She looked for the red dog that had long ago bitten her, but it was probably dead. The sycamore shrugged off more of its bark, flakes of it tangling in Rainie's hair. Approaching the fence, she held her hands in front of her the way Anita used to, not a gesture to restrain the dogs but an invitation to bite her. *My abu learned how to dream from a dogbite,* Anita once told her. *She was bitten by a dog in the city and had a fever for a week. She dreamed of the dead for the first time in that heat. She talked to dog-headed women, or woman-headed dogs. I don't remember. Anyway, that's how she learned to dream, and I want to learn too.* But the red dog had chosen to bite Rainie, which Anita must have perceived as a betrayal. She had always wanted to be baptized by a dogbite.

The largest of the dogs was white, with eyes that were silver in the light. It barked at her through the rusted fence of the lot, and Rainie backed away. It swung its head from side to side, a gesture that looked so human, Rainie almost repeated it. Then it faced her directly, and in the dark of its jaw was not a tongue but a stone, an egg-sized pearl that pried its maw open, propped it wide. The dog spat the pearl through the fence and turned, running back to the corner of the lot. Walking slowly, Rainie approached the fence and kneeled beside it, the other dogs dancing away. She picked up the egg-stone, lightning-white and matching the one given to her by the red dog a decade ago, the one she had not bothered to hatch. Turning it in her hands, Rainie realized that only one end of it was rounded. The other end was pointed, chiseled into a spearhead. The egg-stone was warm only where her hands had touched it.

A heart, Rainie said, and slipped it under her shirt, harboring its cool weight. A heart for a gutless girl. The white stray barked at her again, its neck straining as if it was chained to something, though Rainie could not see what. The bark echoed down the street and returned, the sound thinning into a voice she still remembered: *between gone and grieved, gone and grieved.* Rainie wondered if she had really heard the dogs' voices all those years ago or if it had been Anita the entire time, puppeting their mouths, her fist in their skulls. Without Anita, Rainie no longer understood their language. She lacked a translator.

Guts, Rainie thought, I need guts. Guts for Anita. There was a story she remembered, about a snake god who created the world and whose intestines turned into ten gut spirits that wormed their way into new worlds. But she didn't know where the gut spirits might have been scattered or how to sew them into Anita's abdominal cavity. The white dog approached again, this time with its head lowered, its ears upright and stiff as fence posts. It paced silently along the length of the fence, a yard away from her, and Rainie decided to follow it. Return to doghood the way Anita must have wanted.

The pearl-mouthed dog slipped through a hole in the chain-link fence and trotted down the street. Its tail had been severed halfway, but the bone was regrowing. Rainie followed, treading its shadow, until the dog approached the strip-mall laundromat that her aunt used to operate on her own. She washed and folded clothes, cinching them into canvas bags and stacking them in a cart by the curb for people to pick up. Rainie was the watchdog, guarding the cart until the owners came to claim their skins. Her aunt folded clothes with careless grace, tucking in the sleeves, surrendering the waist. Rainie sat on top of the washing machine as it bounced her bones and marveled at how her aunt folded a dress so delicately that when you unfurled it, there wasn't a single crease in it, no sign that it had once been any shape but standing.

Rainie pushed open the laundromat's door, the bell on the handle jangling against the dogtooth in her wrist. Outside, the white dog paced the sidewalk, weaving between two parked cars in the lot. From this distance, in the tinted glass of the laundromat, the dog's head blurred into a woman's. Its profile was hauntingly familiar, and she realized only after turning away that it was her own. She had been looking at the reflection of her face in the glass, overlapping with the dog's body. That must be it, a mirror trick. The dog could not have her face.

The white stone throbbed against her belly. *Do you need*

change? the woman at the back counter said. Rainie shook her head, feeling suddenly out of place. She doubted the dog for leading her here. The woman at the back counter was not her aunt. She had dyed red hair, dogtooth studs in her ears. *I know you,* she said to Rainie. *You're that girl who was bitten by a dog and went to sleep for a month.*

Not a month, Rainie said, *a week.* The woman laughed. *You were a victim of that family. Now it's their daughter that's asleep. Karma, I call it.*

Rainie felt the stone beat steadily against her stomach. She pressed her hand to it and approached the counter. The aisles were empty, but all the machines were full and foaming like rabid mouths. It was ghostly, all those skins without a body. *Is it true she's been asleep for years?* the woman asked. *Her mother was always dreaming for other people. That's not right, you know. Sometimes the dead don't want to be spoken to, dredged up like that.* But Rainie shook her head: Why else would the dead speak in dreams, if not because they wanted something?

Lowering her head to the register and wrestling with the tray, the woman said, *Who do you know who's dead? If you've got nothing to clean and don't want change, why warp my floors with your weight? There's a sidewalk out there.* When the woman raised her head, her face was placid. She was a threshold god, her features divinely derived. She looked out the windows and saw the shape of the white dog pacing. *Take that thing with you. Those strays know how to desecrate a place.*

Rainie turned to leave, then walked to the closest machine and pressed her palm to the vibrating surface, remembering its hum between her legs, how she sat on top of these machines and pretended to be riding them. Outside, the white dog whined at her, lay down on its belly. Rainie flashed the dogtooth on her wrist and asked, *Do you know what mouth this once belonged to?* But the white dog didn't listen, instead running toward the shade of the strip-mall sign.

When the dog bit her all those years ago and she fell asleep, she dreamed of a dog chorus that could speak. They were a sea. Their voices scrubbed her like salt. They were re-membering a time when mountains itched like mosquito bites and could be scratched open, spilling rivers. She rode the sea of dogs, endlessly reaching. But that was a dream.

The white dog shimmered ahead in the heat, so pale it was almost sheer. Its belly swung as it walked, and Rainie wondered if it was pregnant, but the belly glugged as if full of water. She wondered how the dogs drank, if they lapped up the puddles or had some direct source of rain. It was noon and the sky sank. There was no one she recognized, not the dead sycamore, not the newspaper ad at her feet, the cutout face of a woman offering to sell you a home for cheap so long as you didn't mind that it was once a herd of worked-to-death oxen and you didn't mind vengeance.

Rainie refused to return with nothing but a stone. She felt her jaw expanding in her mouth. The white dog barked again. The echo ricocheted off a row of parked cars and returned only to her left ear: *Carry us away,* the echo said. *Release us.* She understood now what they'd told her when she and Anita were little, the story of being hunted and being hunters. She understood which she would have to be if Anita needed a body.

The white dog had her eyes, which would make this more difficult. Those eyes. Wide and bright. But the dog's placid face seemed to say, *My belly is big because I've grown the intestines of two dogs. I mean to share myself.*

At the dollar store, Rainie purchased a can of luncheon meat. She hadn't yet asked Vivian or Anita's mother for funding, but she knew they would give it to her, anything to build Anita's future body. Outside, beneath the awning, Rainie slit her thumb while opening the can of luncheon loaf. Her blood sprinkled the pavement, and the white dog was summoned to it. That would make it easier, she thought—it smelled her blood and wanted it. It was a hunter too.

Sliding the luncheon loaf out of its tin sleeve, Rainie sucked the sting from her thumb. She held the jiggle of meat out to the dog, backing up when it lunged forward. Then she walked home, back to the duplex and its shadowed side yard, the dog with her face following her all the way.

When she flung the luncheon loaf against the concrete floor of the side yard, it bounced twice and landed at the dog's feet. The loaf disassembled into foam, and as the dog's head was lowered, Rainie removed the egg-stone from under her shirt and knelt over the dog, slamming its head into the ground and driving the edged end of the stone into the back of its skull.

The stone parted its fur, and beneath its pelt was a human face. Like a reflection in the pavement, the dog's face mirrored her own, wincing as she lifted the stone again, burrowing it into the back of that human neck, twisting it in like a screw. Its tongue made a fizzling sound, put out against the pavement. Rainie's tongue mimicked the movement, flopping out of her mouth. She unpinned the stone from the back of its skull and saw the hole she'd made there, boiling over with blood. The Rainie-headed dog was shuddering, its eyes open and brightening. With the sharp point of the rock, Rainie sawed off her own head from the body of the dog. It was surprisingly easy, like tearing through wet paper. When she was done, the body of the dog sprouted a new head, blooming like the transparent bulb of an onion. It finished growing the tips of its ears and bounded away, wagging its tail in gratitude, relieved of its burden, and in Rainie's hands was a severed human head, a white-haired copy of her own. Rainie peered into the hole of her neck, admiring the bowl of her skull. Inside it was a boiling soup of intestines.

When Vivian and Anita's mother walked into the side yard, Rainie lifted the head and said, *I've got her guts.* The intestines were boiling away in the skull, releasing the scent of pickled mustard greens and vinegar. These intestines were cooked to last. In Rainie's other fist was the bloodied stone, red as a heart. Vivian applauded Rainie's brave butchery, but Rainie promptly turned around and vomited all over the pavement. Anita's mother sighed and said, *Too bad it doesn't rain here; we have to clean everything ourselves.* Then she brought the severed head inside and stirred the intestines that simmered in its skull, ladling the guts out of their preservative soup. *I was hoping you'd get something a little more sturdy,* Anita's mother said, *like something made of an artificial material. But if this is what the dogs told you to do, it will do.*

Rainie, exhausted by her own violence, sprawled on the sofa and went silent. That night, she dragged herself to Anita's sleeping side and said, *You should do some of this work yourself. Look what I've done for you.*

Did the dog speak to you? Anita's mother said, slipping beside Rainie. *Did the dog say anything?*

No, Rainie said, *they always spoke to Anita, not to me. It grew a new head and ran away.*

Go back and listen, Anita's mother said. *You need to go back and listen.*

I can't handle any more beheadings, Rainie said. But how else could she build Anita a new body without taking apart other bodies? This is what the dogs had tried to teach her to do, she thought, this was what they wanted too. But if she said it aloud, she was afraid that her echo would contradict this.

Anita's mother kneeled beside the mattress. *If it was just about killing,* Anita's mother said reverently, *I could build her any body in a second.* She turned to Rainie, tapping her throat in the dark, and said: *You hold the other end of the thread, I'm sure of it. She made her knot around you. She needed you to come back to.*

The History of Our Hair

Dear Rainie:

It sounds paranoid, but Abu says it's important to always wear detachable hair in case a man comes along and attempts to kidnap you by yanking you into his car by your hair. (That's what I'll do to you someday, if you don't come back to me willingly.) What I really want is the doll with the mermaid hair I've seen in commercials: the wig is blond when it's dry, but if you dip it into water, the hair turns purple, blue, an extraterrestrial green. When I told Abu I wanted hair that changed color in water, she said, *Why don't I just keep you in the bathtub until you shrivel up*

and turn purple? If you're in the water long enough, every body
changes color.

Abu says that some people's hair is not rooted to
their head, tearing out easily as a handful of leaves.
But our hair is seeded deep in our scalp. Once, when
Abu was little and her great-grandmother died—
blown out of her house by a vengeful wind that
had begun as minor flatulence—they buried her up
on a mountain that grew tea leaves. The tea leaves
grew black that year, black as her hair had been,
and after seven years—the time it took for the body
to become only bone, all its meat meandering away
in the mouths of worms and mushrooms—Abu
and her siblings hiked up the mountain with a long
pair of chopsticks. They dug a hole where they had
buried her and reached in to pluck out her bones one
by one with the chopsticks, but they came up with
nothing but a sheaf of hairs. They dug deeper and
realized that their great-grandmother's hair was still
growing, that the pitcher of her skull was pouring
out hair, an underground creek of black. Her hair
had a current to it, a texture like the oil that men
go to war for, and when they followed the stream of
her hair all the way down the mountain, they found
that her hair was growing in the direction of the sea.
They decided she must want her bones to be brined
there, but when they tried to pick up her skull with
their pairs of chopsticks, her hair weighed it down.
No one could pick it up, not even Abu's oldest and
only brother, and so they tried to cut the thicket of

hair off her skull, though the blade bent against her strands. Her hair had the tensile strength of time.

They left her skull embedded in the mountain, growing its canal of hair, and plucked up the bones of her spine and feet instead, dropping them into the urn they had brought. One summer after that, my great-grandmother's hair snaked beneath the soil like roots and breached the ground, knotting into trunks, emerging as trees made of hair, black and leafless, split-ending into branches.

You and I were almost kidnapped once. Probably. We were at the park our mothers told us not to go to because there'd been a fight there last Christmas (Christmas!) and two boys died. Luckily, they were both reborn in that nativity scene outside the corner church. (Very helpful, mangers.) Another time, there was a car accident and a man was flung from his seat and into a tree. Three firefighters had to come with a ladder to carry him down from the branches, completely intact but filled with leaves.

At the park, we liked to talk to the three women who lived in the trees. The women knotted ropes around the branches so that they could shimmy down whenever they wanted, which was not often. One of the women wore sparrows in her hair, and another ate leaves, and the third woman evolved toes that were like fingers and could clasp around branches, so sometimes she dangled upside down from a thigh-thick branch and spoke to us. Her name was Noon, and she said it was because she'd been born at 12 exactly (though how did she know it wasn't at 12 in the morning?). Noon's lips were shiny as larvae, and she hid behind branches when she spoke to us: *The trees are safer than down there,* she said, though we told her about the wildfires, how her bones were bred for kindling. She laughed and said there would be no wildfires here.

With our necks craned and our eyes wide, we were hypnotized by light. Noon's teeth were silver-plated, and we saw only her mouth flitting between the branches. Her braid of hair descended from the tree, clear as rainwater, thick as drool. We could smell her bitter breath in its thread. *Come up with me,* Noon said, and tickled us with leaves. Another reason why we were not allowed to go to the park was that once, there'd been a body pulled out of the pond. No one could identify it. For weeks everyone wondered how someone had drowned in so shallow a pond, if he'd been drunk or was pushed, and it was Noon we came to. We asked the trees if they'd seen the boy drown, and Noon spoke from behind a cape of hair: *Yes. He agreed to live in the trees with me, so I told him he had to give up his body. He drowned himself in that pond and now he lives up here. He could have any body, but he's decided on being a squirrel. He likes to run under the wheels of cars.*

Now Noon was lowering her braid to us, and you were the one who touched it first—I was surprised too—even though I tried to slap your wrist away. I understood why you wanted to touch it. It looked sentient as water down a drain, and I wanted to drink from it like a faucet dream. But when you began to climb the hair, crawling up to the skyline of her scalp, I pulled you to the ground and rolled on top of you, spat in your face: *Stop*, I said, *we can't live in the trees. We won't have anything to eat but air. Aren't you afraid of that?* But you elbowed me away and got up and kept climbing, your feet winding themselves up in Noon's braid. Then you gasped and let go.

Noon dangled her hand like an apple. You flinched from it, your legs still woven into her braid. In the center of her palm was a razor blade, its corner embedded into her hand, attracting flies. You reached out and touched your thumb to the blade—I think you've always been attracted to embedded objects, dogteeth and razor blades and me. I yanked you down and we ran from the trees. Abu would later say it was my fault you got lockjaw from the rust, loosening only after your mother made a key with a paperclip. She inserted the key into your mouth and miraculously unlocked your jaw.

After meeting Noon, my dreams are all about raining hair, strands of hair that connect soil to sky, and when you tug on them, the sky winces like a scalp, and if you dream of climbing a strand of hair all the way up to its root, then you know you will die soon, you know the strand will snap while you're halfway up and what is there to catch you.

You said lockjaw was a small price to pay for climbing halfway to paradise—a woman named Noon—and I was impressed by you for the first time in my life. Then you told me that hair keeps growing after burial and I believed you again. So

we snuck into a funeral of some woman who had
so many granddaughters it was easy to impersonate
them, and when it was our turn to walk up to the
body and bow three times to the sound of the bell,
we ran forward instead and reached into the casket
and grabbed a fistful of her hair, intending to tear
out a clump of it so that we could observe its growth
at home. Would it grow faster now that it belonged
to the dead? But the women in the front row stood
up and threw us out and whipped us with the straps
of their purses and their shoes and their hair too.
They all had waist-length hair that could be whipped
around like a horse's, and instead of smacking flies
with a swatter like the rest of us, they just whinnied
and shuddered and shook out their hair, flogging the
flies. We checked our fingernails, but we never got
any of the old woman's hair, and we were surprised
by how strongly the strands were screwed into her
scalp, while ours tore out easily as grass, and we decided then that when we died, we wanted our coffins
to be full as fish tanks, full of dark and deep water for
our hair to sip and grow thick as trees, denying the
light a look at us.

Rainie Seeks Out the Reviving
Properties of Red Thread

To replace Anita's hair and blood, Rainie decided on red thread for both. It was what first knotted them together. It was their origin. At the kitchen table, Rainie sat and probed her throat with her fingers, praying for her old thread to surface like a bruise. She would tie the next knot herself. She would trade fingers with Anita if she had to, sawing off her own like branches. When Rainie told Anita's mother about her thread idea, Anita's mother replied that red thread was no longer permitted in the house, after watching how Anita playacted with it, tying it around her neck and Rainie's. Red thread was serious, used to entrap banana ghosts and knot promises, and thus it was removed from the radius of their surname.

After the skull's bowl of intestines was sun-dried outside,

Rainie checked on Anita's room. Ants caped Anita's body, dressing her warm for the winter. The ants were not in tune with the seasons. The skin on Anita's knuckles was sloughing off, revealing the bone beneath. Her eyebrows had migrated down to her cheekbones, perched there and inching like worms. Soon her bones would soften into batter, and Rainie still needed to collect most of her new organs. Rainie tried to coerce her heart into understanding the urgency of this mission and beating more rapidly, but it rolled around lazily.

That evening, standing outside where the intestines were now drying in a plumber's bucket, she watched her hair come undone from her scalp and spiral into the bucket. Her hair, so easily detachable, was not the source of the strong thread she needed.

Neither Vivian nor Anita's mother had volunteered any suggestions for where to obtain arteries. Thick red thread, the kind you could climb if you were lost in a dream. *That kind of thread is procured by wounding something*, Anita's mother said. But Rainie didn't know of anything alive that bled thread.

Rainie walked to the sycamore and grasped the lowest branch. She snapped it. Holding the sycamore branch like a spear, she used it to probe the silver fence beside her, the way Anita would have done. The dogs were absent from the lot: It was hot and they had scattered elsewhere, perhaps sleeping in the dry creek bed, where at least the mud was cool and clammy against their bellies.

Circling the sycamore, Rainie looked up into its branches and asked for its guidance. It was leafless, but on its trunk was a single pearl of sap. Plucking it off with her nail, Rainie placed the sap on her tongue and swallowed. She tried to re-member Anita's voice, the color of it different when she wore her collar, but she could only hear Vivian. Vivian stood behind her, startlingly close, offering her a bottle of water. She was wearing low-waisted jean shorts and a pink T-shirt with Snoopy on it, one of Anita's old shirts, and the bird's beak was sketched over with a Sharpie, reshaped into an eye. *Come home,* she said.

But Rainie kept circling the tree, and Vivian followed her, looking up into its branches. *Do you remember,* Vivian said, *when Mr. McDonald's and I used to take you out in his car? And we'd go through the drive-thru again and again, only ordering one thing at a time, just because you and Anita loved ordering so much?* Rainie laughed. Anita loved rolling down the window, speaking to a clown's mouth, eating while moving, watching the houses and strip malls blur away, all of the world orbiting the gravity of her belly.

I'm walking back now, Vivian said. *It's too hot.* She walked with her hips at the helm, jutting slightly forward, a step that reminded Rainie of the strays, their hipbones nudging the sky.

Rainie stayed with the sycamore awhile longer. Its silhouette reminded her of Anita's, but the familiarity ended there. Its shadow no longer recognized Rainie, receding whenever she moved. It seemed more lopsided than before, its roots withering. Anita once said that mountains were more related to the sky than to the earth. The sycamore tree looked like it had decided the same thing: It wanted to side with the clouds and not the ground, transferring more and more of its weight to its uppermost reaches.

Rainie heard a rustling above her, and when she followed the sound, she saw a woman crouched in the high branches, her hair dangling like rain. Rainie resisted sticking out her tongue to lap it up. It was not Noon. The woman smiled, revealing the teeth of a dog. Her nails were shellacked red. At the base of her throat was a patch of ruddy fur that changed shades like oxidizing blood. *Who are you?* Rainie asked, but she already knew. It was the red dog, the one that had bitten her and planted its tooth into her wrist. The woman had the same eyes, the same planetary pupils.

I'm one of Anita's mothers, the woman said. Her tongue, marbled with silver veins, unraveled from her mouth and flicked at the leaves. *Which one?* Rainie asked, but the woman just laughed. She shifted, and the skin of her legs flaked into bark, scattering at Rainie's feet. *Remember I gave you my tooth as a gift,* the woman said. *A pebble for a pulse. A reminder of the many dogs you could be. My daughter has always been different from you. She has always been more of a jaw than you. Both of you have begun a journey of return. She to me. You to her. Do you understand?* Rainie nodded, though in truth, she hadn't understood a word. Mesmerized, she lifted her hands and stroked the woman's hair. The woman scuttled higher up the tree, climbing past its branches, scrambling up invisible rungs until she disappeared into the sky.

Rainie backed away from the tree. Apparitions would only thwart her. She set down the thin branch in her hands, no longer remembering why she'd wanted to snap it off in the first place. She looked around for something to tie the branch back to the trunk, or at least maybe some spat-out gum to use as glue. But she saw only crushed soda cans. She kicked them with her feet and heard them ring. What organs would Anita have called these cans? Rainie wondered. If she'd believed in the beasts Anita invented, believed the spinning soda cans could be real jaws, or even bothered to pick them up, then their lives would not have diverged so much. Anita would not be buried in sleep, foreign to any future.

Anita would be walking beside her right now, and she would be pointing at the glimmer of a beer bottle filled with piss, the light strained through it, and say it was the gold-feathered neck of a bird that had lived long ago, that had taught flight to all the other birds. Rainie turned back to look at the sycamore tree, its swaying shape the size of a pinky finger, waggling up from the asphalt. If it was still alive after all these years without rain and a quilt of real dirt, fed by handfuls of gravel and glass, then it was possible for skeletons to breach the asphalt and stride out. It was possible that Anita's future was buried here, in fertile ground. Rainie decided what she would say to Anita when she woke up: *I believe you. I see that the sycamore tree is the skeleton of a god who no longer walks, waiting to wear you, waiting to be prayed to.*

When Rainie returned to the house, she helped Anita's mother weed away the basil blackened by dog's blood. Chopping the basil in the kitchen, Rainie asked Anita's mother about a woman in the sycamore tree. *What kind of woman?* Anita's mother asked, head jerking up. *Describe her.* Rainie tried to describe her: unripe eyes, not very much skin, rain-like hair. *One of my great-grandmothers, then,* Anita's mother said, but she sounded unconvinced. *Or someone in my past who I've wronged or not thought enough about.*

You know, Anita's mother continued, after a few moments of silence, *I found her.* Rainie said she knew. Anita had told her an abridged version of the story: The bottom-bunk woman left a baby on her bed, according to eyewitnesses (the moon and the window). *But I dreamed,* Anita's mother said, *that the woman in the bottom bunk would come back and take me away in ex-*

change. That must be what happened: That woman met my daughter in a dream and lured her away from her body. I should have found that woman and killed her when I could. Or I should have gone away with her, followed her wherever she went. I don't know. Maybe she's just another version of me.

She said it casually, half to herself, as if it were the stanza of a song. It was almost a love song: *I should have gone away with her.* Anita, when she was a baby, had cried in another language. *You don't believe me, but she did, I swear she did. When she cried, no one else could understand. She slept in another language too. When she was asleep, I didn't recognize her. The way she is now, since she left her body—I don't know that face. I see the shape of her, but I don't see her. Do you know what I mean?*

Rainie said she did. When her mother spoke to her about marriage, when she showed Rainie the duct-taped kitchen drawer where she kept Rainie's wedding gold, Rainie could see the outline of her life but without her body inside it. She knew the trajectory of her future but forgot her own name, her mother's face, everything familiar, until all she could see was the gold hovering in the air, empty circlets of metal, not her not her not her.

Where is she, Rainie asked, *the bottom-bunk woman?* Anita's mother dried the same dish twice. *I don't know,* she said, *I don't know. Maybe she's the woman in the tree. Maybe she's me. I should have known her name. I bet you I would know it if you said it.*

That night, Rainie woke to wailing. It was coming from Anita's room, but when she entered, all she saw were the shadows of dogs against the white walls and ants sleeving Anita's arms. They were going to eat her free of her bones. Rainie backed away from the mattress and realized that the wailing sound was receding too, that she was the one making it. She pressed her hands to her mouth, but the sound could not be muffled.

Vivian ran into the room, brandishing a flashlight, but Rainie kept wailing. *Stop it,* Vivian said, *you'll scare her soul away,* and then she dropped the flashlight, kicked it back toward the doorway. She ringed her hands around Rainie's neck, wrenching. The wailing stopped, and Rainie folded to her knees. *Thank you,* she tried to say, but the sound wouldn't come.

Vivian eased her grip, letting one hand go. *A nightmare?* she said to Rainie. Winny stood in the doorway, barefoot on the carpet, staring at them. *No,* Rainie said, coughing into the hinge of her elbow. *I don't know what that was.* They left the room, shut the door, squeezed the wet T-shirt back into the crack under the doorframe: Anita's mother always said she was afraid one day there'd be a carbon monoxide leak and they'd all die in their sleep, so she sealed all their doors that way. Vivian said, *Why don't we just buy a carbon monoxide alarm?* But Anita's mother said, *I don't like alarms. When they scream, they sound like women. Or pigs.*

Vivian told Winny to go back to bed. *We're going outside,* she told Rainie, and they stood in plastic slippers in the side yard, no stars, a half-moon, the basil growing slow as bone. Rainie bit her bottom lip to prevent herself from crying out again. There was no dream she could blame, not even ghost dogs licking her in her sleep. She forgot the face of the woman hanging in the sycamore. Rubbing the dogtooth in her wrist, circling it with her thumb, she turned to Vivian, who was tilting her head to the night, open-mouthed as if she were catching rain. Her mouth had the depth of a day.

Vivian held her hands in front of her too, offering them to the sky. *I'm trying to catch blessings,* she said, laughing. The way her thumbs curled inward—oddly shy, like sproutlings, the understory—made Rainie lean forward and kiss her once on the side of her neck. The skin there was cold. Vivian was still. She didn't turn her head. *Sorry,* Rainie said, though she wasn't sure if she was apologizing to Vivian or to Anita.

Vivian kept looking upward. When she was younger, Rainie liked to observe Vivian's posture, the worldly way she stood with her legs slightly apart. A dog on the hunt. *Anita used to tell me the moon is an ice cube. And it melts a little bit at a time. That's why night is colder than day. And that's why you don't want to cut your finger under moonlight, because your blood will freeze,* Vivian said, laughing again. Rainie lifted her finger. For once, she didn't want Anita's name to be invoked. She wanted to be free of all duties, alone with Vivian and the night, nothing waiting for her. There was a streetlight above them, but it was no longer alive, glazed over with flies. Vivian leaned over and tugged Rainie's finger to her mouth, biting it once, so quick Rainie almost believed it was an insect. When she was released, her finger throbbed like a bitten plum. *You see what a lie that is? You're not frozen at all,* Vivian whispered, though there was no one to overhear them. She reached up and drew her finger across Rainie's throat and around her neck, a circlet of red where the thread had once dwelled.

Vivian stepped forward, aligning their chests, and licked Rainie's neck, her tongue tugging at her pulse. Gasping, Rainie leaned back against the wall and looked up, searching for the rain Vivian had been anticipating, but all she saw was the outline of feet swinging above her. The remnants of a dream. Vivian took Rainie's wrists and lifted them to her mouth, suckling at Rainie's inner wrist until a root-ache radiated down her arm. *Not that,* Rainie said, but she couldn't even hear herself. Vivian gripped the dogtooth between her own teeth, scraping it gently, and Rainie reared her head back, knocking it hard against the wall.

Did you blame Anita for the dog that bit you? Vivian said, adorning Rainie's wrist with spit. *No,* Rainie said. *Only a little bit. And she waited for me. Just like I've decided to wait for her.* She didn't remember the fever that followed. Her tooth pulsed, radiating pain through her fingers.

Maybe you'll regret waiting, Vivian said. *Who knows what she's become in her sleep? Who knows who she'll be when she wakes? She'll always be my blood. As long as she's still got any. But she might not be the dog you remember or who remembers you.*

It was a risk, Rainie knew, and she generally avoided those. She wanted a world where she could be weightless. But Anita multiplied her, duplicating their human lives into dog lives, their dog lives into dream lives. They had been together for so many species. Meeting again as strangers would only mean another life together. *Then I'll choose her again,* Rainie said. *I'll choose to know her. As many times as I can.*

Vivian bent her head, dragging her toe through her shadow, smearing it thin. *It's not too late. You could still stop now. You could go the same way you left before. So easily, and without leaving behind even a shit. Who could blame you?*

I would, Rainie said. What she felt for Anita ran through the ground, beneath her feet, like those dogs racing on the underside of the pavement, erupting through a rain puddle. She wanted all the miracles of being near her. All the births she beckoned.

I've chosen, was all Rainie said. She touched the center of her throat, where a knot once bobbed when she swallowed. Anita once told the story of choice as an illusion: The red thread reeled you into every life, every meeting, and you couldn't resist it. But that was only one of many versions, one narrative thread among many. *She would respect me,* Rainie said, *for making my choice. For sewing my own story.*

Vivian nodded. She looked at Rainie, unblinking. Her eyes without whites. A dog's eyes, all pupil. *Good,* Vivian said. Rainie wondered if this had just been a test: It was possible that Vivian would've stoned her and slit her open and dismembered her for the remaining organs if she abandoned Anita now.

The first thing anyone needs is teeth, Vivian said, smiling to show her own. *Do teeth count as organs?*

Rainie said she didn't know.

I think Anita will need teeth, Vivian said, then brought Rainie's wrist to her mouth again and bit down on the dogtooth, ripping it out at the root. Rainie cried out as the tooth cracked away from her wrist, the roots wrenching with a sound like a wet branch breaking. Vivian walked backward with the tooth, tugging the blood from Rainie's wrist in one long thread, until she was at the end of the side yard and then on the street. Rainie kneeled and watched her blood unspool like a magician's trick scarf, a tooth knotted to the end of it. Shutting her eyes, Rainie folded to the pavement. She didn't want to watch as Vivian disappeared beyond the horizon, walking backward until she reached the end of Rainie's blood. As Rainie lost consciousness, she repeated to herself: *I must stay. I must be the one she returns to. I must not let my blood mislead me.*

In the morning, when Rainie opened her eyes at last, red thread lined her inner wrist, stitching shut a hole in its center.

Next to her was a coil of red thread with a tooth tied to the end of the strand—an anchor. She reached for it, weighing the tooth in her fist. It was heavy, drilling into the meat of her palm. The red thread slipped between her fingers, and she wondered how her body had contained the length of this life.

The History of Our Hearts

Dear Rainie:

In our family, we have five-chambered hearts (I say
our, even though I know your mother would say we
are as far apart as toes and tongue). Two chambers
on the bottom, two on the top, and one extra room
in the center of us. It's shaped like a pearl. The fifth
chamber is where we keep extra memories, spare
blood, and mosquitoes. The mosquitoes are the
small kind, the size of sesame seeds, and they whir
inside our hearts and sip on neighboring blood,
and when our bodies are burned, they will fly out
of us and bead the clouds, fill them with black rain.
Owning a fifth chamber means that our hearts are

fully renovated and (up to) the size of a horse's. My
great-aunt's was twenty pounds and took months to
burn, and even then it didn't translate well into ash.
It burned into a pile of slivered red fingernails. Abu
said we evolved a fifth chamber in our hearts so that
we could never bleed out the way slit-bellied pigs do:
If we were ever beheaded, our blood would spill out,
but the fifth chamber of our heart would open its
locked doors and refill us again.

Abu said that if I worried too much, I would
grow stones inside the fifth chamber of my heart and
one day I'd take a bath and drown, dragged down
by the rock-sack of my chest. I didn't believe her, but
still I did jumping jacks in the bathroom every night,
believing that it would loosen whatever was bar-
nacled inside me and keep my ribs from rearranging
into a coral reef.

When we were dogs, I asked you to puncture
my chest so that we could find the fifth chamber. We
played a game called nurse, in which the patient lay
naked in our bathtub. I was the patient, waiting for
you to pry my heart open with a shaving razor.

You said: *If we find the fifth chamber of your heart, I
know what to put inside it.* From the waistband of your
jeans, you pulled out a stuffed sock and said it was
filled with money your mother had told you to save.
I agreed that my chest was the best place to put it. I
splayed out in the bathtub while you punctured the
drum-hollow center of my chest. *Deeper,* I said, so you
pushed it all the way into my custardy heart.

My two aunts visiting from Reno, First aunt and

Second aunt, got up from the kitchen and ran into
the bathroom and saw a thread unraveling from my
chest and kneeled over me, trying to knot it. My first
aunt hoisted me up like a bride and ran me out into
the hallway, scurrying from one end to the other, unsure what to do, and my second aunt said, *PUT HER
DOWN, you pig,* and grabbed at my ankles and my
hair. It was Abu, asleep in the bedroom, who plucked
me out of her arms and rolled me like a log up and
down the hallway carpet to confuse the blood—when
blood is dizzy, it can't stand up and run, it doesn't
know what direction to exit you—and then she tied
a blanket around my chest as a tourniquet and said,
*You rice mites, that's not even where the heart is located, it's not
in the center of your chest, the center of your chest is air, it's a
wind that rattles your ribs,* and you said you were sorry,
you were just trying to hide some money. *You want
to hide something, you eat it,* Abu said, and that was the
reason why, later that week, we all woke up and ran
to the window. You had eaten the sock of money, and
your mother was chasing you up and down the street
with a long cooking chopstick she wanted to insert
into your ass and stir around.

　　Your mother was yelling, *SHIT OUT THE
MONEY, YOU DEVIL,* and Abu said, *Some dreams are
a laxative. Put a girl to sleep and she'll release all sorts of
things: missing nickels, swallowed earrings, severed thread.*

Rainie Makes a Stone of Anita's Heart

C ontrary to her name, Rainie knew rain mostly as a rumor or when Winny watched the Weather Channel and helpfully pointed out each pixelated icon and explained its corresponding message: *This thing with the spikes is the sun—the sun doesn't really look like that, it looks more like a bald head, but that must be what the sun looks like before everyone else sees it. And those dash marks, slanted kind of like knives, that means rain. And the clouds mean it's going to rain. Except not the clouds here, which are more like beards. More decorative. And then there's this one with half a cloud and half a sun jutting out of it. That means the cloud is going to give birth to the sun and we better be out to catch it in our hands.*

Okay, Rainie said, *okay.* She knew what the symbols meant and also why they hovered in their particular order across the days of the week but decided that Winny was uninterested in proper names, in the names of weekdays or cities. Sometimes she was literally light: a beam of light striping the room when she walked down the hallway to Anita's bed. There were accounts of many gods who were born as beams of light, and this meant that inevitably they would sacrifice themselves. Winny told Rainie she hoped this did not happen: *I don't want to die before Anita wakes up. I don't want to reunite with her when I'm dead or in a dream and she won't even recognize me.*

Rainie wanted to say that even in waking, Anita would not recognize her, or either of them. With the dogtooth wrenched from her wrist, she was no longer marked, and maybe this meant Anita would not remember her promise. *I will scar you into my memory. We will meet again like the boy and the girl in the story.* Now, when Rainie thought of the story, it seemed tyrannical rather than tender, the boy throwing a stone at his fated wife, scarring her for the rest of her life. Rainie no longer thought it was about the boy, who believed he could flee his fate; she now thought it was a story about the girl and what a shame it was that she could not escape him.

It's just a story, Winny said. Winny was leaning into her, pressing her ear to Rainie's scalp. She liked to listen to the amplified sound of Rainie chewing as she ate, loved to hear her orchestral jaw.

For Anita's new heart, Rainie decided on the white stone that had been given to her all those years ago. She didn't want to use the dog-beheading stone, which was now sullied in her memory. Remembering that the white stone was in her mother's apartment in another city, Rainie took the bus home. Her mother opened the door and said, *Thank god you got rid of that sycamore branch, it was sickening me, that ghost limb.* Rainie said, *Yes,* but she missed its heat between her legs, the rough skin of its bark.

The stone was in her room. When she brought it back to Anita's duplex and said to Vivian, *Look! A heart,* Vivian laughed and took it in her hands. *A stone for a heart? Anita doesn't deserve to be this cruel.* Rainie sat down on the sofa beside Winny, thinking of dogs in the sea. It was evening and there wasn't yet anyone predicting the weather. *But what about all the people who want to know what the weather will be like at night?* Winny said, before shutting off the TV. The moon dragged its tassels of light, licking the windows bright.

We should drop the stone from the roof, Rainie said. She'd always suspected there was something inside to be hatched, a reason why its original dog owner had been harboring it in its mouth. *No,* Vivian said, *we have to keep it whole, for Anita.* She was as stubborn as Rainie remembered. When she'd given birth to Winny, there was a rumor that she held on to the umbilical cord like a leash and refused to let Winny be severed from it. *I don't let things go,* Vivian had said, and even now she collected Anita's shed hairs, sweeping them out of the room, saving the strands in a suitcase. She was planning to knit a rope for Anita to follow home to her body: She would tie it around Anita's ankle but hadn't decided where the other end was supposed to go.

Rainie laughed: *How are you going to pull her home if you can't even give her the end of the rope? What are you going to do, flush the end of it down the toilet and hope she's somewhere down there?* Vivian stood up and slapped her. It was gentle, a warning rather than an actual reddening, but Rainie rolled off the couch and knelt in the dark. *Don't forget whose house you're in, and don't forget Anita's always listening,* Vivian said, then walked down the hallway to the bedroom. Winny sat and watched, reaching out to pet Rainie's cheek and say, *Don't worry, she's just afraid she won't be able to find a new body for Anita before she rots away, before the ants eat her.*

Rainie said, *I'm building her one.* She took up the white stone, left on the dining table by Vivian, and went outside. Kneeling in the side yard, she bashed it again and again against the ground, praying for something to break.

At last, it split open. Inside, the stone was the texture of an apple. Rainie dug her nails into its flesh, coring it while Winny watched through the window. There was something inside its white meat, a small and bitter bulb. Unsure if it was living or not, Rainie refrigerated it overnight, and in the morning before going to work, Anita's mother identified it as an orchid bulb. *Plant it,* she instructed, so Rainie buried it among the basil, tending to Anita's heart-bulb with leftover bathwater.

Eating orchids, she read once, was an ancient method of conceiving desired sons. The word *orchid* was derived from the word for *testicles,* she'd read. Rainie uprooted the bulb a few times, rolling the scrubbed sac between her palms, its weight warm in her hands. She wanted to eat it. She wanted to beat it. Make it a heart.

That night, while the orchid grew its furred petals, Anita came to her in a dream, nine years old and with her hair greased back in two braids. *I want to show you something,* she said, and in her fist was a ball of raw ground pork. Rainie followed Anita to the sycamore tree, but there was no empty lot beyond it, no fence or dogs. The sycamore foregrounded a mountain, a gondola strung along its spine. Rainie had been there before, when she was six and visited a mountain where one of her dead was buried. She and her mother and brothers were on a gondola, the mountain below spewing milk like a breast. In the distance was an orchid field. The farmers cross-bred their flowers, panda and phoenix and peacock, and were so secretive about their breeding practices and their special varieties that dogs defended the fields from trespassers. One man—Rainie's uncle, possibly the dead one—once snuck onto the orchid farm to steal a rumored rare-dollar orchid, white with spotted gold petals.

He wrestled each of the dogs to the ground and strangled them, buried them in the orchid fields to feed the next generation of flowers. Then he unburied six bulbs from the field and placed them in egg cartons. He placed the egg cartons into two canvas sacks and ran from the farm, leaves attached to the bottoms of his boots to disguise his footprints. But strangely, when he was home, down the mountain where cities inched themselves higher and higher to shirk floodwaters, his egg cartons were empty. No soil, no bulbs, though he swore he'd placed them in his sacks, swore he'd felt their weight on his shoulders as he ran. The air inside his sacks was heavier than the air outside them. And every night until he died, he heard dogs. He recognized their faces as they lunged at him, as he wrapped his hands around them. They were so camouflaged in the dark that he would have thought he'd strangled bare air if not for the tongues that flapped in front of their faces. He saw them all in a row, standing before his bed. He was so fearful of the dogs that he held in his urine and no longer visited the outhouse at night. As a result of this—drunk as he was, or so Rainie's mother always asserted, though no one knew if it was true—his bladder burst one night in his sleep, during his dream of those orchids opening in the dark, dogs' eyes blinking wide in the soil.

The History of Our Bellies

Dear Rainie:

As a girl, my abu was a grief-eater. Your mother doesn't want you to eat processed foods and even gave us that lecture about how McDonald's uses embalming fluids in all their products, which only made me want to eat more of their meat—would my organs get pickled after eating, and when I was buried, would my belly knock against the underside of the soil like a balloon against a ceiling? Would my liver immortalize into light? But *my* abu ate grief, processed or not. This was before she became my mother. Our mothers before us: They were miraculous. In Abu's particular building, when someone died, families hired grief-eaters to enter the deceased person's abode and eat everything they owned. That way, the dead person's belongings could be reincarnated too, carried in Abu's belly and rebirthed through her intestines. Grief-eaters are always women, Abu says.

I've eaten everything. Belts, clothes. Dishes, knives. Furniture takes a while. It wears down your teeth. That's why mine are silver-capped. I've eaten cats, snakes, fish tanks. Bed frames, mattresses too. I've eaten every species of shoe. I've eaten clocks, watches. I went to bed with my belly ticking. I could tell the time without even looking at anything. Something was counting the hours inside me.

To audition for grief-eating, Abu had to walk to a place of worship located on the scalp of a mountain and sit in a room damp as the inside of a mouth and wait for monks to bring her an assortment of objects on wooden trays. She had to eat each object in the dark and defecate into a copper tray that was located in the corner, gleaming red-black like a picked-open scab. The room was empty except for a cushion to kneel on and a teacup of water that carried her reflection. Abu was first brought a glass frog the size of her fist, which she swallowed whole to prevent shards in her throat. For a month before, she'd trained herself to swallow her own fist by first probing her throat with her pinky, then with her forefinger, and then her thumb, until at last she was able to wedge her entire fist inside without even bulging her neck. After she swallowed the frog made of glass, the monks brought her a tray of matchsticks as long as her arms and so

sensitive to friction that they could be lit by breathing on them. Abu knew they were testing to see if
she could swallow them without striking their heads
and setting her throat alight, so she broke the sticks
apart in her hands and mixed them into the teacup
of water until it was a dust-thickened porridge. Then
she drank. Her intestines were silt-lined rivers.

The monks brought the final object, a mirror
the size of her body, and Abu could not see herself
in the dark, could only see an image scattered and
flung like salt, a shadow cast by some unnamed species. The room was dim as a nostril and Abu reached
out a single finger, stroked the mirror like the spine
of a wild animal she was trying to tame. She'd been
practicing how to dislocate her jaw and then relocate
it, to unhinge the bone so that she could fit large
objects inside herself, but this mirror was too large
for any mouth. So she beat the silver pane with her
fists and her forehead and her knees until the dark
of her blood replaced the dark of the room and the
mirror was battered into island-shaped pieces. Abu
sucked the shards like candied rain until each piece
dissolved, said her tongue was in tatters afterward
but it had been worth it, because the monks opened
the door and sound renamed the room and there was
a light looming inside her mouth, miraculous and
deadly.

Grief-eaters were paid by the pound, so Abu
learned to eat the heavy things, necklaces and rings
and jade cuffs and statues of lions and stone like-
nesses of national leaders and paperweights of

resined butterflies and books, so many books, and this was when she discovered that every language had a different taste, and that when we spoke we were so used to the taste of our native languages that we were numb to them. The way you don't know what the inside of your house smells like until you leave it for a long time and return. But if you ate the page of a language you didn't know, it would taste of all kinds of things: sweat on a wrist, wildfire ash, muskmelon, grape juice, piss, porridge.

In the bedroom she shared with my aunts, Abu liked to keep a shelf with books stolen from the dead, and some nights I stood in the doorway and watched as she took down a book and tore out a page, folding it into a neat shape and then pressing it to her tongue to dissolve it. At night, in the dark, she eats. She eats the sheets, the cotton trim of her pillow, the calluses on her palms, the dark itself, the curtains, the moldy moon, the wind. Her own hair. Plaster from the wall that becomes crumbs when you pinch it. Once, she woke with a doorknob plugged in her mouth, and my aunts had to reattach it to the door, except that it had melted in her mouth and was now shaped like the inside of it, a mold of her mouth like the kind you can get at a dentist's. Every time I turn that doorknob, my hand learns her teeth.

Grief-eating, Abu says, is something I can never try. She says my stomach is calf-soft and will be slaughtered by anything not starch-based. She says once as a baby I swallowed my aunt's disposable lighter and farted little fires all over the house that had to be beaten down with a wet mop and a blanket. Grief-eaters were supposed to bury what they excreted, but Abu and her sisters collected the jewelry she expelled days later and pawned the pieces off, saving for plane tickets to America. They pried the pearls out of earrings, snipped necklaces into bracelets, hammered gold cuffs into sheets to be resold and redistributed as daylight.

Because they'd technically thieved from the dead in order to fly here, Abu and my aunts went to the temple every other week to pray to the deceased they had stolen from and atone for their bad karma. At the temple, the names of the dead are written on slips of white paper and pasted to the walls, which are so thick with slips that the room resembles wind, mist pasted to the walls, and when you walk to the front of the temple/rec center where the deity sits with its shoulders half-melted and its face a gorgeous gold, the slips of paper flutter up like a flock of breeze-whittled wings, waiting to flee.

I like to hold Abu's hand and look at the walls and ask which ones are our dead. The names are written with dogs' paws and are illegible to me, so Abu reads them aloud as we move across the wall, the translucent paper slips layered like onionskin, each black-inked name overlapping another until the entire wall resembles the map of a planet where water spreads the same way as night, everywhere at once. Abu brings plastic bags of oranges to leave at the altar, which is just a dog dish at the foot of the deity, its scalp shedding metallic dandruff that I

collect on my tongue. The nuns are seated behind a
glass counter at the back of the temple, writing side
by side the names of everyone who died in the latest
wildfire, the one northeast of here. There are too
many names that need to be updated on the walls of
the temple, so the nuns write all day and all night,
some of them even learning how to write in their
sleep or with their feet or with their mouths, brushes
growing out of them like antennae.

After the names live on the walls for one hundred days, the nuns take them down and burn
them in a bucket in the parking lot, dousing the fire
with water so clear it could reseal a wound. After a
hundred days, the souls move on and their names
are uninhabited. They are other matter now. I have
attended three burnings in the parking lot for three
dead people's hundredth day. The men die first in
my family, proving the existence of justice. The men
in our family are susceptible to the voices of trees
who said things like, *Better to do all your dying while you're
still alive.*

Another time I witness the burning of a name,
it belongs to an aunt I've never met, an aunt who
lived near the sea and raised silkworms in a shoebox
and fried them alive and ate them until she began to
produce silk from her mouth, her saliva stringing into
silver-white threads that were fine as light and could
be spooled and sold. This aunt died of a species of
sadness—we keep an index of melancholies, but I
forget their names—and believed that the sky was
the skin of an animal and that we were all inside the

belly of an ox. There was another world outside us, but the skin of the sky could only be cut open from the outside, and my aunt would stand on her roof for hours and shout to be let out. She slipped one day—or jumped, Abu never told me—and inside her house they found all her dresser drawers and kitchen cabinets full of silkworms that rattled like handfuls of teeth.

When the nuns pasted my aunt's name to the wall, the clouds grew pairs of legs and pedaled across the sky, and I asked Abu if she was sad too, if she believed there was a knife large enough to cut open the sky. Abu didn't answer, just lit a cigarette and smoked it and then put it out on a dish, sticking the butt upright like a stick of incense. The wall of moth-textured names made me feel like we were living in the heart of the onion, that the temple itself was shedding its snakeskin.

Another name I recognized on the wall was my great-grandmother's, a woman Abu says lived so long because her heart was a jewel of coal, and she swallowed matches to keep it lit and never drank water for fear of dousing her blood, and she lived like a fire for over a century and had been alive to see the president apologize to her tribe, which she said was worth a mouthful of shitflies. On her hundredth day, the nuns took down her name and marched us into the parking lot as we chanted words that sounded to me like the language of gnats, and they folded her name into the flame as we looked down and droned the oldest words still living.

One day at the temple, the dead go missing
from the walls, though if you listen to certain neighbors, like the Hsus, they'll claim that the names of
their dead had long since fled, that they had always
suspected the nuns of embezzling names, of stealing
them off the walls and eating them or reselling them
at wholesale price to the not-yet-born. But we don't
believe the Hsus, who also claim to be related to
several emperors, though the only history they have
is a history of heart disease—the oldest Hsu sibling
had veins full of chicken fat—and we believe that the
slips of paper were awakened to their moth nature
and batted off the wall like translucent wings, that
each stroke of ink feathered into flight. (But now I'm
talking like the dogs.)

Abu says to me when she hears: *Names can take
flight. That's why we don't say them unless it's an absolute
emergency. The more we say our names, the more they learn
to love the air, and then one day they'll leave you entirely. You
shouldn't let a bird out of its cage. You shouldn't let your
name out of your mouth.* It was true we never called
each other by name, that it tempted fate to do so.
We called each other by the names of what we ate
as babies: Fishbone, Penny, Television Antennae.
We called each other by zodiac, by eye color, by the
shape of our shadows, by the skin of our armpits, by
the number of hairs on our cheeks, by the way we
curled when we sleep, by the kind of apples we liked,
by the frequency of our hiccups, by the breadth of
our hands, by the whiteness of our lies, by the number of children we have had or lost, by our appetite

for bitter things, by our preference for wet weather, by the men we had married once and outlived.

The day the names took flight from the temple, only one girl saw it. She had been in the parking lot with another girl—for the purpose of pleasure, not prayer—and they were in the back of their 2006 Honda Civic (the exterior a green-beetle sheen) when she saw the doors of the temple buck open. A flock of paper flapped out of the dark, translucent wings without bodies attached to them, each of the names saddling a different light. Some names sailed out over the street, others mounted the sky, others beat their bodiless wings across the lot and out toward the Pacific. The girl—the witness—said she thought they were moths at first, because they were white and seemed to seek light, but then she realized that each of the wings bore a black name and must therefore be seagulls, and the girl who had been with her—her torso tattooed with cloud formations—said no, seagulls don't have names on their wings, and besides, these birds were brittle as ash, and when a wind knifed through the flock, some of them unraveled into cinders and scattered, fluttering down in a gray veil over the car, and when the flock of names crossed over our neighborhood, Abu and I jutted our tongues out the window and tasted their lineage of disintegration.

The names flew toward water, skimming their bellies against an eyelash-shaped creek that cleaves the hills above our houses. We call it the butt crack, that place where the hills meet, where the wildfires start wolfing down on the grass and the city goes on its knees.

The nuns bought laser guns and arrows and stood out in the parking lot, aiming at the sky to shoot down names, but the paper wings whipped higher into the sky and turned the clouds to curd. As the names tunneled through the clouds, their wings folded downward and thickened into legs, their paws made of clustered embers. The legged names ran through the clouds, tearing them down like gauzy curtains, and then they started to chase their own tails of ash, creating funnels of air that whirled and vacuumed up cars and roofs below.

A few rolled onto their backs and wagged their tails like a smoke signal. Others began to coalesce into packs of dense ash, their many legs churning the air above. It was unclear why they were running when they could float, being made of ash and smoke. The nuns below kept missing, unable to shoot down a single name. When the names thickened the air, I thought at first it must be a wildfire, that the ash was ushered in from the hills, but Abu said she recognized the taste of the ash, said it was almost legible, that by tasting the ash she knew its name, and she recited the names of the dead to me. The opacity of the air caused three major accidents on the freeway, and what was left of the name-flock kept circling the city, looking for mouths to land in, waiting for us to pronounce them gods.[1]

1 (or dogs)

Rainie Stomachs the Sky

Every morning, Rainie knelt by Anita's bed and tried to squint through her onioned skin, tried to discern what inside her was rotting first, but when she leaned too close, her breath fogged Anita's torso and turned her opaque. One morning she felt her own presence doubled, then turned around and saw Anita's mother standing behind her. *See how there's a mushroom plugging up each of her nostrils? Those need to be trimmed daily.* From her pocket she took a pair of silver nail-trimming scissors and hovered over Anita's body, stabbing each translucent mushroom cap with the blade and twisting it out of the nostril. *These can be eaten,* Anita's mother said, and pocketed them.

Rainie raised her head, and her hair fanned the scent of Anita's rot, like soil under her fingernails or a skinned grape sheltered in sunlight, sweet and deep. Furred mold lined the inner creases of her elbows. Her fingernails were completely dissolved now, reduced to ridges of weak light. Rainie tried to detect rapid eye movement beneath Anita's lids, a sign of the kind of sleep where Anita could dream, but she must have been alive beneath her body, because her eyes were still and sunken. Anita's mother pocketed her scissors and placed her hand on Rainie's shoulder. *Almost a body,* she said, which Rainie interpreted as encouragement. She and Anita used to wake up early and sneak into Anita's mother's room and look down at her sleeping body, lifting the hem of her shirt and shining a flashlight onto the skin to better detect any movement. They wanted to see what she had swallowed, and so they'd kneel and stare at her belly and watch for movement, like the flash of a silver tail in the dark water of a fish tank, any sign that beneath the skin was a living sea of swallowed things. Rainie asked Anita's mother if she'd just pretended to be asleep all those years ago, and she laughed and said, *Are you still wondering about my belly? You girls.* Rainie almost smiled. *You girls, you girls. If you want to go belly-watching,* Anita's mother said, *you need to leave this house.*

After the dogs in the lot began their seasonal process of sloughing off their skins, wearing only their skeletons, Rainie walked to the temple for belly research. She remembered that there'd been a statue of a bare-bellied god with a snake through its tongue, but she wondered now if that had actually been one of Anita's fossil descriptions. Anita was the one who knew how to worship, or at least believed herself capable of doing it. Rainie wondered if remembering counted as prayer. Wasn't she tending to Anita in that way, retouching her in every story?

At the temple, she watched the nuns lead a procession of women to the parking lot, a bucket swinging from the head nun's wrists. The women cinched around the bucket, feeding wisps of named paper to the flame. From the sidewalk, Rainie watched the nun closest to the fire, her head freshly shaved, her bald head blue. It reminded her of the white stone, the substitute for Anita's heart, the orchid crouched inside it.

Rainie snuck in after the two o'clock service, past the card tables spread with anti-gambling pamphlets, past the rows of red cushions to kneel on, the prayer books that were winged in her dreams. The walls of the temple fluttered with white flocks of paper, their names overlapping like veins. She tried to read them, but it was dim inside the temple, minus the deity elevated in its alcove: It was a woman, with a flat nose and a gold face refracting the room. A few feet in front of her crossed legs was a smaller statue of a boy, his belly lunging forward into the dim, a belly round as an orchid bulb. There was something maternal about the boy's belly, as if he had swallowed something secret and was harboring it from harm. His face was splayed wide in a smile, rioting with laughter, shoulders raised. Before today, Rainie had never noticed how a face contorted in laughter looked the same as a grimace of grief.

Rainie saw her mother attend a service only once: It was to pray for her dead brother, Swallow, the man she claimed to have killed. She bought a bunch of green bananas and brought them to the altar, which the nuns discouraged—oranges and apples lasted longer on the altar—but Rainie's mother said she had to offer bananas. Though she and her brother had despised their softness, this was the only way to appease the banana ghost that still leashed him. Anita had said, *If I were a banana ghost, I would be offended to be offered a banana. That's canni-balism, like if I died and you brought me my body to eat.*

The laughing boy was so glossy, his belly seemed to jiggle. Rainie walked up to the statue with her head bowed, feigning prayer, and reached forward across the altar, the apples just beginning to soften. She dragged her finger across the boy's belly, begged it to bare its contents. But the belly was cold and full of bone, and Rainie withdrew her finger when she saw the nuns return single file with a bucketful of ash.

Rainie pretended to bow, but she was still watching the belly. She wondered if it was possible to cleave his belly from his body like a cantaloupe, then shuttle it home in her arms or between her legs.

She backed away from the altar and lingered by the doors of the temple, waiting for the nuns to evacuate again with a bucket of fire, for someone else to require supervision, but the nuns remained. Pacing, Rainie browsed the anti-gambling pamphlets. She remembered when Vivian used to buy lottery tickets from the 7-Eleven every month. She would let Rainie and Anita choose her numbers, and Anita always counted roadkill, while Rainie always chose the birthday of her mother and the number of moles that had appeared on the soles of Anita's feet. *It's because she was punished in a past life and walked on coals for a century—that's why her soles are spotted.* Rainie didn't re-member who said that: Maybe she had, though she didn't be-lieve Anita was being punished. Occasionally, when Anita won a few dollars—because it was always her numbers that won—Vivian split the money between the three of them and said, *I told you we're lucky. How else could we have gotten to meet each other and be together.* Rainie believed it, believed that inside Viv-ian's belly was a god badgering to meet them. Rainie always kept her prayers brief. The shorter they were, the more likely they'd be answered. Her mother said the dead were not patient and concision was key. Walking back to the altar, Rainie kneeled in front of the boy's belly and prayed, *Anita, return. Rain back to me.*

Rainie returned to the duplex and told Vivian her idea to steal Anita a belly.

It's not a good omen to complete Anita's body with a theft, Vivian said, but she was smiling. *So how do I take it?* Rainie asked. She described the statue and its glossy belly, containing an entire world of joy inside it, like the glass orb of a snow globe. She described the vigilance of the nuns with their buckets of ash. *Break in,* Vivian said, but Rainie said she didn't want to steal from them in the night. *Does it make a difference if you do it in the day?* Vivian said, leading Rainie down the hallway to the kitchen, where a slab of fish thawed on the counter. *It does,* Rainie said. *This way we'd just be borrowing it. No breaking in. We won't violate anything. Though I don't think you'd mind violating something.*

Vivian said nothing, but Rainie could tell she was pondering the possibilities. *I'll atone at the temple,* Rainie said. Standing at the kitchen counter, Rainie could see into the living room where the TV played. She watched the woman on the Weather Channel identify the eye of a hurricane, circling it in red with her finger.

By stealing from it, Vivian said, laughing. *Fine. I'll help you. A distraction,* Vivian said, *though too bad that place is run by nuns, not monks, since men are easier to distract, even the celibate ones. Men are digressions.*

Rainie said, *The nuns set fire to the names in the parking lot. We could coax the fire inside, bait it with our own names.*

Too bad they've got no hair to catch fire, Vivian said, reaching out her hand to stroke Rainie's hair. *Though hair doesn't burn, just singes.*

Rainie flinched, remembering Vivian's mouth on her wrist. *We can't set fire to a temple*, she said. *What kind of gods would we be?*

No fire necessary, Vivian said with glee. *You said names. Don't you remember? The day the names fled, flapping off the walls?*

Of course, Rainie repeated, though mostly she remembered Anita's letter recounting the incident. The day the names flurried off the walls and fled the city, the nuns outside with laser guns and arrows, trying to shoot them down.

How do we make those names feather? Rainie said. Vivian replied, *Those names just need to be shown the sky and they'll want to be outside.* Rainie didn't know how it was possible to show them the sky besides smuggling it inside. Or taking off the roof.

Vivian said, *Exactly. Bring the sky inside.* She walked out of the kitchen and stood in front of the television, her back barricading the hurricane, barring it from the room. Rainie asked her, *How do you bring a sky inside? How do we tempt those names to leave their walls?*

Vivian smiled and said, *I knew a boy who could swallow an entire tree—really, he'd unhinge his jaw and swallow the whole thing, the size of a baby. He learned how to do it from snakes.* Rainie flicked a fly off the TV screen and said, *You better not be expecting me to swallow the boy's belly and carry him out inside me.* Laughing, Vivian said, *No, I'm just thinking of distracting the nuns.*

In the evening, Vivian woke Rainie from the sofa, dressed in all black even though it was too bright outside. *We're going to get Anita's belly now*, Vivian said, and so Rainie followed, buckling herself into the passenger seat of Mr. McDonald's's former vehicle. The temple was squat and square, with double doors gilded in gold paint. Even in the parking lot they could hear the symphony of a sutra. Rainie asked again what their plan was, but Vivian only told her to enter the temple alone after the service and position herself for prayer. *Wait for me,* Vivian said.

Rainie entered, pausing before the altar while the nuns tucked the red cushions beneath the card tables. In front of her was the boy, belly rubbed blank. Two other women stood beside her, and Rainie mimicked the incline of their heads. There was a comfort in their uniformity, as if all the women in the temple might be praying the same thing, which Rainie believed must increase the chances that the prayer would be received. *Anita, Anita, Anita,* she repeated, mouthing the name, praying it contagious.

Vivian entered while the nuns were walking around the parking lot with their buckets of ash, burning the names that lived too long on the walls. There was a lit match clutched between each of Vivian's fingers. When she walked up to the walls flanking the prayer area, the kneeling women stood up from their cushions and hissed the same sound. They thought at first that she was a god, which was what Rainie believed too when she turned around and saw Vivian in the aisle, both hands raised into a chandelier, fingers spear-tipped with light. Vivian touched her hands to the walls, the white name slips fluttering. All around her the women gasped, unsure how to address her, and the paper on the walls flared into ash.

Rainie reached across the altar and lifted the boy, her hands gliding along its belly. It was lighter than she believed, hollow, a belly the size of a basketball, its smile spanning her palm. *Run,* Vivian said, as ash seasoned their hair. The women

kneeled under the card tables again, as if this were an earth-
quake drill. Down the aisle, Rainie ran for the double doors,
flung open by the nuns who streamed in, crying out. Vivian
and Rainie shouldered past the nuns, who were beating the
walls with the sleeves of their robes. Vivian's hands were still
on fire, twin torches, though later they could find no burns on
her, and Vivian said she hadn't felt heat, only a pearl on her
tongue.

They raced down the block, the belly tucked under Rainie's arm, and together they ran for the bus, panting smoke into
each other's face. Behind them, the temple was haloed in ash.
The whole way home on the bus, they could not stop laughing, the boy on Rainie's lap made of some kind of stone or
ceramic, its belly smoothed by hundreds of hands.

At the duplex, Rainie rinsed the boy underwater, suspect-
ing that it had wanted all its life to be clean. The water rippled
its skin. *Hold him on his side*, Vivian said, setting down the cutting board. Rainie pinned the boy like a bread loaf, cupped his
head in her palm. Beside her, Vivian raised her watermelon
machete and brought it down, attempting to cleave the boy
from his belly. But it held.

Let's throw it from the roof, Vivian said, and Rainie said, *I
considered that, but I'm afraid of heights.* Vivian shook her head and
lifted the boy from the cutting board, swathing it in a dish
towel, cradling it in her arms. She walked outside to the side
yard and lobbed it to the concrete, but it bounced instead of
breaking. *It's hollow, I swear it is*, Vivian said. *Let's just use the entire
thing*, Rainie said, lifting the boy into her own arms. *After all, it's
okay if there's a god attached to her stomach, as long as she has a stomach.*

The orchid bulb pulsed in the soil at their feet, and Rainie
bent to uproot it, closing her fist around the heat of Anita's

surrogate heart. *Now we build the body,* Rainie said, and kissed the belly, imagining that it was Vivian's. She struck her tongue against its skin, lighting her tongue like a torch. Ash filled the sky, swelling it pregnant.

Rainie looked down at the dirt where they would map Anita. She licked the sore coin of her inner wrist, the place where Vivian had extracted her tooth. Beneath soil and the pavement, Rainie felt a pulse that synced with the one in her wrist, a dull pain that prodded at her heels. Maybe it was true, Rainie thought, the things Anita believed, that there were fossils beneath their feet, skeletons waiting to be reinvented, draped with meat, given eyes and mouths.

The pulses in her wrist and the pavement began to beat out of sync, the rhythm of dogs running in a pack, their legs drumming up blood, narrating every story. She bent to the cement and pressed her sacrificial wrist to the pavement, heard the chorus of dogs running along its underside, pounding it soft as steak, the pavement rippling and bulging with the force of their paws almost punching through to the topside. The dogs were straining against the skin of a dream, their voice shimmering up from the street: *Rainie Rainie Rainie. Anita Anita Anita.* Their paws snagged the underside of the pavement, gathering it like cloth, contracting the distance between cities, between countries. They drummed Anita's name as they ran, a beat Rainie decoded with the soles of her feet and mirrored back, stomping on the concrete. She wondered if Anita would recognize a scavenged body as her own, if she would be able to invent a life from the fossils Rainie had foraged for her. Once, Rainie would have called this a scam, but now, as Vivian stood in the side yard with the belly and the thread and the tooth and the stone, ready to assemble the present, Rainie called it possible. She lit a candle and watched the smoke taper into string. As she folded forward and felt the pulse of dog feet, bruising her knees and echoing the dash of her own blood, she prayed for Anita to remember the syca- more, the dogs, the thread that once looped their lives to- gether.

Vivian Recounts the Building of Anita's New Body, with Minor Digressions, and the Rest of the Hsia Family (and Rainie, and a Ghostly Pack of Ancient, All-Knowing Dogs) Witness an Awakening

It's dogshit talk, everything they say about how bodies are all the same on the inside and we all bleed the same blood, etc., etc. Anita is made of flaky pastry. She crumbles under my breath. Abu is made of rain that's actually made of little screwdrivers. It rattles around inside her, that rain. Rainie girl is made of rinds, all kinds of rinds, banana rind and lemon rind and cantaloupe rind. She is the outside, all the way in. She keeps touching her neck, and I know it means: *Anita, tie a red knot around me.* She walks hungry, her feet fertilizing the concrete when she walks, so that now there are cracks all through it, with caterpillars of moss crawling out. That girl reminds me of another girl I used to know, Sunny. Funny how their names are antonyms. Rainie, Sunny—I didn't plan any of this. Sunny used to work with me at the denim factory. There are these big silver tubes that open like coffins, and inside are rubber balls, stiff and the size of eggs, except they're very hard and don't crack or give birth to anything, and then you toss the jeans into them and the coffins fill with acid and it bleaches the jeans so that they can sell them and they look streaked at the knees. Ayi always says she never understands why people pay more for their clothes to look damaged, most people didn't want to stitch their pants from old flour sacks, but I told her this way, it's like your ass is buddies with the sun, light-bleached, and that's the look people go for, like all is my throne. This girl Sunny and I used to go home together—I didn't want to go home with her, but she was always asking me for a cigarette, even though I don't smoke, and we took the same bus and she would sit next to me and talk up her own ass about all the boys who had loved her, even though to me she looked like another breed.

Though Anita and Rainie once wore threads around their throats, at least that was a choice. Sunny to me seemed sad, and I told her that. But she also gifted me apricots from her tree at home and limes too, and I thought that was nice, except the fruits always had worms in them, living laces, and once I bit into the apricot and it was full of larvae, tiny pearls that squirmed open, and I couldn't even see a hole it had entered through. On the bus, I was mostly tired, but sometimes I pretended to be asleep so that she wouldn't talk to me, though she always talked anyway. She would say things like, *I don't like my neighborhood because it's full of other people,* and even though I was pretending to sleep, I'd wake up just to say, *I think you're full of larvae.* She laughed at this. She was like a stick of butter, and I wanted to melt her onto the blacktop. But one time when we passed a street full of sycamores, she said, *Those trees remind me of the gorgeously cosmopolitan city I was born in. That's why my mannerisms are so high-class and my business sense is like a dog's sense of scent.* I almost pitched her head out the bus window, but then she said, *There was this tree outside my apartment building where dead people used to appear. Underneath or in the tree.* And I listened and said, yes, I knew a tree like that too, its elbows and knees. Under that tree, she told me, she saw a woman with eyes on top of her skull, looking up at her window. The woman said, *Don't you want eyes on top of your head too? That way you never have to look anywhere but up, and only the trees will speak down to you.* And Sunny said, *Yes, I would like eyes on top of my head.* So the woman said, *Okay, then what you need to do is snip out your eyes and reglue them to the top of your scalp, but shave your head first so that you know where to place them.* That's why Sunny kept her hair short, in case those eyes ever grew on the top of her head. I asked if she succeeded in snipping out her eyes, and she replied that I was stupid. But I knew a tree just like that one, a tree secretive about its sap, branches snagging ghosts like plastic bags. One day she stayed behind at the factory, probably meeting one of the boys whose story I didn't listen to, and the next day they found her body inside one of the bleaching tubes, rubber balls in her mouth and eye sockets, her skin bleached to bark. She resurrected two weeks later at my bus stop—mine and not hers—and she laughed at me and said it was all a big prank, she staged her death because she was too afraid to quit and has a general fear of disappointing people, and I said, *Just seeing you is a disappointment to me.*

Rainie reminds me of that girl, not because she pretended to be dead but because she listens to women in trees, listens to everything, when really nothing is worth listening to, except the dogs who love you. I prefer silence. That's what I tell Rainie: *Don't build a room for all that noise. Don't give her body an excuse to fill itself with only that.*

In the side yard, we arrange the organs in the correct order: the orchid-bulb heart, the dried and rinsed dog-boiled intestines, the thread of Rainie's blood with her dogtooth knotted at the end of it, snipping the length into hair and arteries and their tributaries. A cantaloupe for a head, a good one from another galaxy, fly fodder. The holy belly rolling beneath the orchid-heart, a surrogate stomach. Kidney beans I found at the bottom of the pantry. Rainie fills a sandwich bag with water for the bladder. The organs of hunger have all been collected. We visit Anita's rotting body in the bedroom. Her skin is the surface of a lake, knitted with eggs.

We gather in the side yard and admire our arrangement. *Your new body,* I say to the soil, the basil, Rainie. *Anita, come home. We're waiting.* All evening her organs are sprawled in the side yard, but still no souls return to collect them or at least heist them from our hands.

We can't just wait for her to come back, Rainie says, and lifts the coil of red thread I've arranged on the pavement. *Don't tie it around your neck,* I say, but Rainie says she won't. Instead, she tapes one end of the thread to the pavement and unravels the rest behind her as she walks down the street, me following like a stray, mouth panting open. The thread behind her tautens and hums. She reaches the sycamore, kneeling to knot the other end around the waist of the tree, enough thread to wind it three times around the trunk. I tell her what she's doing is cursed, but Rainie doesn't listen to me, so maybe I'm wrong in believing she's the kind who listens. She ties the knot with the solemnness of an execution, and I look up into the branches, waiting for some woman to descend. That time I kissed Rainie, her wrist, the side of her neck, her eyes tossing and turning in the dark—

That night we follow the thread back to the duplex, Rainie's hand on my back, guiding me like I've got no legs of my own. We watch. Together we sit cross-legged beside the arranged organs of Anita's body and wait, and I tell her stories the way Sunny used to tell me stories, and in the bedroom, ants anchor Anita's body to the mattress, steering out her eyeballs, carrying them on their backs like a pearl to present to their winged queen.

We wait and flick the red thread with our thumbs, and it makes a sound like singing. Then, in the night, it flickers on, the thread, it glows white and thrums as if plucked from below and above by a million thumbs, and we beat away the owls that try to land on it: This thread of blood is for Anita to follow.

It's nothing like I dreamed, though Ayi always says dreams are not memory, are not the future: They are failures. What we have failed in waking will follow us like the dead. Rainie stands and says, *I'm not going to wait.* She runs along the thread, back to the sycamore, and I trot behind her, saying, *Be careful, we don't know what this night is made of,* but she is already circling the trunk of the tree.

The machete, Rainie says. *Bring it to me.* I bring it. I remember her tender wrist in my mouth, and it churns me, ripens my belly. The melon machete is long and the handle is wood and Rainie wields it. She lifts it above her head in the dark, a dark as dense as water that opens only to the blades of our hands, and then the machete lands. The tree bone-glowing, beaconing for the blade. The trunk splits and shudders away in two white halves, folding to the pavement like clothing without a body.

Crouched inside, shedding the trunk like a cocoon, kneeling on a copper coil of roots: Anita. Anita with her eyes shut and then opening. *Are you one of those banana beings?* I ask, but Anita doesn't answer. She's wearing the jeans I gave her, defects from the factory, with buttons that don't open unless you bite them, and so I always helped her, kneeling to undo them. Her hair in two tight braids, so tight they make her cry. Anita, younger than her body eaten by ants, somewhere between the girl she'd abandoned and the one laid out on the mattress. She stands, eyes shutting and silked with sap, and with one hand gliding along the red thread, she follows us home.

We walk in silence, but then Anita laughs and I turn back to her. Her eyes are dull as stones. *If I were a banana ghost, I'd ask you to let me go,* Anita says. *I'd ask you to snip me free.*

But we're taking you home now, Rainie says, *home.*

At the duplex, we open the gate to the side yard, both of us now flanking her, unable to touch her. She tugs on the thread, the loose end of it trailing behind her, no longer tied to the collapsed trunk of the sycamore. She yanks as if fishing for something, and when she enters the side yard and sees her collected organs on the ground, she laughs. *You did this for me?* Anita turns to Rainie, and that's when I know it's her, not a banana ghost, because she fingers the skin at her throat, the place where she tied a knot. She's looking for the one around Rainie's neck, but it was severed so long ago. Anita lowers her head, then kneels and plucks up each of the organs—the dog's intestines, the thread, the belly, the orchid bulb—and swallows them in size order. The thread balled in her fist, strung down her throat. The orchid bulb, warm as afterbirth, then the dog's intestines, heavy as a mophead, then the statue-belly. Her jaw unhinging, widening into a doorway: You could step into that dark. *I was telling the truth,* I wanted to say to Rainie, *about the one I knew who could swallow cantaloupes.* It was possible: Anita was a city full of trees. Each of her organs collected by Rainie's hands. Each one a lost word for love.

Where did you go, who did you see? we ask, we beg, but Anita says, *Abu, Abu.* Abu in the doorway behind us, her arms aimed like spears. *Go back, banana ghost,* she says, but Anita touches her throat, and it's a gesture we recognize, the one that returns all our voices to our mouths, the one that reminds us we're bound.

I met two women, identical, Anita says, looking at her mother. *Inside the tree, I spoke to them. One of them gave birth to me and the other brought me to you. They had my face but banana hands, peeled and bloodless.* Abu steps forward, kneeling on the concrete, the shadow of dog blood pooling around us. *And you chose to come back to me,* Abu says, but Anita shakes her head and says to Rainie, *You cut me open. I promised to scar you to see you, but you didn't need a scar. You didn't even need skin. You built me from within. I home in you.* She touches her own throat again, then walks to Rainie and presses her thumb to the skin above Rainie's left eyebrow, relocating her pulse there, pinning it. We hear rain inside her body. She carries her organs like bells, goldening her gut, ringing us awake. Her innards rise into so many islands, everywhere we are born to.

Final Testimony of the Dogs
as They Run on the Underside
of the Pavement

(As Read by the Soles
of Rainie's Feet)

In the beginning we bayed our blood and ported in the past, shored to ourselves. We sank the ships by spitting into them, holing their hulls; handless, we could hold everything. We carried ourselves in triumph, climbed the throat of trees, labored into seas. We left the remains of men overhead like mornings. We eat our feces and trees breach our bellies. We know you daughters, you dogs, who see the dead too, who dilate puddles into doors, innovate pores. We know the mountains like our knuckles and use them too. Expose every face beneath our face. We take our teeth to the trees.

Make axes of our ankles. Bruised backside of the moon. We know that too. The stories say. Not the moon that shoulders the waves but us running beneath, carrying all water on our backs, all worlds, this word we run all the way off the page: *gone*. It's true that we ran and run still, some into the water, some into cities, some back into our mountain. Our hind legs house us. The sun full. We jump and nip it and spill every day onto our pelts. Back home is ahead of us and we run through the sleeve of a wave we run out of land we live into the sea.

Acknowledgments

I feel so lucky and so grateful to have completed what feels like a mythic triptych: *Bestiary, Gods of Want,* and now *Organ Meats* to complete the cycle. This trio feels like one body of text, and to see all three of them side by side will truly feel like a beautiful rebirth. The closing of one cycle and the beginning of another. Every book, I realize, is the overflow of the last, waiting for me to catch it. To my editor, Nicole Counts, who has guided me through the journey of all three books: Your enthusiasm and eye for possibility always excites me. You see me as all the writers I want to be, not just as the writer I am. To my agent, Julia Kardon, who I trust with my first drafts, good or bad: Thank you for seeing my work with more clarity and generosity than I could have ever imagined, and for being the constant uplifter, problem solver, and voice of reason in my writing life. My deep gratitude to Hannah Popal: Your early enthusiasm for this book was so heartwarming and motivating, and I hold on to that often. To Carla Bruce: Your ways of describing my work make me want to continue writing into the horizon and deserve those words. Your kindness and expertise are always inspiring. To Oma Beharry: Thank you for all your work and encouragement, for championing all of us One World authors, and for tolerating all my double-emails. Thank you to Lulu Martinez and Tiffani Ren for their expertise, care, and creativity. To Chris Jackson and the whole One World team: Thank you for believing in my books in the first place. To Michael Morris: Thank you for designing yet another stunning and gorgeously off-kilter cover. Thank you to Susan Turner for designing this book's beautiful interior.

To Amy Haejung, Kyle Lucia Wu, Pik-Shuen Fung, and Annina Zheng-Hardy: Thank you for reading the first pages of the first draft of this book, and for sustaining me throughout the journey. You have all taught me to honor the inherent value of living and creating. To Hairol Ma: Thank you for our café writing sessions, our meditations on suburbia, and our laughter-filled friendship. I'll never forget that moment when we were driving through the fog and you mistook a neon sign for the moon: ordinary magic! Our habit of texting in-progress paragraphs and sentences to each other has shown me how to bask in the unfinished beauty of what we create and how to feel a sense of ownership over it. To Maya: Thank you for always reminding me that we're not alone, and that there are so many more adventures to come. To my mother and brother: Thank you for your love and care and constancy.

About the Author

K-Ming Chang is a Kundiman fellow, a Lambda Literary Award winner, and a National Book Foundation 5 Under 35 honoree. She is the author of the *New York Times Book Review* Editors' Choice short-story collection *Gods of Want* and the novel *Bestiary*, which was longlisted for the Center for Fiction First Novel Prize, the PEN/Faulkner Award, and the VCU Cabell First Novelist Award.

kmingchang.com

About the Type

This book was set in Baskerville, a typeface designed by John Baskerville (1706–75), an amateur printer and typefounder, and cut for him by John Handy in 1750. The type became popular again when the Lanston Monotype Corporation of London revived the classic roman face in 1923. The Mergenthaler Linotype Company in England and the United States cut a version of Baskerville in 1931, making it one of the most widely used typefaces today.

From the Lambda Literary Award winner and National Book Award Foundation 5 Under 35 honoree

In her bold, surreal storytelling, critically acclaimed author K-Ming Chang captures myth, migration, queerness, and multigenerational narratives in her "signature precise and enthralling prose" (Shondaland).

"[K-Ming] Chang . . . rewrites the world as a place of radical transformation."
—*The New York Times Book Review*

"Chang has a special talent for forging history into myth and myth into present-day fiction." —*Los Angeles Times*

Learn more at kmingchang.com